is the pseudonym for Molly Keane. She was born in Kildare, Ireland, in 1904 into 'a rather serious Hunting and Fishing and Church-going family' who gave her little education at the hands of governesses. Her father originally came from a Somerset family and her mother, a poetess, was the author of 'The Songs of the Glens of Antrim'. Molly Keane's interests when young were 'hunting and horses and having a good time': she began writing only as a means of supplementing her dress allowance, and chose the pseudonym M.J. Farrell 'to hide my literary side from my sporting friends'. She wrote her first novel, *The Knight of the Cheerful Countenance*, at the age of seventeen.

Molly Keane published ten novels between 1928 and 1952: *Young Entry* (1928), *Taking Chances* (1929), *Mad Puppetstown* (1931), *Conversation Piece* (1932), *Devoted Ladies* (1934), *Full House* (1935), *The Rising Tide* (1937), *Two Days in Aragon* (1941), *Loving Without Tears* (1951) and *Treasure Hunt* (1952). She was also a successful playwright, of whom James Agate said 'I would back this impish writer to hold her own against Noel Coward himself.' Her plays, with John Perry, always directed by John Gielgud, include *Spring Meeting* (1938), *Ducks and Drakes* (1942), *Treasure Hunt* (1949) and *Dazzling Prospect* (1961).

The tragic death of her husband at the age of thirty-six stopped her writing for many years. It was not until 1981 that another novel— *Good Behaviour*—was published, this time under her real name. Molly Keane has two daughters and lives in Co. Waterford. Her latest novel, *Time After Time*, was published in 1983.

Virago publish *Devoted Ladies, The Rising Tide, Two Days in Aragon*, and *Mad Puppetstown. Full House, Taking Chances* and *Young Entry* are forthcoming.

VIRAGO
MODERN
CLASSIC
NUMBER

194

MAD
PUPPETSTOWN

M.J. FARRELL

With a New Introduction by
POLLY DEVLIN

Published by VIRAGO PRESS Limited 1985
41 William IV Street, London WC2N 4DB

First published in Great Britain by W. Collins Sons & Co. Ltd. 1931

British Library Cataloguing in Publication Data

Farrell, M.J.
  Mad Puppetstown.—(Virago modern classics)
  Rn: Molly Keane   I. Title
  823′.912[F]   PR6021.E33

  ISBN 0-86068-588-8

Printed in Great Britain by
Cox and Wyman at Reading, Berkshire

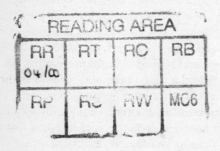

INTRODUCTION

Mad Puppetstown published in 1931, was the fourth novel by the new young writer, M.J. Farrell, who had already established an avid following with her previous horsey, housey romances, starting with *The Knight of the Cheerful Countenance*, begun when she was seventeen, finished not long after, and, she says, best forgotten. This first book was published by Mills and Boon and had attracted the attention of the head of Collins who then published her next two novels, *Young Entry* and *Taking Chances*. This last had blown her cover. Until then, though everyone knew that M.J. Farrell was a pseudonym, her real identity was a well-kept secret.

There was speculation about this writer who was obviously not just privy to the world she wrote about but an integral part of it. She got the details right; nothing got past her; not a foible, not an affectation. She wrote with an amusement that was amusing; she wrote affectionately but pounced on base motives, dishonourable actions, mendacity and pretension. She had a kind heart and a sharp pen; and there was the glimmering of the wit that later became so evident in her writing. The huntin' shootin' Anglo-Irish society who had read about their own activities in *Young Entry* with intrigued delight were more ambivalent about

Taking Chances. It was thought to be going it a bit, to be somewhat risqué and cynical. Reading it now it seems so innocuous and whimsical that one can scarcely believe this.

"One of my best friends let out that M.J. Farrell was me" says Molly Keane ruefully. There was astonished reaction: and acerbic reaction too. Yet it was not surprising that young Molly Skrine, as she was then, should be a writer, as well as a horsewoman of skill. Her father, Walter Skrine, was a fanatical horseman and rider to hounds and her mother was famous for her poetry written under the pseudonym Moira O'Neill— "the poetess of the seven glens". Her sweet, sentimental and touching poems about the "people" of Ireland were an acceptable product of "scribbling" and caused no shivers in polite society. Not so *Taking Chances*.

"I'd kept the writing thing a secret really rather well until then. I hadn't set out to be a writer. I'd really only started because when I was seventeen the doctor said there was a threat that I might have T.B. and I had to stay in bed. There was absolutely nothing to do, no-one paid me the least attention and I started to write." She told herself stories: and the first one was *The Knight etc.* "An awful book, but I thought I was Shakespeare—I wrote it—and all the next books—under the name of M.J. Farrell" (a name she saw over a pub on her way home after a day's hunting) "and no-one connected them with me. I didn't want to be recognised as a writer. I only wanted to be good in the hunting field and to be popular at hunt balls. I was so *starved* of fun when I was young, and loved fun so much."

She'd grown up in a rather isolated way in her parents' house in County Wexford. They all had one passion in common, her parents, brothers and sister— horses and hunting—but otherwise there seemed hardly any of the normal family connections of laughter and shared pursuits. Even in riding the children were simply expected by their father to be able to ride well and stylishly, as though through some genetic inheritance. One just rode, naturally, as one walked, which made for many a terrified child. "It was extraordinary," Molly Keane recalls, "at dinner, people would tell about some incident involving a small child shrinking at a wall, blue with terror, or taking it clinging on for dear life as though it were the most amusing thing." Molly Keane's brothers and sister went to school in England, which she refused to do. She was educated by governesses, by her mother, and for a while at a school outside Dublin, and as soon as she was old enough escaped to Woodrooff, a lovely house belonging to the Perry's, where for some years she spent the greater part of her time, hunting and generally living the sort of life that her nature craved. She was a good horsewoman, so much so that she caught the eye of Snaffles, an assured and faithful recorder of the pain and pleasure of foxhunting—and no-one had a more discerning eye for a likely horse and exhilaration. His drawings of her taking a fence at speed are among the few to have survived the war, when many of his plates were destroyed in air raids.

But her life at Woodrooff was productive in other

ways—it was here that she first saw how life was lived in "civilised" houses; here she met sophisticated, charming people who, best of all, liked her; here that she met those who could and would introduce her to London life; and here that she began the friendships with the children of the house, Sylvia and John Perry, which would later lead to the collaboration with John Perry on her plays, two of which had a great success in the West End. There was a great gap of decades when she ceased to write, partly as a result of the death of her husband Bobbie Keane, partly because her work seemed to go out of fashion. "Bobbie couldn't have liked my books more. He was very sharp though and wouldn't read them until they were published. I think he was afraid he would suggest things and influence me. He was quite right."

She speaks with reluctance about her writing. A reticence springing from a mixture of modesty and the ethos of her class and times in which talking about oneself in any obsessive way was quite unthinkable, and in which being *décontractée* was and is far more acceptable than appearing to be vain or earnest. Art was a word not much used in her society, "scribbling" was an unembarrassing way to describe writing. Such debunking has its charms but it's a difficult way of living and of thinking to transcend.

What seems to have happened with Molly Keane was that she started each novel through expediency and need, but as soon as she started, became obsessed by what she was writing and didn't leave it until she was finished. The artistic imperative in fact, though she would anxiously eschew such namings. She was, and still is, reluctant to recognise herself as a writer, and every time, what began as a racy, lightweight novel about hunting and houses and the only way of life she knew, ended up as something more than the sum of the parts of it. Her books are, in some ways, an indictment of her own social milieu, portrayals of a vicious snobbery and genteel racism, a world where philistinism was a virtue and horses were gods and the native Irish were heard with amusement but never seen at all. And more; her books became social testimonies, accurate in their detail and made more valuable because the way of life they recorded had vanished, though their memories and effects still play a part in the Irish *Zeitgeist*. Indeed the privileged way of life she recorded as the ordinary daily life of great houses still pertains in atavistic pockets of Ireland; but as a whole system it vanished, as did the Raj in India after 1948 or the *ancien régime* with the French Revolution. In Ireland it came to an end after the Troubles and the Treaty of 1922.

What was extraordinary about Ireland of the time in which and about which M.J. Farrell was writing was that the two classes, some might say the two races, Anglo-Irish and Irish, each considered themselves to be living the "real" life of Ireland in which the others played bit parts. For the gentry, the native Irish supplied the local colour and the local labour; for the Irish the Anglo-Irish were their erstwhile masters, there by default and remaining only on sufferance, a sufferance that in *Mad Puppetstown* comes to an end.

The two ways of life were so closely linked that to tear one from the other was to rend both almost to pieces.

Puppetstown is a large, fictitious house in County Westcommon owned by the Chevington family. Open any book on the ruined houses of Ireland, or on existing great houses, and you will find its match. It is based, as so many of Molly Keane's creations are, on a composition of houses she knew and admired. Though by 1908 when the book opens the great period of the Irish demesne, when a house belonging to the Anglo-Irish gentry stood in thousands of acres, had ended, life still went on undisturbed in these houses. Their time was running out, but no-one within these enclaves seemed to realise it. Puppetstown was, like so many other houses, left standing in a little isolated island of fantasy, a marooned dream of tranquility and largesse with the lodge keepers at the gate there for show rather than protection.

In *Mad Puppetstown* we are shown the life of these houses in the sweet years before the two great upheavals of the time—the 1914 War and the Irish uprising. The two are linked in the book, as they were in life in Ireland. Indeed it was the fact that the Irish "took advantage" of England being at war with Germany to start their own war that made so many English and Anglo-Irish particularly bitter. Molly Keane conveys the sadness of the ending of that ostensibly tranquil way of life.

> All the servants at Puppetstown looked back on the days
> of the Major as on a golden age—a splendid time the
> like of which they were never to see equalled again.

They would tell tales of fox-hunting and racing; of days
when all the quality would be gathered from the
country round to ride schools over the fences at
Puppetstown; of the winners the Major had bred and
trained and ridden they would tell; of the wine in the
cellars, the horses in the stables, the foxes in the coverts,
and the notable runs they provided. They had scores of
stories wherewith by contrast to darken the leaner years
that followed the Major's death and the Great War and
the little bitter, forgotten war in Ireland.

This is a setting and a cast with which Molly Keane is
utterly familiar. She marshals the organic throbbing
life of the house, its servants, horses, stables, old Aunt
Dicksie overseeing its smooth running, the delicious
food; the pretty, selfish widow, sister to Major
Chevington the owner of the house and mother to Basil
and Evelyn the young cousins all of whom live at
Puppetstown. There are the officers from the British
army, in and out of the house for dinner, tea, supper,
for boating, bridge and tennis. It is Somerville and
Ross territory, but mapped with less of the heavy irony
which they employed, less of the stiflingly patronising
tone which suffuses their books. And then there is
Easter Chevington, the daughter of the house, an
appealingly gawky child with a secret life of her own,
who sounds remarkably like Molly Keane herself,
growing up with the century. It is through Easter's
acute sensual observations of her environment that
Puppetstown's atmosphere and gardens are so vividly
conveyed. "Silence burnt like a still flame behind
green grass." It is these sense-memories that exert their

pull on Easter when she has returned to England and all but forgotten Puppetstown.

The decay and disintegration of the way of life that seemed so true and certain to Easter as a child, happens in kilter with her personal chronology; and her gradual realisation that she cannot take her security for granted, and that the house she loves is a place of danger, synchronises with her own lack of confidence in herself. All of this has its counterpart in Molly Keane's life, save that she did not leave to live in England.

"Today the house we lived in would count as a big house—oh lord, what is a big house?—and it was burned in the Troubles. It was a god-awful shock for my father who was a belligerent little Englishman. Everyone had warned him, had said you must come back and live in England and bring the children there, but he said 'I'd rather be shot in Ireland than live in England.' He wouldn't leave when they came to burn down the house. The top man in the I.R.A. bunch who had come to burn the house down said to him, as he hopped about, shouting and threatening. 'If you go on like that we really will have to shoot you.' They tied up both my parents and left them sitting on the lawn outside the house." Her father's defiant cry is echoed in *Mad Puppetstown* when Basil and Evelyn, grown-up and living in England, try to explain to their English hostess why their old aunt had stayed on in the decaying Puppetstown. "She'd rather be shot there by accident than live here on purpose."

In *Mad Puppetstown* the house is not burned—it is

saved because old Aunt Dicksie's glimmering presence as she flitted like a moth from room to room persuaded the Sinn Feinners waiting to fire it that it was guarded by the militia. This story too had many precedents in reality. Ballynatray House, for example, was guarded all through the Troubles by the wife of the owner (who had taken his pack of hounds for sport in England); Elizabeth Bowen gives a vivid description in *Bowen's Court* of how her own house survived. "The Republicans took over the house, mined the avenues, wired the house to blow it up and then waited." They waited for four days and, as Elizabeth Bowen says, "Even prejudice must allow they behaved like lambs, were great readers and especially were attracted to the works of Kipling. Then Aunt Sarah, vexed by a series of circumstances, drove to the house, moved in and sat down to consider what she would say to the Republicans when they came back from their daily reconnaissance. They never came back and Aunt Sarah remained convinced that it was her presence that deterred them—that, or the 'nice feeling' she attributed to all Irishmen. In the matter of the Troubles and Ireland and houses and behaviour on both sides no fiction could improve upon or exaggerate reality."

The book moves in episodic fits and starts and when the whole setting decamps to England the movement of the book becomes more stilted and awkward. Basil and Evelyn go to Eton, thence to Oxford. Easter comes of age and they all grow up locked into the convention of English upper-class life. It is hard to believe how stifling the atmosphere is, especially in the country house setting of Lady Anna and her exquisitely beautiful, exquisitely boring daughter, Sarah, with whom the by now unspeakable Evelyn is in love.

The portraits of Lady Anna and her daughter Sarah are drawn with an unerring eye. They are prigs of the first water: so is Evelyn with whom Easter, alas, is in love; they are archetypically high Tory English and regard Ireland as a wild, savage and far-away country. Both Easter and Basil are far more likeable characters, more romantic, unpredictable, amusing, unconventional—they love Ireland, long for it and return home. People as representatives of a country: often in Molly Keane's books the characteristics of the characters dovetail with what she sees as the characteristics of their country. And in her book the Irish are far more sympathetic—whether they are Anglo-Irish or native Irish—than the stolid, pedestrian, perfectly beautiful overlords. Basil and Easter seem ineffectual, but in fact act far more decisively than either Evelyn or Sarah who diminish life. Basil and Easter, insecure as they are, are on the side of passion and so, always, is Molly Keane. Her portrait of Lady Anna and her life is gently done, but it reveals the real lack of life and art in such a life; what might seem like a facade is in fact the same the whole way through; quite unlike the Irish, whether epitomised by Patsy, the servant at Puppetstown, or Easter and Basil on the other side of the social fence. The only time that Lady Anna seems to be in touch with the hidden life of dreams, emotion, yearning and spirits is in her recognition of the ghosts in her house.

It is a theme that Molly Keane returns to again and again—the way that the spirit of a house is comprised of the remnants of lives lived there. Her great friend Elizabeth Bowen, writing about her own house, Bowen's Court, once wrote ''I was not conscious of the lives of the dead there . . . but the unconsciousness, the unknowingness, the passivity, in which so much of those finished lives had been passed did somehow reach and enter my own. What runs on most through a family living in one place is a continuous semi-physical dream.'' In many of Molly Keane's books the spirits play even more of a role than this: and in Puppetstown itself, the whole house is animated by a spirit which resists the efforts of Basil and Easter to change it until they have found the magic route into the heart of the house via its guardian, Dicksie.

This old woman, who is, in her quiet and sometimes quaint way a memorable Keane heroine, has in effect turned Puppetstown into a hermitage; or has become an exile whilst never leaving the place she calls home. Most important of all, and most telling of metaphors, she has learnt how to survive by co-existing with the other marooned outcast, Patsy, the ''pure'' Irish kitchen-boy, whose terrible position in the miasma of Ireland, ripped apart by civil war, is revealed in all its pitiful and painful ambiguity. It is because he trusts in, and believes the words of his masters, and, at horrible cost, tries to protect them, that tragedy strikes. Nothing could be more ironic than this bitter twist, not of fate but of venality, which brings what Thomas Hardy called ''the cruelty of circumstances'' into the story and is the sign of a fine novelist. The point is never laboured. As Molly Keane peels away the layers and the wounds seep, the reader can only read on, appalled at the toils the people of the place, both the innocent and the cynical, have got themselves into. And it is, as ever, the innocents who suffer most. Like old Aunt Dicksie, Patsy learns to shift within the ruins of his life—he can do no more than be silent, collude and survive, and it seems that their hungry existence during the years of the children's absence, in a displenished house built for luxury, has had a shriving effect. Divested of its voluptuous input, it gains, as does Aunt Dicksie, an ascetic, almost savage, quality. Many of the houses in Molly Keane's novels are invested with this anthropomorphism. Here Puppetstown lies waiting for Basil and Easter, a new, nervous generation and, it would appear, an ultimately sterile one, rendered so by their frightened retreat into romanticism.

For they too, in an instinctive way that may be their salvation, seem to recognise that the house has been scorified. Lovely, ordinary, level-headed living is, as yet, beyond them and so they reach for a precious way of life that will leave their violence and passion undisturbed, will leave them unattached to anything other than their semblance of Irish life, on Ireland's surface. Basil, Easter and their like will take nothing for granted in Ireland again. Those days are over. It is as though at some profound level, a level operating beyond the reach of their intelligence, they recognise that the bubble world of Puppetstown has been shaken too hard for the atmosphere ever to settle peacefully again. The new Treaty is based on qualities new enough to the Anglo-Irish—compassion and respect and finally fear. Love has always been there. It is a far cry from the arrogant takeovers of earlier days. These Anglo-Irish who gave so much and who took so much and never learnt the balance, have crept back home to roost.

Puppetstown has survived the Troubles. Only just: and not because of Basil and Easter, but because one old woman, representative of her admirable, indomitable race, kept faith with the house and the only way of life she wanted to know. Yet, in showing what happened to a great house in Ireland as its way of life perished, in writing of the demise of a civilization, Molly Keane was also pointing out the way to a new dispensation.

Polly Devlin, Somerset, 1985

PART I

I

Then :—

They said : " You *naughty* man ! " They wore hair nets and tortoise-shell combs.

It was more than fast to accept presents from men.

You bought a blood four-year-old up to weight for £60.

There was no wire.

They talked about " the ladies " and " motor-cars." " By George ! " they said, but never used Americanisms ; such were not known.

Their top boots were shorter and their spurs were worn lower down on the heel.

You loved with passion.

You did not trouble to keep your sense of humour ready in the background.

Love mattered.

Manners mattered.

Children mattered.

Places and dependants mattered too.

Money bought much more.

People drove about in dog-carts and pony traps. Invitations were issued to tea.

5

Tea parties mattered too.

Women who powdered their faces were fast. Women who painted them—bad.

Hunting, low wages, feather boas, nipped in habit coats, curly bowlers, bunches of violets, black furs and purple hats were much in vogue.

A book called *Three Weeks* was both enjoyed and abused.

Champagne was a very frequent drink. Women never drank whisky.

And in those full-blooded days Easter Chevington was a child—an unattractive and intelligent child.

Now at the outset of life the most serious handicaps of the young are—an entirely lacking sense of proportion and the presence of a conscience. Very few children are born with a sense of humour, and very few are born without a sense of guilt. While age does not invariably develop humour, advancing years may generally be considered to endow the possessor of a conscience with the faculty for keeping that unhappy commodity within better control.

Easter Chevington reached the age of eight years, and had not even yet worked off either of these two distressing handicaps. She still repented her crimes almost with agony of mind and saw little to amuse, though much to interest, in a serious world.

Easter was a small, mousey-looking child. Her nurse scraped all her hair straight back off her forehead and away from her ears, plaiting just a very little of it on the top of her head, and tying

this unattractive morsel with an infinitesimal piece
of brown ribbon. The rest was allowed to lie in
straight uninteresting strands down her back. This
unbecoming method of hair-dressing laid bare every
inch of Easter's forehead, which was high and in-
tellectual and bulged hard and round like a cricket
ball. Her eyes were grey and very shortsighted so
that they always appeared to be screwed up into
slits. However, Easter's father, Major Chevington,
hated to see children in spectacles, and therefore
attributed Easter's headaches to over-eating or
imagination. Easter's mouth was large and at the
moment very untidy, what with teeth coming and
going and with the difficulty of breathing through
adenoids. However her nose (though full of adenoids)
was the tidiest thing about her (if one excepted her
feet and hands), and her laugh was splendid. She
would roar with laughter sometimes, though not
often, as her sense of the ridiculous was limited.

She wore blue serge sailor suits nearly all the
year round, with a flat square collar ornamented
by three rows of white tape and a white anchor
on her chest. She wore long brown stockings
and black or brown laced boots. In the winter
months she wore a round blue cap with H.M.S.
Victory written on it in gold letters, and in
the summer months a white straw hat that sat on
the very top of her head and was held in place below
her chin by a very much bitten piece of elastic.
This hat had H.M.S. *Dreadnaught* written in gold

on its blue ribbon—by way of variety, perhaps.
She wore, too, a white cotton petticoat made of
stoutly embroidered calico beneath her blue box-
pleated skirt.

Easter's clothes were chosen for her by her aunt,
and did not, in those far-away days, appear nearly
so horribly grotesque as they sound now. Even if
her mother had lived long enough to select more than
the first garments (which were luckily ready in time
for Easter's premature appearance), it is improbable
that her daughter's clothes would have reached a
higher artistic standard. Almost every little girl in
those dim years wore a sailor suit, and had Easter been
dressed in any more becoming garment she would
have suffered agonies of embarrassment. Nor would
her companions have spared her their criticisms.

Easter had many young friends. Although she
was an only child her life was far from lonely. She
lived in a large house called Puppetstown in County
Westcommon. She saw her father quite often;
while he was shaving in the morning and sometimes
before he went down to dinner, or, as was more
usual, went out to dine with a neighbour or in the
officers' mess four miles away.

Before he drove away in his tall dog-cart he
would come into the clean half dark nursery and
kiss Easter good-night as she lay in her bed—a
plain little shrimp in her thick flannel nightdress.
Easter's kiss smelt of the bath she had just had,
with a faint added flavour from her blue mug of

milk, and there was about it, too, a lingering crumbiness of *Marie* biscuits. Major Chevington's kiss was much more exciting and left a memory of eau de Cologne, Egyptian cigarettes and his last drink. His chin was smooth because he was one of those unhappy unfortunate men who must shave twice a day—and often do.

" Hallo, Daddy ! "

" Hallo, Easter ! Been a good girl to-day ? "

Easter would roll her head upon the pillow in embarrassed silence.

" Well, good-night, darling. Sleep tight——"

" An'-don't-let-the-bugs-bite," Easter would finish all in one breath. It really was an excellent joke and one that made her shout with laughter. Major Chevington appreciated it religiously too.

" Ha ! Ha ! Good-night, my mouse ! "

" Good-night, Daddy. Don't go yet. Daddy, Daddy, *Daddy*."

" Miss Easter, if you don't stop roarin' and bawlin' an' tearin' on the red raw minute ye'll be gettin' tally-whack an' tandam where ye'll not like it." Nanny would put her head round the day nursery door to say this and Easter would subside before such a dark and quelling threat.

Besides her father and Nanny and all the maids and Patsy Roche (the boot boy) and Paddy Fortune in the stable yard, Easter had her two young cousins, Basil and Evelyn, and Aunt Brenda, their mother, and Great-aunt Dicksie who was by way of doing the

housekeeping at Puppetstown and sometimes did—
when she could spare time from the garden.

Basil and Evelyn were very grand and grown up.
Their age was nine, one year older than Easter.
They were twins and, though inclined to be indulgent
with Easter, preferred their own villainous pursuits.
They had not been sent to school yet, but it was time
they went, for their brogues already rivalled those
of the National School children.

Major Chevington, who was their guardian, urged
their mother frequently to let the boys go, but there
was always an excellent reason why their departure
should be postponed yet another term. Last time
it was because they had caught ringworm in their
heads through kissing the calves, and you cannot
let people embark on the most cruel adventure of
their short lives while their heads are shaved as
bare as marbles. Not that Basil and Evelyn seemed
to take their leprous condition in a properly sensi-
tive spirit. Each had painted a face of alarming
ugliness on the back of his brother's shaven head,
artistic achievements lacking merit only to the eye
of authority. Thus for one sweet summer more they
kept wild holiday at Puppetstown.

While Aunt Dicksie thumbed and prodded with a
small fork that accomplished much about the garden,
and their mother bought lovely new blouses and
swaying skirts which were worn with much grace
and success at local tennis parties and entertain-
ments at the camp and picnics by the river, Easter

played with Evelyn and Basil (out of doors,
"Remember, Miss Easter, don't go too close to
them or you'll ketch that dirty disease too," warned
Nanny).

The days slipped past, bright ships, sailing out
far beyond remembrance.

.   .   .   .

It was morning, a very faint young morning, cold
and chaste past belief. The sky was as flat as wax
and as green as a leaf. The day had only just
forgotten its last pursuing star and the birds' July
singing strained like tiny, creaking wheels in the
stillness.

Easter sat up in bed, waking immediately and
unregretfully. The alarm clock on the chair by
Nanny's bed could have told her that two hours
must still go by before it was time to get up, but
Easter could not *quite* read a clock and tell the time
by it—an ignorance of which she felt ashamed and
concealed with feverish duplicity.

But it was light. Easter sat upon the edge of her
bed swinging her bare shanks. Why at this enchant-
ing hour was everything forbidden ? Books, pictures,
toys, walks abroad, everything that failed to dis-
tract or amuse in its proper hour would entrance at
this live forbidden moment.

Easter sighed. A wary eye on the heap that was
Nanny slumbering, and her foot reached down to the
linoleum—colder than glass. A small shrill wind
blew in at the open window, billowing the thin

curtains, coming like a knife through the thick
shrunk placket band of Easter's flannel nightdress
and setting its long skirts to skirl round her legs.
There is a time of life when we do not feel the cold,
when adventure is high and purpose dares to win
fulfilment.

The day nursery was dead still. John-the-
Clarney stood in his corner immobile, his eyes
glassily stony, the very scars which Easter had dealt
him had lost their kindly familiarity. Easter passed
by the rocking horse. He was not friendly.

Fritz-Max-Hums sat stiffly with his back to the
wall, his long red-trousered legs flat before him, his
Teutonic solidity unimpaired by the near presence of
lovely Angelina, who openly languished towards him,
her flaxen head drooping, her apple-blossom com-
plexion surviving even the day's most disenchanting
hour. Easter passed them by. She passed, too, the
Young Mechanic, leaving this intricate and baffling
pastime shut still in its red cardboard box.

Good bed toys are difficult to find. A book, now,
with satisfying detail of pictures, pictures that told
you lots and suggested more. Easter had such a
book, it was large and heavy, bound in brown and
gold, and within, enriching the tales of "Bluebeard"
and the "Sleeping Beauty," were illustrations of
surpassing choiceness and exactitude. In one picture
a macaw swung in a thin hoop of gold, while Fatima
and her girl friends sat gossiping and eating sweets
(drawn and coloured so plain that one could

count them where they lay in their dishes) and fruit,
each seed of which was clearly to be seen. The very
rings on their fingers, and the embroidery of their
clothes was painted with unstinted labour.

But this was a Sunday book ; together with *The
Life of a Chinese Baby*, it diverted the long after-
luncheon hours of the Sabbath day. It certainly
was not a book to be brought to bed of a Tuesday
morning. But what was this to Easter lusting
unbearably after its enclosed delights ; after the
fruit that she could touch and the rings that she
could count ? Nothing. It was the work of a moment
only to scramble on to the heavy table from which
she could, with a certain amount of effort, reach up
to the top of the book-shelf where the Sunday books
were kept. *The Youngest Girl in the School*, *The
Madcap of the Lower IV*, even the entrancing
Dora's Doll's House and *Cushions and Corners*,
each brimful of entertainment for a week-day morning, she left in their places, and with the chosen
prize heavy between her hands, lowered herself
into a sitting posture upon the table. The chill
of its American cloth covering struck unpleasantly
through her nightdress, but Easter heeded it not.
Her fingers were red and bulging with cold, her feet
blue and shining, but what matter ? The pages she
turned satisfied even her longing. Faintly sniffing,
Easter gazed upon a fairy godmother in a white
dress that shone like stars. She swung on the dark
bough of a fir tree and discoursed with a messenger

whose seven league boots curled frantically behind him.

Turn over : A wicked godmother in apple-green and russet gown laid her comprehensive curse upon a richly-clad baby princess, while the queen fainted, and court ladies screamed by the dozen, their jewelled hands held up in execration. " *Sweet* little baby." Easter touched the picture, stroking the baby gently with a forefinger that traced round the back of its shawled head. Her eyes gloated on the magnificent furniture that surrounded this infant princess.

Turn over : A prince hacking his way through a forest. Dull. She knew the end. *Ah!* here was the unfortunate merchant who must give his daughter to the beast. But this was one of his lucky moments so happily immortalised. He sat alone, while before him was spread a feast so delicious, that Easter's eyes bulged as she counted the many exotic dishes. Roast peacocks jostled heaps of pomegranates, grapes and bursting purple figs. Long-necked flagons of amber wine were set to cheer the guest and a ship for spices, each thread of its rigging and each porthole distinctly to be seen, ornamented the centre of the table. The merchant's nimble fingers (used to cracking nuts and selling the shells by retail) peeled with a curling gold knife a fruit of surpassing richness and delicacy, while his eyes and his brown face glistened with quite excusable greed at the prospect of the good things in store. Was there a baby monkey chained in a far faint corner ? Oh, there *was* !

Rigid now with cold, Easter turned page after page, lost, indeed, to all sense of time and place. A faint, at first only half-heard creaking hardly penetrated her understanding, till in sudden wild panic she realised what it meant.

Nanny was waking up.

Softly Easter closed her book ; back on to its shelf it went ; and without accident she slid to the ground, padded across the floor and fumbled her way carefully through the door that divided the night from the day nursery. One more minute fraught through with anxiety, and her grimy, icy heels were kicking down through the bed-clothes. She was safe. Warmth stole upon her, easing her to comfort, betraying her at last to sleep.

"Waken up now, Miss Easter." It was Nanny, another incarnation of the slumbering heap that you never *could* quite think to be the same person.

"I declare you got a great sleep this morning. That's better for ye than to be persecuting me to let y' out o' the bed from six o'clock on, to go out to yer scheming for the day."

Easter assented. Yet as (hampered this time by prosaic blue felt slippers) she approached the wash-hand stand for her morning ablutions, there was born within her a sense of guilt that endured maddeningly even after her boiled egg and a second cup of milk had been despatched where they belonged.

" Can I go'n see Daddy ? "

" No, dear, no." Nanny untied the strings of the cotton feeder. " He's asleep yet—why wouldn't he and him not in the bed at four o'clock o' the morning "—(but this was an aside). " Take a race round and look for Master Evelyn—and mind and don't go strealing off to the farmyard now," was Nanny's parting warning as her charge, equipped in the H.M.S. *Dreadnaught* hat, and a Holland smock that strained viciously round her neck, opened the nursery door and sallied forth.

Puppetstown was a large house, large enough to permit of the nursery wing being situate at a vast and peaceful distance from the rest of mankind. Not that Easter was of a noisy or in any way riotous disposition ; but, as generations of Chevingtons had been brought to maturity in that dismal locality, there was no reason why Easter should not do as her forbears had done before her.

To-day her brown sandals carried her quickly down long clattering passages, past the chosen haunts of housemaids' pails and cans ; past dusty forgotten windows looking out, God knew where, for only the all-seeing eye looked in or out through them or noticed their dust ; past box-rooms where forgotten trunks, bulged grossly with long forgotten clothing, and legions of pictures kept their faces turned to the dark walls ; down a bare staircase and along a winding, twisting passage, until a heavy door swung to let her out into the blaze and glory of a July morning.

Easter trotted below a long line of windows, her head not quite so high as their sills : dining-room, drawing-room, billiard-room, study. Outside the study Daddy's two terriers, Max and Kit, sat aloof on the shadowed window ledge, outraged in their finest feelings that at the hour of 9.30 their breakfasts were still to beg. They paid no attention to Easter beyond a faint uninterested sniff as she trailed her fingers along the rough stone beside them. Easter trotted on—she knew of a better dog.

The garden came first on Easter's list. She crossed the lawn, starting out at a line of green footmarks through its heavy white dew, plunging from the clear burning morning light into the soaking shadows of trees, along a straight turf path between clipped yew hedges, where the rabbit, the peacock and the elephant (there was an old wren's nest in the elephant's trunk) lent a charming zoological variety to the aspect.

The worn iron latch of the garden door was set low, well within Easter's reach. Tall shrubs leant over the archway shading it darkly. The high garden walls were green and dark behind them. The way into the garden was as cold as a deep well. There was a creeping sense of adventure as you lifted and dropped the heavy latch and passed through the last shadows into the glorious garden.

By the gold fish pond, his legs straddled bravely from the island in the middle to the stepping-stone half-way across, Evelyn was standing. And Basil was not there. Easter's heart quickened. Separately her cousins made allowances for her feminine mawkishness and squeamishness, together they affected to despise and combined to outrage her nicer feelings.

Easter's legs quickened, keeping pace with her heart.

" Hello, Easter ! "

" Where's Basil ? " Easter asked.

" Gone to get his toof out in Dublin."

" Ooo ! " Easter's face grew pink, partly from pity for Basil, partly from pleasure at his absence.

" Yes. Aunt Dicksie took him and he's to go to the penny bazaar, too. I wish I was."

" Why didn't you, Evelyn ? "

" I roars more than Basil roars," Evelyn confided with pride. " So I'm to play with you." He stepped ashore.

" You've got ringworm.   Yah ! Who kissed the calves ? Who kissed the calves ? " Easter chanted and ran, setting the time for the first act of the day's play. She fled down a long garden path. Between flights of columbines and spires of larkspur, her brown legs streaked, faster and faster, till, with Evelyn not a yard behind, she whirled round screaming :

" *Pax. Pax.* I said *Pax*."

After all she was only a girl and could be forgiven when she did these blatantly mean things.

" I caught you, though," Evelyn grasped her

hand firmly in his own dry and grubby one. *Now,* have I got ringworm ? " He thrust his round stubble-covered head at her.

" *No.*"

" All right. Let's go'n find John O'Regan. Shall we ? "

John O'Regan was stooping in the strawberry bed, his vast red beard sweeping the plants, while his careful blunt fingers picked the fruit after the niggardly and grudging fashion of a really good gardener. He affected not to see the children as they stood on the path, still hand in hand, watching his slow, unimpatient work. It was almost unbearable to them to see the ripe prizes he affected to ignore, and the more perfect gems that dropped from his earthy fingers into crisp cabbage leaves.

" Good-morning, John."

" Good-morning, John."

Slowly John O'Regan raised himself from his delicious task.

" Begone, now ! " he commanded. There was no conciliation about him, only a deep mistrust of Evelyn and all his works, matured and seasoned through the years down which he had suffered much at the hands of that innocent child. Neither had he much toleration for Easter. " Some calls her Pesty, an' more calls her the Devil's Needle, but *I* calls her the Ferret," he had confided to a fellow-sufferer upon an occasion when he had been most devilishly outwitted. O'Regan was meaner even than

most of the tribe of gardeners, and it was on this
weakness of his and on his inordinate personal
vanity that Evelyn (one of the world's thinkers)
played, as an artist plays his chosen instrument.

" Isn't John's beard gone a great colour ? " he
demanded of Easter.

" I think he dyes it." Easter knew this was the
proper response. She giggled and rubbed one
sandalled foot against her leg while John stooped
once more with majesty to his toil.

" He does not, then." Evelyn's brogue was really
deplorable ; especially when he was delightfully
engaged in joining in wit and repartee with the men.
" He does nothing to it at all scarcely, only to run a
fine tooth comb through it on a Saturday evening."

" Who told you ? " Easter perceived that the
conversation was to be kept going as far as possible
on its present lines.

" Mary Josie told me," said Evelyn simply.
But his wary eye took notice of two things. The
colour that bloomed in John O'Regan's cheeks above
that carefully cossetted growth of whisker had turned
a livelier iris and, three rows away, a cabbage leaf,
growing limp now in the sun, sheltered the first of his
pickings.   Had Easter seen it, too ?

" If John O'Regan got ringworm in his beard the
same as what you and Basil got in your heads,
he'd have to shave off every hair and get painted
with iodine, too." Easter's contribution was a flash of
sheer genius.

" Did you see my ringworm, Johnny ? " At the approach of that unattractive head, John O'Regan leapt backwards and Easter sidled unobtrusively towards that leaf-ful of ripe strawberries.

" Away, now ! Out o' me garden the two both o' yez. G'wan now, Master Evelyn, I can see ye well enough where y'are." Thus John, retreating step by nervous step.

With a yell of artistic savagery Evelyn was upon him.

His beard divided in two golden wings on either side of his head, his dignity swallowed and forgotten in the maw of personal vanity, John O'Regan departed in full flight for the pea stakes with Evelyn in hot pursuit.

. . . .

Seated side by side upon the slanted perches of a dark and deserted hen house, Easter and Evelyn shared the fruits of their success. The stuffy smell of long past poultry lingered still in their retreat, but the bouquet was nothing to these adventurers. For the moment they were in harbour and the fruits of their piracy, strawberries, small and honey-hot from the sun, were sweet in their mouths, and the triumph of victory hot and present with them.

" I knew he'd make for the pea-stakes before he chased me," said Evelyn, the thinker. " An' Nanny said my last ringworm was dead, too. I *do* wish I could keep it alive till the greengages is ripe."

" He'll tell Daddy," Easter warned.

" Tell Uncle Dick he ran away for fear he'd get
ringworm in his beard ! No fear, he won't."

" Won't he, Evelyn ? "

" Uncle Dick'd laugh at him. Easter, let's go to
the yard an' see if Jim Deacon's pig has calved yet."

Her desire to investigate this enthralling mystery
of nature quite overcame Easter's wavering sense of
obedience to Nanny.

" 'S let's." She slid to the ground, licking a faintly
sweet stain on the filthy palm of her hand.

Outside the hen-house (which had been built
years long ago for fowls too choice to lodge with
the commoner of their species), the July sun stared
hotly down, bringing out the smells of tarred felt
and the faint choking incense of the nettles that
grew round lush and high. Easter and Evelyn
stepped through them cautiously, going single file
down the little beaten path that led from this secret
spot of theirs back to the more vulgar haunts of man.

Through a tangle of elder and laurel and twisting
rhododendron they penetrated with the effortless
accuracy of complete custom, to find themselves
in the long dim aisle of the Nut Walk. Here silence
burnt like a still flame behind green glass. No bird
sang. The children's sandalled feet padded without
noise up the loamy path. The day was kept without.
The golden July day was defeated. And beyond
this darkness Aunt Dicksie's own strip of garden
lay like a bright sword of colour beneath the sun.

In the autumn the Nut Walk was the jolliest

place of all to play. Filberts lay on the ground,
splitting their creamy green jackets ; round hazel
nuts, polished like so many brown boots, were
there to pick up. And walnuts, all ready to be
crushed with enticing messiness from their coating
of black slime, awaited the adventurer. But to-day
the Nut Walk was withdrawn into itself, in a green
and secret spell of quietness. Without words the
children hurried down the length of it and dropped
themselves from a sun-baked four-foot wall into the
cheerfully brazen field below.

A slippery thread of a path spun its way across
the field to an unseen gateway, where, under the
trees, the air trembled, laden blue in the heat. Here
two young horses barked a beech tree with merciless
avidity, pausing sometimes to hang their noses to
the dry ground and to stamp at the incessant flies.

As the children drew near the gate opened and a
little man with a wry neck and a quick limping step
came into the field. He wore an old pair of breeches
and leggings and a striped, collarless shirt. A
battered straw hat shaded eyes as blue as a crow's
and an awkwardly broken nose. Paddy Fortune
had been a steeplechase jockey in his day, and there
was not a racecourse in Ireland over which he had
not met with disaster and success. In his elderly years
he was groom at Puppetstown and intimate friend
and ally of the children. The grass swished smart-
ingly round their bare legs as they ran towards him.

Now they were deep in the shade, watching in

stilled enthralment the application of a mixture
smelling principally of paraffin oil to the horses'
backs, while Fortune answered their questions
with the divine, endless patience wherein the servants
of Ireland are, with rare exception, steeped and
endowed—at any rate in so far as their employer's
children are concerned.

" What's that for, Fortune ? " Easter balanced
with her back against the gate and her heels stuck
through the second bar.

" For to keep away the gad-bee and the dirty-
fly, Miss Easter."

While he explained to Easter the instincts, habits,
hibernation, birth and probable future life of the
warble-fly, together with a brief summary of the dis-
comforts caused to the horse in whose back its eggs
lodged and hatched, Fortune acceded amiably to
Evelyn's request that he should be permitted to
hold the end of a head-stall and proceeded quickly
and painstakingly with the dressing of his horses.

The conversational possibilities of dirty flies and
gad-bees at length exhausted, Easter cast her eyes
upon the ground in ruminative silence, and found
there fresh matter of interest.

" Lovely new boots you've got, haven't you,
Fortune ? "

" I'm easing them to me feet this two days,"
Fortune told her. " New boots is nice, Miss Easter,
but they'd prey on ye for the first. What price
would ye say I give for them, now ? "

" Two pounds ? " Easter hazarded.

" Sixpence out of a quid as God is my judge."
Fortune resumed his ministrations to the horses.

" Did Johnny O'Regan ketch yez ? " he inquired
casually at the end of a peaceful minute. " Well, he
ran mad into the yard to know did I see Master
Evelyn. I did, says I, himself and Miss Easter
made off for the ash grove but one two minutes
ago. Likely they're playing themselves with the
little dolly-house they has in it. Didn't I see yez, the
two-both o' ye—creepin' up the Nut Walk at
the same time. Well, boys ! He took a dart down
to the ash grove and him fit to drink Master Evelyn's
blood. Sure he left the old hat after him in the
garden and with the ginger hair and the ginger
whisker stuck three foot out after him in the breeze,
well, he was like nothin' only a man was run through
hell with his hat off. It must be he got great hardship from ye, Master Evelyn ? "

The children told ; Easter shrilling the tale in
an excited treble ; Evelyn joining lustily at the
salient points.

" Well, well, well ! O'Regan is a mountainous
man and mountainous men is very passionate."
Fortune slipped the halter off the young horse and
immediately it sunk its head, thrusting against his
shoulder. " Hold up now, the big fella ! Woa,
boysie ! " He pulled the tongue up in the buckle,
making the halter fast on his second horse, gave the
tag to Evelyn to hold and set to work once

more. Quick and quiet, his work was pleasant to
watch.

" O'Regan has thousands of strawberries in that
bed, anyhow," Evelyn said suddenly.

" Millions," amended Easter.

" Well, what length would strawberries go for a
tea-party. Them's what the ladies use. Now I'm
as nice meself I wouldn't care about them if they
were throwing after me. Them's nothin' only old
wish-wash and maggots."

" Is there a tea-party to-day ? " Easter said.
All the strawberries she had eaten seemed to rise
through her with a small bitter shivering. The first
grim panic of a party darkened the fair earth.

" Is it a tennis party ? " She slid slowly off the
gate on which she had been swinging and fidgeting
with such unthoughtful enjoyment. " Oh, do tell me,
Fortune." Easter sank all in a doleful heap upon
the ground, her white straw hat dropping to her
knees, excessively forlorn.

" Ah, well, Heaven for comfort, Hell for society,"
Fortune comforted her with benign tolerance for
the eccentricities of her elders and his superiors.
A moment later his voice held shocked reprimand.
" Get up, Miss Easter ! Sure it's as dangerous as
blazes for you to be sittin' there among them owld
phis-phires. If them devils got up yer legs there'd
be no cure for it only the bath ! "

Easter removed her person from the ants' nest
whereon she had sunk herself, shook out her petticoat

and dusted down her knickers. If the tennis party was truly inevitable then it must be faced. But its presage cast heavy shadows across the bright hours.

" Come on, Evelyn," Easter said. They left Fortune behind them in the blue gloom of the beech trees and struck forth once more into the day.

High noon towered a pillar of heat over the farm-yard. A turkey cock scratched pompously in a heap of manure, jutting his wings and protesting at the children's armed approach. In a bath of dust beneath the roots of three untidy elder trees a white hen wallowed, struggling the sand through her feathers. The dark doorways of cow byres and farm stables showed black and empty at this hour. The children went through one door. They stood a moment upon the threshold, their thin eager bodies soaked in the bright heat, before the gold and purple gloom of the dark stable received them, folding them away from the daylight. Above their heads a hen dived out strident and hysterical. Easter could not see over the edge of the manger whence she had flown, but by reaching up the full length of her arm she succeeded in closing her hand about the hot solid circle of a newly laid egg. She rolled it against her cheek, smelling its warmth through the cloudy thickness of the stable's air.

Evelyn was in the next stall. She could hear him moving slowly, rattling a chain, climbing upwards with an effort a very little way ; she heard him gasp and squeak with excitement, and putting

down her egg went in to see what he had discovered.

"Nothing," Evelyn said. "No, I didn't find
anything." His stubbled hair was full of hayseeds
and his eyes were full of dust. He stood in his blue
Holland blouse a rock of obstinacy before the hay-
rack, and to all Easter's entreaties for a share in
that mystery he guarded, he replied with taunts
as to her sex's well-known incapability for the
keeping of secrets.

"Miss Easter——" It was almost a whisper,
this interruption from without. Easter turned to
where a boy stood in the moated shaft of gold light
which struck through a slitted window. A very
thin boy, light on his bare feet, with ears set and
pointed like a fox-cub's or a faun's, a dark, neatly
balanced head in which blue eyes were set surprisingly
and a mouth that suited his quiet speech.

"I beg your pardon, Miss Easter," the boy said,
with enormous gravity. "May I take a pluck at
the paycock?"

"*Patsy—what for*? Yes. Come on!" Easter
flamed towards the pale boy, forgetful of Evelyn,
of Evelyn's sulks and Evelyn's secret nest of kittens
—for what other animals spend their young lives
in hayracks, used and disused?

"Me da has a black fly dressed for the Major only
for a sign o' paycock in the wing," the boy said
quickly in his soft voice. "He says surely he should
kill a fish on it to-night with what wather is in it."

" Is there enough water in the Kilcurry burn to catch trout on a worm, Patsy ? " That was the only form of angling as yet known to Easter.

" I'll tell ye when there's a yella flood and ye may slip off to me then. We'll murder them in it."

Patsy, son and grandson of a poacher, walked quickly through the respectable domesticity of the farmyard with half an eye on every doorway. The newly gathered hazel switch in his hand was a slim defence against the onslaughts of the farm dogs who broke from their sun-induced languors to rate and bate this outcast who had slipped like a shy dark fish into their still day. Dimly they perceived that, although for the moment he was, like themselves, a servant to man, yet he came of the spirit and clan whence are raiders.

Evelyn rubbed hayseed and grime into his eyes, and at the same time worked himself up to a state of chaotic anger at Easter's desertion of him for the company of Patsy Roche. Mingled with his anger was a growing sense of jealousy, a sense of having been abandoned, a very present and painful sense of injury. Evelyn felt left out. Even his hidden nest of kittens (and there was one half Persian and a Tortoiseshell), failed as a solace for the secret and illicit delight of stalking through the green coverts of the shrubbery under the masterful direction of Patsy Roche. But the thought that he could report Patsy Roche to authority for the neglect of one and all of his manifold duties never crossed Evelyn's mind.

Supposedly employed at Puppetstown to clean boots and knives, chop firewood and carry coals for the nourishment of that all-consuming furnace, the kitchen range, in point of fact, Patsy was seldom at hand when any specific duty was required of him. He could, nevertheless, fulfil with a certain wild competency the work of almost any servant on Puppetstown's vast and ever-changing staff. Mrs. Kelly, the cook, in the intervals between the comings and goings (principally goings) of her long flights of kitchen maids, had instilled into his strangely receptive mentality such knowledge of cooking lore, that he had been known on one memorable occasion, when the presiding deity in the kitchen had sunk into a whisky-induced stupor, to cook an entirely eatable dinner for six hungry young soldiers brought in at a moment's notice by Puppetstown's impulsive master.

" Is it soup," Patsy had said, regarding with scorn the efforts of the cook's cousin, Mary Josie (whose proper sphere of activities were limited to slovenly house-maiding). "Arrah, what soup ! Sure ye'd think t'was a mouse ye had drowned in it. Get out from under me feet the lot o' yous and be dashing the cream for the trifle."

In a perfect storm of artistic construction that dinner was, course by course, produced by Patsy. Mary Josie's soup he flavoured with ducks' feet and giblets, and stiffened with what the cook's thirst had left in the bottle of sherry. The salmon cutlets he grilled were paragons of stiff flakiness. Melted butter swam in the deep old silver sauce boat. The ducks and the trifle alike were testimonies to an inspiration which had divined even the correct end of a duck at which to insert the stuffing.

"Ah, what use is women," said Patsy, as he departed that night for his bed in the boot room. Nor did he forget, on his way thither, to visit the four snares and one trap with which he combated the armies of rats that found in Puppetstown such pleasant quarters.

Yet on the day following this achievement, Patsy was picking grass from between the cobbles in the yard, without any feeling of rancour towards the cook who had skimped his breakfast and set about his ears with a wet dish cloth because he had seen fit to enliven the previous night's trifle with the remaining half of her last "Baby Power" whisky bottle.

Patsy ghillied for Major Chevington. He had the sure eye and the swift unerring hand of one whose father and father's father have had fish out of the river in ways more illicit than warrantable.

The children loved him. That they were entirely forbidden to play with Patsy Roche lent a charming excitement to hours spent in his society. Whatever he did had about it the authentic stamp of artistry. Whether it was cooking a dinner or working a ferret, killing ducks, or marking out the tennis court, he did it with the soul that was in him, and the children, perceiving here a singleness of spirit that

matched well with their own, gave him the strong
friendly liking of the young—friendship neither to
be dimmed by years nor sated by daily familiarity.

When (oh, *years* ago, now) he had discovered them
digging desperately hard in order to reach Hell
and put out the Devil before the bell rang for their
midday nap, he had joined them and dug too until
his iron spade struck a spark off a flint. Whereupon
they abandoned their wooden ones, and quenched
the devil and all his works with three buckets of
water before they marched in to their beds.

Patsy it was who found and gave them Edward.
Edward was their pet worm. He flourished before
the days when Basil and Evelyn and Easter took
to such manly sports as fishing, and they loved him
exceedingly. Edward was a handsome fellow of a
deep pink colour with peculiarly neat hoops of
mauve encircling his body. His length almost
exceeded that of the perforated lozenge box in
which he lived. His career was nothing if not
varied. His *debut* as the Blind Cobra, guardian of
Aunt Brenda's jewel box, did not meet with signal
success in the eyes of authority. Neither did he, in
spite of an exclusive diet of mulberry leaves, manage
to enrich his lozenge box by so much as one strand
of the rich straw-coloured silk which other worms
we read about produce so generously. Edward,
on his diet of mulberry leaves, only grew hard in
the body and wiry-looking, while his purple hoops
faded sadly in colour. A little earth revived him.

So, perhaps, did the walks for which he was taken day by day, Basil, Evelyn and Easter taking it in turn to carry him. They shared him with scrupulous fairness and even thought it right to give poor Nanny her turn at carrying Edward. But Nanny's turn proved disastrous to Edward's life as a pet. So damned refined was she that she must carry the worm in a piece of paper instead of comfortably in her hand. When the time came for the paper to be unfolded Edward had disappeared. . . .

On the morning that saw Evelyn, an open rebel to the authority that sought to physic him with castor oil, betake himself for one wild and lovely day to the woods which hemmed Puppetstown darkly on two sides, it was Patsy who stayed his deranged stomach with rhubarb tart, cold pig's cheek and acid drops. But at the gilded hour of two o'clock on a fine day, he wisely spoke no word to the rebel touching a return to domesticity. Not while the May sun struck hot on tall pale rocks. Not while the colour and the scent of bluebells flowed like a song through the warm peace of the day, lightening the darkness of the woods with bays and fiords and small secret lakes of blue. Not while the young leaves were like a green fire-magic in the blood and the egg of a golden-crested wren (taken with scrupulously mud-smeared fingers) waited still its pinprick and blowing. Not while a long romantic spy-glass, that morning abstracted from the hall, lent its last touch of realism to the

outlook post in a Scotch fir. Not then do you abandon
a life of furious outlawry. No, you do not. Rather
do you say : " Sneak out the air-gun to me, Patsy.
This pig's cheek can't last for ever." With your air-
gun you will kill small birds and roast them on
spits of green wood. You will sleep in the disused
culvert where last year's leaves lie rustling dry.
Indeed, when the sun is high, a determined outlaw
will plan wild deeds to pass all man's believing.

Patsy waited until the evening. He stayed the
hand of authority, panicking now and demanding
that search be made through the woods.

" Ye'll not ketch him that way, ma'am," said he
to frenzied authority in a purple tea gown. " Master
Evelyn's as wayward and as perverse he wouldn't
let a one near him. If he took the notion he'd cod
the lot of us, and himself'd hook it like blazes
through the woods till morning."

" Well, may God punish you, Patsy Roche."
Nanny, tears coursing one another down her cheeks,
uplifted her voice in hysterical rebuke. " You that's
no better than a little tinker's herring, ye have
the child dragged from me. Ye have him enticed
the way he'd go out the highest ditch that could
be built to escape me or one belonging me. Me that
rared himself and Master Basil as nice, eveny I
kept little woollen gloves on them and took them a
drive each day in the ass-car along with Mary Josie
and the baby, till yerself come around them with yer
sneakin', poachin', sootherin' ways to entice them."

" For heaven's sake stop that old woman talking,"
said Major Chevington, emerging, napkin in hand,
from the dining-room. The hall, the dim spaces of
its twilight defeating the orange glow of a single
paraffin oil lamp, seemed full of his servants. They
faded into the farther shadows at his approach,
with sibilant excuses and affectations of extreme
uninterest.

" Brenda, go back to your dinner. Now, that's
all I want to hear from you, nurse—that will *do*.
Patsy Roche, what the devil d'you think you're
doing, standing there in your bare feet ? Put your
boots on, young lad, when you come into the house.
Oh, you might run up to your father's and tell him
to meet me at the head o' the Phucka's stream at
ten o'clock in the morning. What's this about
Master Evelyn ? Out in the woods since morning
is he ? And a good job if he stayed there. (Now,
go back to your dinner, Brenda.) And go out you and
fetch him in, Patsy. Don't forget to give your father
that message. That's important. And send Master
Evelyn to the study when he comes back. I'll see
to him."

Patsy slipped out through the heavy baize-
covered door that led from the hall to the kitchen
passage. On the hall side its red baize was thick
and respectable, but on the kitchen side it hung
down in shreds, where dogs had scratched at it with
unavailing optimism and trays and coal scuttles
bumped twenty times in the course of a day. A

series of spring doors wheezed and closed as he passed through them. He avoided with the ease of long custom the pieces of disused and broken furniture that languished forgotten and unkept in the dank murk of the endless passages, and making a cautious detour of the kitchen premises, arrived quietly at his own sanctum—the boot and lamp room.

Patsy changed the single handle from the outside to the inside of the door and glanced round the castle of which he was king. A table in the window (a window of large and dignified dimensions— there were no small windows at Puppetstown) took up nearly the whole of one wall. On the table and on a long shelf above stood row upon row of hunting boots. Some were so old that their bucket tops began almost where their bagging ankles left off. Cobwebs draped their stumpy trees. The hunts they had seen were all forgotten now. The faint lightness of an early summer night caught the dusty crystals of a very old chandelier that lay in broken heaps in one corner, and touched greenly the dirty brass of innumerable disused oil lamps. It was not light enough to see where Patsy and his predecessors had scribbled their names (together with their low opinions of all immediate domestic superiors) in the soft damp of the walls. Nor yet the details of a series of delightful old coaching prints that bulged, mildewed and decaying, from their frames. A white ferret with her spawn came out from the shadows.

They hooped their long backs in the dimness, brushing their bodies across Patsy's bare feet. Patsy put them back inside an old sedan chair that lolled across a corner, stopping up their bolt hole with a few of the heavy pear-shaped drops of glass which lay round the chandelier. The ferrets had been imported presumably as a deterrent to the hungry hordes of rats which, according to Patsy, leapt upon him nightly to cut his throat for their pleasure, and suck the blood up through his ears. On the subject of propagation, authority had laid down no rule, the fertility of ferrets being supposedly in direct inverse ratio to that of gate-lodge-keepers. But Patsy, being an artist, had sympathy in him even for the moods of ferrets.

To-night he lifted the sash of the window, propped it to the height of a boot tree and slid out on to the brown twisting branch of a Portugal laurel that grew below. His bare feet dropped to the hard, worn path that led intricately through overgrown shrubberies to an avenue of tall beech trees. A dark thick wall of stones grown full of moss and ferns fenced the avenue behind the light shining beech stems, and in the sloping fields beyond, cattle moved, shrouding themselves in a mist of breath. An old white ass brayed suddenly with hideous effort. Patsy climbed the wall and struck out across the field, the dew on the grass shrill and cold against his bare legs and feet.

Sitting on a rock at the very outmost edge of the

woods he found Evelyn. His small face glowed pale
out of the darkness like a piece of dead white wood.
His hand in Patsy's was very cold, and his wet black
boots dragged and struck weakly one against another
all the way home.

" *Well*," said Uncle Dick, when the weary sinner
was arraigned before him in the shuttered, lamp-lit
study. " Well—— ? "

Evelyn's face was like a piece of pea-green china.
His wet black boots looked enormous and his shins
most meagre. He had nothing to say. The day's
high deeds were forgotten. A moment later he had
accomplished childhood's most successfully dramatic
act. He had fainted away on the hearthrug.

He came to without being sick and much enjoyed
a liberally sugared glass of Uncle Dick's whisky and
hot water. Later he sank into a gently drunken
slumber in the bed reserved for himself and Basil
when either of them enjoyed such poor health as
to warrant a night's lodging in their mother's room.

A bed other than your own is delightful. Thoughts
of discovery and adventure crowd to the head lying
strangely on an unfamiliar pillow. The blue bed
in their mother's room (a couch it was really)
always seemed to Basil and Evelyn like a strange
ship wherein they sailed out to new dreams. To wake
with the light coming in from an unaccustomed angle
began the morning surprisingly. Slowly thoughts
crept into your still mind. You remembered Her
coming the last thing to tuck in the slippery blue

silk eiderdown. You remembered : Now it's To-
morrow. You saw your red dressing-gown hanging
on the knob of the big bed. You stretched down a
hand for the jam-pot wherein your minnow usually
swam by your side through the night. It was not
there. The disadvantages of invalidism jarred
suddenly upon you. It might well be that the law
which forbids the solace of a minnow's company to
those who have yesterday been sick past conceal-
ment should to-day distress and inconvenience existence with legislation no less arbitrary than idiotic.

But first there was the excitement of early morning
tea. The bright clatter of a tray at the door—Mary
Josie drawing the curtains back in a hushed and
subdued manner much at variance with what
Evelyn and Basil knew of her private nature. You
smiled and made a face at her and she smiled back
secretly. You knew that it did not do for Mother in
her bed to realise the depth of your intimacy with
Mary Josie. Embarrassing and complicated fact.
Difficult to say when the knowledge of it was first
born in you. Always it was the same thing. Fortune's
hightest flight of wit or profoundest word of wisdom
when quoted to Authority met with inevitable
criticism. The latest information current in the
kitchen touching Mary Josie's flirtation with O'Regan
was greeted with a quelling lack of interest. Even
the high deeds done by Patsy in the capture of rats,
the slaughter of rabbits, or the outwitting of the
cook, you knew were best left untold . . . which

brings us back to the matter of Evelyn sulking with feigned indifference round the farmyard while Patsy and Easter stalked a peacock through the dark, green jungle of the shrubberies.

Who can forget the shrubbery smell ? The peculiar air heavy with small flies hanging where a rare open space grows weeds that reach up towards the light on long pale stems. The varying denseness of the covert ; brown, twisting stems of rhodo-dendrons, their good honest bark (unlike the slippery green laurel) leaving no mark behind upon the clothing. Monkey puzzles, with their South Sea Island stems and dying branches that never drop ; berberis impenetrable—here's the path where we shoulder round their evergreen unpleasantness. And now the sticky aromatic green savour of that sea-recalling shrub. It has insignificant pink flowers, clusters of small bells stood upon their heads. Another thing—liking its share of sunlight it grows only on the last edge of the thicket ; a landmark then, to tell us we are back upon the bounds of the grown-up world again.

Hunched near a lonely sun-dial, standing up faced to the sun in its sunk green strip of mossy grass, that's where the peacocks were mostly to be found of a morning. Near Aunt Dicksie's garden they slept, roasting their tortoise backs in the sun, picking down the length of a green breast feather. When Aunt Dicksie (who looked so like the white variety of their family) appeared they would scream with harsh expectancy and follow her up the little path back through the laurels towards the house. And she would turn back and fling them small handfuls of Indian corn out of her gardening basket, and laugh as they picked and pounced along the path behind her, their vast dignity forgotten.

But to-day Aunt Dicksie had put on her mauve blouse and hat and her long tussore silk coat. She had tied an elegant veil, composed of small black dots and dashes, over her face and hat, and had buttoned on an inconceivably narrow pair of black glacé kid boots, and had gone to Dublin with Basil, who was to have a tooth out, and later to visit the penny bazaar. There was undoubted method in Patsy's selection of to-day as suitable for the rape of peacocks' feathers.

Easter and Patsy stood together on Aunt Dicksie's walk as it was called They looked down into the narrow green alley where the peacocks waited on the shallow steps round the sun-dial. Through a slit in its bounding beech hedge they could just see into her garden. So still, so burning bright it was there you'd hardly dare to walk through. No, and never would you dare to cleave again the stillness that lay bound and kept behind the garden within the Nut Walk. Aunt Dicksie's garden was like a piece of water between you and beyond. Water too deep to wade. Water that you were too young to swim.

But before the garden came the little lawn and
there the peacock awaited the vengeance. The
peacock who, in former days, had been known to
come quietly up behind and peck the young just
above their short socks—a smart thrusting snap
with his strong beak, which a creeping, sneaking
method of delivery rendered ghastly in its suddenness. In those days you armed yourself with a short
rope, the deadlier for two or three stout knots in
the end of it. It was a satisfactory weapon with which
to lay about you, and lent a feeling of security to
its wielder. Imagine then how sweet to see your
tormentor spoiled of his most boastful plumage—
to watch his long neck twist and writhe and his
dark legs kick impotently in Patsy's secure hold
was exquisitely satisfying and amusing.

" That'll *punish* him," said Easter, staring avidly
at her discomfited tormentor. " Pull some more out,
Patsy."

" I have enough taken, miss." Patsy had passed
the age that finds a primeval satisfaction in the
infliction of cruelty. He stooped to the grass and
picked up his bright feathers, marrying them one
against another with slow, careful fingers. " Ye'd
love to see them fellas catch hardship ? " he asked
her. An assertion more than an inquiry.

Easter nodded. There was no doubt about it.
She would—just what she would like to see.

" Wouldn't you ? " she asked.

Patsy shook his head.

" The cook above's the only one I'd wish to see beneath me sway." A shining leapt into his eyes at the imagined prospect. " I wish I'd see the day that ould one'd get her dues. That'll be the quare change for her! That'll be the day she may sing woe!"

Easter, poking holes in the mossy lawn with a stick, agreed. She could perfectly understand Patsy's attitude towards Mrs. Kelly. It was so entirely on a level with her own sense of subservient animosity towards authority.

" Where will you hide the feathers? " she asked. " Miss Dicksie said you weren't to pluck the peacocks any more. If they catch you, it's *you* may sing woe."

" Ah, never fear will they catch me." Patsy took off his coat and poked the feathers into the back, through a two-inch rip in a seam of the dirty lining. " That's where they'll lie snug till I'll get to slip them to me da."

Easter regarded his coat awestruck. The possibilities of such a garment slowly unfolded themselves to her. Thus could one import to the nursery such forbidden delicacies as sloes and nuts ; perhaps, even blackberries (certainly apples) for secret nocturnal consumption. There was a touch of intrigue about the business which took excited hold of her mind. Pockets might (and certainly would) be turned out, but a lining, the lining of your coat, Nanny in her most probing and suspicious mood could scarcely think to pry there. The consideration of the prospect was exhilarating in the extreme.

" Well, I has me work to get done," Patsy announced with a sudden and intense access of virtue. " Is is what has I to do, Miss Easter ? Only to be tending the One Above, noon, night and morning. Look at, I'm bet up going hither an over dashin' cakes for her pleasure, and draggin' every big rock o' coal in Ireland to the kitchen range. I'd not get me health in that kitchen, Miss Easter. I do have to cry, sometimes, with every little dirty little abuse she'll give me. Oh, that one's the finished tartar surely." Patsy paused while Easter murmured sympathetically of pigs and their deserts.

" Ah, well, sure what is it all only passing through life ? " Patsy summarised the little disadvantages of existence philosophically and proceeded to outline his plan of retreat to the house. " Keep the pat, you, Miss Easter, I'll take a prod out through the bushes now till I'll see a chance to slip it in at the boot-room window."

Easter was left all alone. Patsy had vanished completely and utterly, not even the stirring of the shrubs told which way he had gone. Aunt Dicksie's garden shivered beneath the sun. The peacocks returned, slowly pacing up the sunken strip of dark grass towards the sun-dial. Easter walked away equally slowly along up the curly, evergreen shaded path, furiously curbing her desire to run from the loneliness abiding there in Aunt Dicksie's garden.

Almost it was a shock of joy to meet Evelyn
again. With a pleasantly trivial companion no
wandering is aimless, no half-filled hour too long.
Easter, forgetting that hidden nest of kittens, had
equally forgotten her prompt desertion of Evelyn
for another. Her grey eyes, with all the flat green
of the surrounding laurel leaves changing their
colour, brightened. She ran forward instantly, her
sandals beating hastily up the smooth path. But
Evelyn who had an excellent memory for a grievance
turned and ran faster far than she could follow.

" Oh, *Evelyn*—stop ! " Then with reproach and
dismay changing to ribald taunts, screamed so that
the unseen might not be spared the hearing of them :

> " Charley-barley, oats an' *hay*,
> Kissed the girls an' ran *away*."

> " Cowardy cowardy cowardy *custard*,
> Wouldn'y eat his father's *mustard*."

But all the same it was lonely as you wandered back
to the house ; out of the narrow tunnel of a path,
back to the sunlight that soaked the wide grass
in flowing, shaking, midday heat, and leaned its
warmth upon the grey walls of Puppetstown. The
very house looked languorous. It seemed to open
the pores of its stones to the day. As comfortable, it
looked, as a wide-lapped woman, sitting blue-
aproned in the sunlight.

Below the drawing-room windows three flights

of terraces led peacefully down to the indifferent
grass tennis court, where embowering copper beech
trees lent their varying shadows to embellish the
hazards of lawn tennis in the year 1908. From the
court came now the grunt and whine of the roller
and a faint rattle from the marking machine.

"Tommy"—Easter paused, listening, as
O'Regan's voice was raised ; it came from the tennis
court. "Have ye them rabbits' holes level yet ? "
it asked.

And the respectful murmur of Tommy the slave :
" I have them done, sir."

Silence hung about their occupation for a farther
minute ; then O'Regan's voice as though in prayer :

"Well in God's name, where did I leave down
that measure out o' me hand ?—— Likely Master
Evelyn have it whipped—ah, step it out you,
Tommy—— My feet is big."

Easter, slipping like a sun-baked lizard round
one hot corner of the house came suddenly on
Aunt Brenda. She was sitting with her feet over the
side of a long striped linen deckchair, and seemed
quite amused about something. At Easter's appearance she swung her feet back again, resettled
the angle of her white parasol, and said :

" Good-morning, ducky. Easter, dear, run into
the drawing-room and fetch me that ivory thing
with a measuring tape in it. You know it—a snake
thing. On my writing table, I *think*. . . . Thank
you, sweetheart. Trot off and tell O'Regan he can

measure the lines with it. But he's to be careful not to let it get broken."

It was a flat ivory box whereon birds had been carved with breathless acumen (but that was in China ever so long ago) that Easter carried down to O'Regan and his satellite on the tennis court. She walked nervously, sniffing at the box which smelt strongly of darkness and sandal wood ; and pulling at the weak spring of the faded silk measuring tape as she went.

O'Regan received it from her with silent dignity. He would not, Easter knew, forget to remember, and the truce in hostility she rightly regarded as sinister. Because it gave him the more time to think.

Easter turned back up the terraces slowly counting each step as she took it, and stood again below the windows where Aunt Brenda still lay in her long striped chair.

Aunt Brenda's hair was pale and finely gold. It waved back from her face in two wings supported symmetrically by fuzzy yellow pads. Its length was brushed up from the back of her neck and trimly coiled on the very top of her head. The fashion suited her neat, heart-shaped face and sloping shoulders very well indeed, as she knew. She spent far more time over her hair-dressing than she did over the manicure of her nails. In spite of the multitude of chocolates which she consumed her figure retained the absolute proportion of an hour-glass, and her skin, the unassisted bloom of which

one sometimes reads in the more dashing novels
of the past century. Aunt Brenda was as indolent
and careless and charming as she could be. She
spent her entire jointure on clothes and scent,
relying with unquestioning complacency on her
brother for the support of herself and her two young
sons.

Of course, in the future, there was Tattingham—
Tattingham, the old place in Wiltshire that Evelyn
would come in for when his great-uncle died. And
for herself there was that second marriage which
some day she supposed would happen. But in the
meantime . . . well, there was a tennis party here
to-day, and to-night dinner at Temple Connol.
To-morrow the puppy show at the kennels—
Heavens!—*had* she remembered to let the cook know
that there were eight extra people for tea? Aunt
Dicksie had left so early this morning on her way
to Dublin with Basil, that there had been no time
for her to do the ordering. Well, even if she *had*
forgotten, Sally Lunns and strawberries and cream
ought to meet the case.

" Easter—*Easter*! "

" Yes, Auntie Brenda ? "

" Run into the house and tell Mrs. Kelly there
are people coming for tea. Wait a moment—here's
a chocolate."

" Thank you.   Auntie Brenda—Fortune knows
and Patsy knows and O'Regan knows, so don't you
rather think Mrs. Kelly knows too ? "

" Run in and find out." Aunt Brenda relapsed into a book called *The Rosary*.

Easter obediently climbed up the three wooden steps, set against the window ledge for the convenience of dogs and humans whose young legs might prove inadequate for such heights, and dropped into the drawing-room.

After the hot daylight the drawing-room was still and cold. A faintly musky air hung about it, not an air of disuse, for the drawing-room was much inhabited at Puppetstown, but rather the scent of old things put away. Papers and shells, old pieces of ivory and bits of china, a little broken, hidden and lost for ever in among the shelves of lovely shining cupboards and the drawers of the gently bow-fronted tables and bureaus that filled the room with their crowded elegance. On the walls a thick Chinese paper of almost priceless value had somehow survived the zeal of Victorian redecorators. There were strange blue colours in it like the swaying shadows in deep and foreign waters. It had been brought back to Puppetstown by that sailoring Chevington, whose ivory and dark-scented lacquer boxes grafted their choking Eastern fragrance on to the air of the drawing-room. A very pretty gentleman in a blue coat saw himself reflected in an oval mirror of Chippendale's. He had died for King James at the battle of the Boyne. But before he died he had spent a cheerful youth fox-hunting and drinking and sky-larking at Puppetstown. His young

son they had brought up in France—a wild gosling—
and he had come back to Puppetstown with a
French wife. Her picture was painted on chicken-
skin and hung near the fireplace in a round gold
frame. A pleasing, silvery likeness of great-great-
grandmamma Marianne : powdered curls bound
up with a blue ribbon and a faintly irregular nose,
and in her lap a dog whose curls were as extravagant
as her own. Poor little French *bourgeoise*, she did not
live very long at Puppetstown, but her *dot* was a
generous endowment to a place she can never have
loved very much. Cold and grey she must have
thought it and the servants and natives—but
savages ! In a glass-fronted cabinet lies still her
greeting to a son she hardly saw. A white satin
bonnet of surpassing smallness and stiff as a little
helmet, and an oblong satin cushion about four
inches long and stuffed seemingly with sand, on
which is inscribed in an elegantly traced pattern of
steel-headed pins :

" WELCOME SWEET BABE—RICHARD OR CAROLINE."

Probably Marianne brought from France the carpet
that covers the drawing-room floor still, all wreaths
of flowers joined by chains of roses, strong enduring
colours, faint only where ceaseless feet have plied
from door to fireplace. The little painted China
clock, its business hushed this long time, was certainly hers. Perhaps her year at Puppetstown was
not such a grey affair at all. There is a marble

tombstone in Aunt Dicksie's garden and on it is written : " Fifi, died 1731," which shows that this Chevington cherished a little curly dog to a riper age than he was able to do its mistress.

But great-great-grandmother Marianne is really only a slipping pale shadow in the drawing-room at Puppetstown, her type did not persist in the family ; and that faintly coloured drawing of her is hardly to be seen beside the portraits of her full-lipped, full-bosomed successors and predecessors. Her year was an epoch in water-colour and crayon like her picture ; rather faint now : easily overlooked.

Easter went through the room with that peculi-arly hushed reverence with which drawing-rooms inspired the youth of her day. She stopped a minute to look at the Chelsea houses, because their complete and brightly-coloured intricacy held her mind enchanted and questioning, before she went on through a wide curtained archway into the morning-room. The morning-room had been redecorated when pale yellow and old gold en-livened by a dash of pea green were colours much in vogue, and it was the room Aunt Brenda usually sat in. A large coloured photograph of her late handsome husband leant upon a wooden easel near the writing table, and innumerable magazines and catalogues of fashionable clothes lay about on the tables. A chocolate box, which might or might not have been empty, was half pushed away behind a sofa cushion. Easter passed it by with a terrific

effort then returned to a hasty and fruitless search
among its dreadfully rattling papers. Aunt Brenda
did not often leave the last chocolate in the box,
unless it was of a kind that she particularly disliked.
Easter felt cheated out of both her chocolate and her
self-respect. She hurried through the hall, the third
of that cool chain of rooms, and in the turmoil of
the kitchen delivered Aunt Brenda's message. With
the tail of her eye she saw Patsy seated in a dark
corner meekly plucking the feathers from a pair
of chickens, while the feminine members of Puppetstown domestic staff sat round the kitchen table with
their elbows up drinking tea.

Easter's message was received in quelling silence
until, as she left the kitchen, the reigning deity
uplifted her voice in an imperious request for a tin of
baking powder and a box of matches from the store-
room.

"Oh, very well," said Aunt Brenda, without
raising her eyes from her book. "Tell her I'll get
them out at lunch time. I heard Nanny ringing your
bell just now. Run in to your nap. Evelyn!
Evelyn!" she called suddenly, catching the glimpse
of a blue blouse in the distance. "Where is the little
boy gone?" Aunt Brenda's voice was rich and
sweet and as bright as her hair.

"Little boy is here," said Evelyn, coming round
the corner. He loved his mother to the edge of
romance. Hardly ever did he sulk at her, hide from
her or keep her waiting his pleasure. Evelyn's hair

was golden like hers and his eyes were as blue and
his skin as fine. He was very unlike his twin Basil—
a blunt and stubby little boy.

" Time for milk and nap," She said.

" Time for chocolate," amended Evelyn. Easter
was given one too before she climbed back into the
dim room that would be her own some time.
(But she did not know that.) She envied Evelyn
with a sudden flashing envy because he was a boy
and could presume with so much grace and success
over matters like chocolates. That was to be a
boy—Easter felt a girl and out of it as her lagging
feet carried her up again to the nursery.

Drink your milk and take off your sandals (and
look what you stepped in, Miss Easter. Can you
not behave like a lady should ?) And lie down
beneath your top blanket, so thin and yellow from
many washings. The bright morning light comes
watered in through the drawn blinds and blowing
curtains. Your eyes (as they have done since ever
you remember) seek the dreamy familiarity of that
picture of Queen Victoria hanging on the wall
opposite the bed-post, a large plain photograph of
a small plain lady. Easter turned her eyes from it to
the more interesting antics of the flies on the ceiling ;
then, pulling the blanket over her head she imagined
herself in a house where every sort of contrivance
existed that could enliven the days of the young.

What a house it was ! Such stairs to lead you up
and down. Such small particular doors to let you

in and out. Such freedom of action and at the same
time such perpetual secrecy. And what excellent
food ! Not surprising indeed that all this perfection
should melt at the last into a dream.

Dinner-time in the nursery came, and Evelyn
and Easter met again. Brushed and tidied they sat
down to a silent consumption of potatoes and gravy
and rabbit. Once Evelyn put down his knife and
fork, drank heavily from his mug of water and said :
" I wish Basil was back."

" Eat your dinner and don't talk," Nannie commanded. Easter breathed heavily through a mouth-
ful of rabbit and said nothing. After dinner she
asked : " Do we have to go down to the party ? "
Yes, she was to put on her blue *djibbah* at four
o'clock and go down to her Auntie on the tennis
court and so was Master Evelyn, and in the meantime
let them try to behave as passable imitations of little
ladies and gentlemen if possible. Let Nanny see how
good they could be for once. With which cryptic
warning they were loosed on the world once more.

The world of afternoon—as different as may be
from the pale, rapturous plans of morning. In the
afternoon solid doing counts. The day is on the go
and we must be up and at it. The stable yard is
not a bad place to begin if you have no definite
plan in view. There at least the presence of Fortune
lends a motive to ten minutes' idleness. Their
differences of the morning tacitly forgotten, Easter
and Evelyn stood together in the sunlight watching

Fortune scrape and rake the gravel. The yard at
Puppetstown was built in a semi-circle—one side
of it being the house itself. Over the open doors of
several loose boxes looked out the heads of young
horses, and the lean, grave face of one favourite
old hunter that never did well out at grass. Yellow
roses and white roses climbed with fervour between
the stable doors, and a large tabby cat called
Portmanteau affected to sleep in the sunlight while
she kept one vigilant eye on a couple of half-grown
hound puppies who had, if the truth were known,
no courage to molest her.

Paddy Fortune desisted from his light and artistic
labours with a rake as soon as the children appeared.

" I'm after wringing the neck off o' th' ould
turkey cock," he informed them with arresting
simplicity.

" Why, Fortune ? " Delightful to feel tragedy
so close.

" God, didn't the fox whip the last o' the hens
e'er yesterday and what good was the cock so ? "

" Why, Fortune ? " More curious and curious
grew this circumstance of death.

" Never mind the why." Fortune raked the
gravel with a sudden renewal of energy. " The cook
has him hangin' in the larder this minute."

" Well, that's great ! " said Evelyn, with immense
satisfaction. Turkey without Christmas was something to which one might look forward.

It was at this moment that the cook put her head

out of the scullery window to announce with intense excitement and barely concealed satisfaction :

" The turkey hen is abroad in the yard this living
minute—and the poor cock dead ! Oh, pity ! "

" Well, the ways o' God are something fierce,"
murmured Fortune, as he subsided upon his rake,
apparently quite overcome by this domestic tragedy.

" Well, whatever change should come on that cock,
I declare to God he could as well be quinched as to
be the way he was," said the arbiter of Fate, advancing her head from the scullery window. " God
help him he was as drooped in himself ye'd be sorry
to be lookin' at him walkin' the yard hither an' over
and he pining always the very same as a Christian."

" God, it's yourself might pine when the mistress
hears 'twas your instigation killed her prize-cock."
Fortune's jocular wink was entirely lost upon the
awed children to whom this was indeed a case
where the ends of justice had reached a sorry skein.

" Now what would serve you better, Paddy
Fortune, is to go out through the shrubberies follyin'
that hen to her nest, in place o' standin' there cuttin'
hints at me—for God knows it's little I'd regard
the like of a little ignorant little savage the like o'
yourself."

" Oh, Jesus—Mary—and—Joseph ! Isn't that
frightful ? " came from an unseen chorus in the
background of the scullery. And with the names of
the Holy Family still vibrant upon the air, Paddy
entered on the combat with sudden fire.

" As for ignorance," he observed scathingly, " a pairson might do the b——y rounds o' the world and they wouldn't meet the aiqual o' yerself for ignorance, unless it's be that little tinker of a husband ye have and he hiding from ye this ten years."

Thrusting her unattractive head and neck tortoise-like from the scullery window, Mrs. Kelly surveyed her antagonist for an instant, an instant fraught through with intense venom and complete scorn. " Well," she returned with deadly calm, " maybe I did marry a rotten little tinker, Paddy. But if I did itself I wasn't as bad a case as your poor wife—God help her !—had to go to the Zoo and pick a monkey——"

After which unanswerable thrust she retreated to the background of the scullery whence a sudden yell of delight from her supporters told that the jest did not go unappreciated nor was it likely to die unrecorded. From the manner in which Fortune raked the gravel it was manifest to the children that a silent retreat was the most tactful mark of sympathy which they could offer. They offered it.

" What will we do ? " said Easter. She swung on a gate, back and forth, and looked to Evelyn for inspiration.

Evelyn had an idea but like most of his ideas the doubtful wisdom of imparting it to a female was uppermost in his mind.

" Did j'ever see a dead badger ? " he asked cautiously.

" I did not. Nor a live one," Easter confessed.

" Well, I'll show you where they buried the badger Max and Kit and Pidgie killed on Thursday."

" Is it in the fox-covert ? "

" No."

" In the wood ? "

" Yes. Listen ! Will we bring our spades and dig him up and look at him ? "

" S'lets ! "

This ghoulish project filled Easter with complete enthusiasm. She sought no fairer occupation for this sleepy afternoon. Like certain of the Athenians she was eager ever to hear or to see some new thing. And the double urge of digging up your discovery put an end of mystery on the affair difficult to resist.

So over a green hill's breast they trotted solemnly, these two, their straw hats planted, it seemed, upon their shoulders, as intent on the business of the moment as two little dogs off for an independent hunt. The sun went in and a little grey wind blew shrill through a field of tattered yellow ragweed and turned the colour of the oats that grew beyond a low wall of round stones from green to silver and back again. Across the little tumbling wall they paused to gather ears of corn for future consumption, then along the headland where the purple-pink of blackberry blossom lay in crowns and long wreaths, they pursued a narrow dusty path, the sun hot on their backs once more. Over the edge of another hill and below their feet, a tangle of furze and

strong growing bracken, lay suddenly the disused
sand pit. Beyond again the woods leaned up their
gradual slopes, while ranks of purple foxgloves kept
watch within and without—tall sentinels of quietness.

The children slid down the steep face of the gravel
pit, their heels digging out separate tracks in the
coarse sand, tracks speedily effaced by that portion
of their anatomy best fitted for sliding down pre-
cipitous slopes. Then they started to dig, labouring
and scraping in the heavy sand, where a promising-
looking mound was cast up. It was slow work
with their blunt spades, but they progressed with
serious endeavour and but few pauses for rest or
speculation. Finally they laid bare a side of the
corpse, very stiff and pig-like it lay, sand and small
stones mixed in its harsh wiry coat. As they gazed
a fiercely coloured blue-bottle dropped and settled
on its flank. Evelyn planted his hat upon the blue-
bottle then incarcerated his captive in a safety
matchbox.

" Bet you I catch a trout on that lad," he said,
peeping at it through a crack in the end of the box.
They caught three more in the same way before
they shovelled back the grave, stamping it down
with terrific energy. Then they turned their minds
and their steps from the freedom and the wild to the
immediate prospect of probable censure and certainly
the abhorred rites of unnecessary cleanliness.

" Oh," thought Easter, as an hour later she minced
shyly towards a group of ladies and gentlemen who

sat beneath the trees and watched four of their kind exerting themselves on the tennis court. " Am I going to cry ? I won't, I won't cry. Oo, I *won't* cry ! " For that was the disastrous and unattractive way that shyness took her. Her face felt stiff and raw after its recent scouring, and her blue *djibbah* stood out stiffly from her shoulders. " Please, God, *don't* let me cry," she prayed fervently, while a bright bed of geraniums wavered ominously before her eyes, a forewarning that her prayer would not be answered. Infinite regions away seemed the bright group of sunshades and white flannel. It was more than Easter could bear. Why had Evelyn not waited for her—why had he not waited ? Unkind, unkind. Easter's mouth shook helplessly. In another moment the tears would come to shame her.

" Ah, ha ! Who is *this* little girl ? " An old gentleman of the colonel sort, that is to say, he had a very stiff moustache and a very bald head, turned round to notice Easter's miserably ineffective approach.

" I'm Easter Chevington," Easter introduced herself in a solemn whine.

" Ah, ha," said the old man, with a facetious ogle. " So *you're* the little girl who couldn't be found at tea time, eh ? You're the little girl who digs up badgers, ah-ya ? Well, well—have a biscuit ? "

But Easter was incapable at the moment of eating even a pink and white biscuit. *Who* had told of their private doings ? Little did she guess that Aunt

Brenda, having extracted an unwilling confession from Evelyn, had proceeded with a burst of delighted laughter to tell the party what those two had been doing: " Digging up a dead badger—dirty little brutes ! "

" So long as they don't roll in it," Easter's father had said tolerantly, and the guests laughed and were so very jovial about it all when Evelyn appeared in his clean white sailor suit, that he had blushed slowly up to his forehead and down to the collar of his blouse and refused even chocolate cake because he felt so uncomfortable. And now it was Easter's turn to answer whether badger smelt good and when she intended to dig it up again to see how it was getting on. She was urged to give it another week, at which point she burst into loud and unbecoming sobs and rushed away to hide in the laurels, anywhere away from this crowd of ladies in large hats and fluffy white blouses and strange men with striped belts that matched the ribbons in their straw boaters. Away from their laughter and chatter and senseless teasing, she hid herself, for among them there was no friend for her. And when she had disappeared the ladies said : " Shy ? *poor* little thing ! " But the old gentleman was really distressed at having caused her breakdown. He ambled towards the laurels with a cake in his hand. But it did not serve to tempt Easter from her fastness. Not till Aunt Brenda called, in her sweet determined voice, did Easter emerge to field tennis balls with sulky diligence at the opposite end of the court to Evelyn.

Then Basil appeared. His arrival created something of a stir, for he was dressed in the first pair of long trousers he had ever worn. Aunt Dicksie had bought them for him that very day, together with a pair of the same sort, exactly, for Evelyn. Basil had put his on in the shop and wore them to go to the dentist. Walking along the streets he had felt the eye of every passer-by must be upon him, and going home in the train, between the trousers and the important feel of that strange new cavity in his mouth, he was sure of it. But now as he approached the group on the lawn he knew the pangs of any shy celebrity. But Basil had one support which Evelyn and Easter had not. He had Pidgie—Pidgie, so much more like a fierce white field-mouse, with her long muzzle and pink and chocolate nose and extra long dock (for she was a working terrier), than a dog. He had Pidgie, and with her he could endure much. Pidgie had slept all day in his bed, fiercely resentful of disturbance. And he had brought her back a present too. Her own name, PIDGIE, printed by himself on a neat tin label, and for the privilege of printing it he had paid a penny. It would look neat tacked to her basket. Basil looked forward to affixing it, but in the meantime wished he could fold himself up into his trousers and disappear for evermore. With an effort at nonchalance, an effort that faltered pitifully with each step he

took across the grass, he came and stood behind
Her chair with Pidgie, like a little white pig, held
upside down in his arms. *She* was talking to a gay
young man who sat at her feet making jokes, so
did not pay any attention to Basil for a moment.
Perhaps, after all, his appearance would escape
remark. Perhaps, if he sat down—and tucked his
legs under him.

" Basil, darling—my lamb, did the dentist hurt
you much ? Say how-d'you-do to Captain Longworth. This is my other son, Captain Longworth.
Date one rather, don't they ? Basil, dear, get up
and fetch that box of cigarettes." Then it happened :
" My precious, what a scream you look ! What
handsome trousers, aren't they ? Go and show them
to Mrs. Longworth, Basil. Mrs. Longworth ! Isn't
he *killing* ! "

A lady with very grave eyes looked at Basil for a
second, then she looked at Pidgie.

" Is that your dog ? " she asked. Then : " Her
poor little muzzle is all scars, isn't it ? When did she
get *that* one ? " Basil told the history of each scar
that he could remember, and showed how a badger
had once nearly bitten her foot off. The lady was as
interested as you like, and Pidgie lay on her broad
back, rolling her little pig's eyes fatuously during
the recital of her bravery.

" And what does she eat ? " asked the lady, and
Basil told. " And where does she sleep ? "

" Between d' sheets—that's where she sleeps,"

Basil answered in his regrettable brogue. "Don't you, Pidgie? But she has a basket too—look! what I got for it——" He produced the label marked with her name.

"Aha!" said the lady. "No common dog will get into her basket now—not when they read *that*."

"No—my God!" Basil agreed heartily, much after the manner of Mary Josie or Mrs. Kelly.

"*Basil!* Didn't you promise me not to say that?" *She* had heard.

"Yes—my God!" Basil clapped a hand to his mouth and turned crimson. It really *was* an accident that time. But She was not pleased.

"Go and help the others collect balls," She said.

.   .   .   .

At last the tennis party dispersed; the ladies put on warm coats with nipped-in waists and large sleeves that puffed from the shoulders, and with their gravy-spoon-like tennis racquets in their hands climbed agilely into dog-carts and on to side-cars and into round-about pony traps for the drive home. Fortune clung to the heads of fresh ponies and horses, touching his cap-peak precariously when he received his tips and running back to the yard to bring round some one else's conveyance as his last charge set off down the long narrow drive, where the straight rows of blossoming lime trees breathed out their very souls to the sweet evening.

Every one but Captain Longworth and the grave-faced small, brown lady, who took an interest in

Pidgie and was Mrs. Longworth, had gone. The gravel in front of the house was covered in scores of narrow wheel marks and only the great excitement of seeing Captain Longworth's motor-car start remained. There she stood in the shade of a chestnut tree, her beautiful red paint and bright brass lamps and fittings forming a splendid contrast to each other. The children hung about, their shyness forgotten, eager to see this giantess of speed in motion. But She and Captain Longworth were walking slowly, very slowly up the terraces towards the house, and Uncle Dick had taken the little birdy lady away to look at a horse in the stables.

" What a perfect evening ! " Reggie Longworth said. But he did not look out to where the mountains sank themselves against the winey stupor of the sky, he did not hear the peace of the evening lapping Puppetstown quietly about. There were great hanging cushions of purple catmint growing as lavishly as love over the grey stone of the terrace walls, yes, and small Irish roses, each with a voice of its own for whispering spells, and the crafty sweetness of stocks that mounts quicker to the brain than the scent of any other flower. Walking ever more slowly by Brenda's side he found this Irish widow as perfect as the evening.

Aunt Brenda wore a blouse the same colour as mauve stocks and as puffed about. She wore a hat in the latest mode for *le sport*, it was of soft white straw, planned on the same noble scale as a cart wheel, and generously trimmed with mauve velvet. She wore black silk stockings, their open-work insteps just showing below her skirt, and thin black leather shoes with red rubber soles. She was completely right and well she knew it.

Now if ever an evening was made for the first stir of a flirtation, this was the evening, and there by her side, six foot of interesting and handsome masculine melancholy, walked one of singular charm and wit and sadness with whom to captivate the hour.

" By Jove ! Yes, a perfect evening." Reggie had to answer himself, he found, for the lovely widow was not wordy. She walked slowly, her skirts swaying and making small, skirt-like noises while the least wind blew among the ribbons threaded in her blouse.

" Isn't it, though ? said Captain Longworth at last, and he had to bend down for his answer, which when it came was only : " Yes, indeed." But the golden voice almost sang.

" Are you going to like Ireland ? " Brenda asked, after another hushed moment.

" I'm going to love the Irish *people*," Reggie Longworth told her in that meaning voice which went so well with the breathless hour. " I've always wanted to be quartered over here—for the hunting, you know. Never met a fellow yet that didn't want to come back, once he'd had a go over this country. I remember dear Tommy Barraster telling me of a marvellous hunt he had here. He

was riding a real clinker—a bright blood bay he
bought for twenty pounds from a farmer who sold
him as a spoilt horse—a real brute he was too, but
he turned out to be a champion. Tommy had a
way with horses, the worst seemed to be a good one
when ridden by him. Anyhow, this horse turned
out good enough to win some useful 'chases when
Tommy brought him over to England. But I was
telling you about this hunt. Yes, a nine-mile point
it was and most of it over the most hair-raising
country—your banks and ditches frighten us
terrible, Mrs. Curtis, you know. I'm very frightened
of them—oh, yes, but I am. I assure you it's a fact.
'Pon my soul, yes, it is indeed. Well, to make a
long story short, out of a field of one hundred and
fifty, only three people besides the Master and one
of the hunt servants were there to see hounds
roll their fox over fair and square in the open. And
one of them was Tommy, one was a young farmer,
and one was a very gallant lady."

"Was that the hunt from Bradey's Bogs to
Raheendaggin, four seasons ago ? " Brenda asked.
Was it the glow of the low sun that had lit that
spark in her eye and flush in her cheek ? Maybe it
was.

"That was it. I remember the names now you
mention them. Were you out that day ? "

"Yes," said Brenda. "It was one of the best
hunts I ever remember. The old Master gave me
that brush and I still cherish it." She said it all in

a hurry, and looked as shy and pleased as any awkward girl.

"Then you are really the lady I've heard about on each of the many occasions when Tommy has told me the story of that hunt?" (What was it Tommy had said? "Jumped slap on top of me six fences running," he had said, "but, by George! I don't forget the lead she gave me over the seventh. A real teaser, too.") And this was the lady ("A Hebe, my dear Reggie, absolutely a Hebe"—he could hear Tommy's enthusiasm still). This was indeed she. And what an evening this to meet her.

Dick Chevington and Doris were coming down the terraces towards them now. "I've really seen a horse at last," Doris was saying in that small thrilled voice she kept for tall strangers. "You must see him, Reggie. Major Chevington tells me he's bred good enough to win the National, and he looks like doing it too, before he's done with! Oh, *thank you*, Mrs. Curtis, but we can't stay, can we, Reggie? We *must* be back by eight o'clock."

"But it is only ten miles from here to the camp. In your motor-car you will *easily* do that in an hour," Brenda protested hospitably. "Stay to dinner— I've promised to take the children to the circus afterwards. Let's all go together. Really it would be killing—do let's!"

"Shall we? You love a circus, Doris. I know your vulgar weaknesses. It is kind of you, Mrs. Curtis."

And so it happened that while the children waited in vain to see the departure of the motor-car, they could not guess that the hour approached when, almost sick with rapturous excitement, they would be pressed between the grown-ups on the back seat of that wonderful machine, and driven at a dizzy pace to the village of Bunclody, four breathless miles away from Puppetstown.

Dinner had accomplished itself with apparent ease—an ease owing more to the determined exertions of Aunt Dicksie than to the hysterical laments of the cook at the sudden additions called for by a menu of soup, cold beef and apple tart.

The dining-room table at Puppetstown was big enough for a banquet. Half a mile of linen it must have taken to clothe it as the decent fashion of the day demanded. Candles in squat branching candlesticks lit down its length; their small flames piercing the dimness of the room. Roses, just gathered and still faint from the heat of the long day, hung their heads a little over the great potato ring of Irish silver that circled them. The glass was Waterford, most of it, and the china old Lowestoft—varied by plain white delf, where gaps occurred in the service.

Aunt Dicksie, her cheeks flushed a pale carnation by her labours, her manners always indefeatable, welcomed these unexpected guests with grave interest, and directed the inapt ministrations of a pair of handmaidens with unruffled acumen. Dinner was good—as good as peas and roast ducklings, and a frothy pudding made of liqueur and beaten-up eggs, with a dessert of strawberries, wild-flavoured and sweet as honey, could make it. Neither did the wine betray the taste of that bottle-nosed grandfather on the wall who had laid it down with due thought and care.

The first nip of sherry with her soup, and Aunt Dicksie was enjoying the party and proving herself the very spirit of it. She was lovely, Aunt Dicksie, with her high cheek-bones and speckled, hazel eyes—quiet eyes, for she was a gardener. Her breeding showed in the faint swift lines of her temples and in her curious hands. There were sad stories about Aunt Dicksie's youth. Her love of Puppetstown was the only love crowned with luck for her. And her service to that love was tireless, but it brought her peace ; also the children of Puppetstown loved her.

Excitement overcame the children this evening. As night draws on children and cats (particularly small black cats) become possessed of a very devil of liveliness. To-night it took the children in the form of snatching food from the dishes as they came out of the dining-room, and savaging the drumsticks of the ducks in the darkness of the back-stairs. Slightly intoxicated by the dregs of the pudding, they removed one of Patsy's ferrets from its lodging in the Sedan chair, and placed it in Nanny's bed before, coated and hatted and good as gold, they stood in the hall to await the coming of their elders.

"God send them home safe," sniffed Nanny woefully as she wrapped them to their quivering noses in defiance of the cold night air through which they were to rush at the unnatural speed of 15 m.p.h. "God pardon a mother who would let her childer run the risk o' death in a hell-car the like o' that." She indicated the red terror that reared its perilous height at the door and cautioned her charges to hold fast to the little handrails whatever.

This was something like adventure. Tearing and hurtling through the air, wind and dust smarting in your eyes, you strained forward against the rushing night. *She* sat beside you and was she, or was she not, just a little bit frightened at the dangers of their pace ? Her trim kid glove had a tiny split in it, so tightly did her hand clutch a brass rail beside her, and she gasped as her hat, despite its anchorage of veils, leaped and rocked on her head.

"Not frightened ? " the tall man asked who drove the devil of speed through the night. "That's right. Now hold tight. I can get seventeen out of her on the straight mile into Bunclody."

The circus tents and bright caravans stood in a field outside the village into which the motor, having triumphantly fulfilled her driver's boast, now ground her way. Everywhere the crowds of barefooted children and shawled women fled before

her, only when she came to a panting standstill did
they gather in an awed circle—a circle dispelled by
Pidgie, who had been hidden by Basil beneath the
rugs and was the only member of the party who
appeared unmoved by the circumstances of her
transit. Now she addressed herself to the business
of the moment—which was to rage with wicked
imprecations at the detested bare legs of little
boys.

Shortly after this Basil was lost. *She* thought the
lions might have eaten him, and indeed there he was
at their cage showing them to Pidgie. He even
boasted that she had put a foot through the bars
to prove she was not afraid. But he did not add
that he had held it there and Pidgie had hated the
whole performance.

At last the party settled down into their seats.
The show had already started and the clown with
his grievous white face was doing his turn with an
expressionless contortionist who folded himself
about like a flexible foot rule.

" How *does* he do it ? " Easter asked her father.
But he didn't know. Basil and Evelyn talked.

The big tent was warm with warm draughts
hurrying across it. It was full to the top, packed
tiers of faces. A low strip of red calico divided them
from the ring and two or three feet of grass.

Plump piebald horses, black and white, and
brown and white, stood with their feet on tubs
while one of them trotted round, lacing in and

out between the others, its movements directed by a tall girl with such a bold, anxious face.

The band played, endlessly suggestive of the tricks the animals were doing. A tiny pony with a head as long as a coffin, grave and very old, jogged round the grass and sawdust, while a little monkey clung to its crimson saddle-pad. A grim and sober pair they were, very intent on their business. A tall Irish boy introduced them and later held the pony's head while the high jumping mule cleared the grave pair.

The delightful clown appeared again but never too often. He turned somersaults, bumping on the hard ground with a most unselfish disregard for his person, and made countless good jokes. For his rudeness the circus proprietor first dismissed and then proceeded to undress him. He scurried out of the ring at last, clutching his shirt to him and pursued by hearty cheers.

A tall young man with terrific shelving muscles in his back and calves, braced his feet on the quarters of two docile, trotting piebalds, while he balanced a lovely acrobatic lady, now on his torso, now on his head, now at the full stretch of a steel wire arm. While he did slip tricks with his feet the audience held its breath, applauding with ardour as he bowed and gallantly left the lady to take all the applause.

Now horses came in. Troupes of girls in jockey caps and brilliant blouses sprang on their backs. Everything was gay except their tense faces as they

ran twisting and jumping across the ring. One girl
was so lame she could hardly stand, but when her
turn came she ran and leapt with the best of them.

A tiny dwarf with a vicious face, dressed in a
black tail-coat and white waistcoat, fought the clown
and delighted them hugely for ten minutes or more.
He danced, a black cane in his hands, mincing and
pirouetting his ridiculous feet, chasséing through
the sawdust with all the skill of a ball-room expert.

An acrobat mounted a tall swing. Gripping the
steel ropes with his hands he swung while the band
quickened unbearably. He went higher, higher,
higher. Up to the lights. Back. Up again. Farther.
Farther. . . . Easter shut her eyes, but over he
went—so they told her. Then there was the mule
that defied every effort made to capture it, kicking
and biting with indefeatable subtlety and in the
end, unsure whether or no to let its trainer catch it.
The clown mounted a high ladder while the band
played a tittuping, vulgar tune; he dipped and
ducked and pointed his toes and climbed to the
top where he rocked and swayed and fell with a
roaring crash, to save himself by magic.

The curliest of cur dogs and a vulgar, smooth-
haired fox-terrier with the monkey chained to his
collar, rode in turn on the back of the sorrowful
pony. He ran through bridges of wood and the
dogs jumped on the top of the bridges to avoid
being scraped off, and looked wisely down between
their forelegs, waiting for him to come through

again. When he did they dropped on his back as neatly as birds.

At last the circus was over, but warm and fanciful its memory flowed through their beings—marvellous fulfilment of all dreams of wonder. One little chord of disappointment crashed momentarily in Evelyn's mind.

" Where was the lion ? " he asked her. " Why didn't the lion come ? "

" *I've* seen the lion," Basil boasted in contentment. " Pidgie put her foot in between the bars. The lion roared——"

" *Basil !* "

" Oh, well, he didn't really roar, only he would have in a minute, I bet."

" It's what they tells me——" Evelyn looked up to see the red beard of O'Regan unmistakable in the pushing throng of faces that swayed out of the tent. " There's one o' them lions loose in the Puppetstown woods. He broke out o' the cage and legged it away from the lot o' thim. That's a fact— now I'll swear a hole through an iron pot, one o' the lads is after showing me where he med flithers of his kennel. Is it where would he go ? Maybe to the fox's burra' would he go——" The voices drifted away in the crowd, and Evelyn, whose mind had halted for a moment almost in panic, remembered with relief how swift would be their journey home—the swiftest, fiercest lion could never catch them.

" Did you hear ? " he asked Basil. But Basil had not heard, and what with the excitement of climbing again into the motor-car, Evelyn quite forgot to recount the news.

Not quite so fast their progress this time. Strange poppings and spittings took the place of the earlier clean roar of the engine. Far from touching her brilliant record of 17 m.p.h., the red motor-car, on the last faint slope of road towards Puppetstown, failed and spluttered and stopped. Her passengers got out and stood about her unable to offer assistance, mercifully unequipped to give advice. For some minutes her owner strove in vain with the mysteries that veiled her life spark.

" I think," said *She* at last, after a hushed conference with Mrs. Longworth, " you children had better run home by the wood avenue. And promise to go straight to your beds. *Does* the little boy promise Mother ? " She thought Evelyn looked the most doubtful of the party—Basil and Easter were only sleepy.

" Come too," Evelyn said. " *Oo, doo* come too."

It was undeniably tiresome of Evelyn. Even his small hand, holding tighter in hers than daylight and manliness ordinarily permitted, did not help Brenda over a feeling of faint disappointment that the evening had ended untimely. She had said to Dick, " If the thing doesn't go bring them back for the night," but she was afraid it would go. Indeed sudden sounds of re-awakened life in its

engine reached them through the night. Evelyn
trotted by her side, Basil and Easter lagged behind,
Pidgie barked in front.

"Send Basil on," Evelyn entreated with sudden
urgency. "Do please, *please* send him on in front."
It was not to be denied, that urgency. The funny
little boy.

"Run on, Basil, and catch Pidgie—why did you
leave her collar on? She'll get held up if she goes
to ground."

"Pidgie, Pidgie, Pig!" Basil darted off to
capture her. On ahead he raced through the tree-
shapes pale in the darkness, and Easter followed
him, blundering useless as a fat moth in all her coats
and sleepiness. And Evelyn, who had trotted so
hastily beside her, delayed now, hanging back and
dragging from her hand.

"Tired?" she asked. "No? Not tired? Why
did you ask me to send Basil on? *Won't* you tell
Mother?"

Out of the woods now. The friendly crunch of
gravel under his boots, the lights shining out one
by one from the windows of the house. Evelyn's
hand in hers relaxed its tenseness:

"I *knew* there was a lion in the wood," he said,
"and if we sent Basil on, his new long trousers
would attract the lion, and while he was eating
Basil, you and me could escape into the house."

"Oh, Evelyn! *Not* very brave, darling, was it?"
Too much for Evelyn. He was in tears, the little

boy, and all his ingenious plan for saving her in
bits and pieces. He was almost more than disappointed that the lion had not eaten Basil and so
justified him in his forethought. In tears he climbed
the stairs to bed. In the delicious sleepy solace that
comes when tears are dry, he wriggled, burrowing
deep into his bed. Nanny, folding up their clothes
when she came in from Easter's nursery, was prepared to hear an account of all the wonders of the
circus and all the dizzy excitement of speed. But
Basil, with his tongue in that still strange and toothless cavity in his mouth, and Pidgie's head on the
pillow beside his own, was already nearly asleep,
for his day had been most immoderately fraught with
excitement, and Evelyn, too, only blinked at her owl-
ishly as he sat up to have his ringworm anointed.

"The—motor-car broke," he said. "There were
lions," and he sighed a small, child's sigh before he
slept.

"Ah, God help them, the creatures, they're bet
up!" Nanny finished folding their sprawling garments and went out, shading the light with her hand.

"I'm after wasting a lot o' good fret over them
this night," she pondered, and heavily closed the door.

.   .   .   .

What hour it was when she woke to Evelyn's
screaming she did not stop to look. Grotesque in
her striped flannel nightdress, she was in his room,
and before a draught from the bellying curtain had
outed her candle, she saw him standing up in the

corner of his bed, squeezed against the wall and screaming—screaming—screaming. Basil, not to be out of it, awoke and roared, and Pidgie barked maniacly.

" How bad yez all are," said Nanny, with calculated and angry calm. " What a nice pastime it is for ye to waken me out o' me sleep. Have done now, Master Evelyn. Hould yer whist, Master Basil. Lions ? There's no lions nor tigers in this nursery. Wait now one minyute till I'll crack a match and ye can see for yourself."

But Evelyn was past seeing, hearing or caring. The lion was *there*, it had sniffed his sleeping face, brushed his body and thumped from his dark bed on to the dark floor. It might eat Nannie or Basil or any one it liked so long as the poor little boy escaped.

" Whist now," soothed Nanny, fumbling for her matches, and then in a snatch of time the candlestick and matches went with a clatter to the floor and Nanny herself was up on Evelyn's bed. " Jesu ! " she shrilled, " there's a great—*big*—RAT—afther—me ! He crossed out over me two feet and the two ears on me lad laid back this way. Loose the dog, Master Basil, before he'll cut our t'roaths."

Another thump and a terrific scattering through the darkness followed by horrid squalls from a cramped corner told that Pidgie had pinned something. It was Basil who found the matches, lit the candle and revealed to sight the sickly, snake-like corpse of one of Patsy's ferrets.

" Leave it, Pidgie ! Good Pidgie ! Brave Pidgie ! "
Basil picked her up ; panting and with blazing
eyes she set her four feet against his ribs. He turned
the ferret over with an unhesitating great-toe.
" That's Patsy's big-buck ferret he paid six-and-
sixpence for," he announced with awful calm, and
went back to bed.

Evelyn was too relieved to be ashamed of himself.
So blessed the relief that he forgot to remember
even how and why the ferret came to be in the
nursery. Its lion-like smell was stilled now for ever.
That was all that mattered. With it the wraith of
a lion was low. But before it had been laid, O'Regan,
did he but know it, had been most cruelly revenged.

But Nanny, because she was a little ashamed
(although of all just causes for hysterics, rats are
the least questionable), scolded with a fury and a
venom that knew no bounds and the object of her
wrath that little stinkin' tinker, the biggest rogue
in Ireland, with his thrashy dirty ferrets and his
lying and his poaching.

" It was me," Basil interrupted, " brought up the
ferret and put it in your bed." He sat up with much
dignity in his pyjamas.

" In *my* bed, Master Basil ? "

" I meant in Evelyn's bed "—no need to waste
good confession—" and I'm sorry now."

" Are you *real* sorry ? "

" Yes, my God ! " And Basil was thinking only
of the impossibility of acquiring the six-and-sixpence

necessary to replace the lord of the boot-room harem, but this only intensified the earnest solemnity of his apology.

So they were forgiven and Nanny left a candle to burn on the mantelshelf, its wavering small dagger of flame a strong link with the safety of honest daylight, and fumbled her way back to bed.

II

THIS is Basil. He is sixteen now—a queer age full of great boastings and great shyness and the discovery that you can sometimes hold a gun straight, but most often don't, and fishing is the sternest art and fox-hunting the greatest of life's importances. So grave Basil was, thinking mostly of his grey pony, Jesuit, and of Pidgie. He knew the name of every horse in training, though, its breeding and place in the handicap. He read Bailey's *Hunting Directory* and *Horse and Hound*, and could tell you all about birds. He and Evelyn were at Eton now. Evelyn liked school and Basil did not mind it when he was there, but going back made him nearly sick with unshed tears and coming home nearly sick with never-told happiness. Basil was still stubby and his dark hair lay well ; but Evelyn was shooting up into the very likeness of his mother, with a thin air of never-told reserve which, had she been given it, her beauty would have made men mad.

The great war had been fought for a year and more.
Easter's father was with the South Irish Horse.
Major Longworth was dead and the little birdy lady
married again. The names of most of the young
soldiers who had come and gone and fallen, at
Puppetstown, in and out of love with Aunt Brenda
were the names of young ghosts now.

Aunt Brenda did work for remounts and went
to dances at the Curragh. She had forgotten that
it was important to marry again. She was con-
scientious and efficient in her work and tired sometimes to a contentment past belief. Partly she felt
the war *must* be over before Evelyn was old enough
to go—and Basil, of course, too—and with a de-
delightful microscopity of vision she saw her work,
as an important cog in the great machine called
Winning this War. The solace and fortification this
lent to her spirit was as deep as it was calming.

The children did not notice the war very much.
Easter felt a pleasing importance when the post
brought her a letter from her father with censor
marks on the envelope, and she wrote to him dili-
gently, telling him about the hunting and the horses
and the dogs, and when Patsy's ferrets had pups,
and Fortune said the Polenious mare had slipped
her foal. She had seen her puppy, Rapture, hunting,
and regretted the fact that she tyed on the line
like a harrier. Happy Days had given her a cruel
fall ; she just folded up coming off a steep drop.
Fortune said her legs were bent. They'd had a right

hunt from Bradey's rocks—two hours and ten minutes—and stopped hounds in the dark. But Basil said they had changed foxes once at least, and Easter suspected they were hunting hare in the end, but the Master's wife was as pleased as a dog with two tails. Very important letters telling of all their doings and about the dogs—how Pidgie and Max and Kit had a dead sheep somewhere that no one could find, and how a badger had bitten out a piece of Max's jaw and a large treble tooth, and now he was very sore but very famous, and Easter enclosed the tooth and ended her letter :

" With love from
" EASTER."

Out of the schoolroom window at Puppetstown you looked across flat water—where Giles, the swan, sat in immemorial calm and the dogs hunted water rats and moorhens—over the Long Acres, where young blood horses moved in a stately decorum of beauty, away to the chill breasts of the mountains yielding themselves only to the slow rapture of a sunset ; thin and stark at any other time and remote as the grey women of the Sidhie that men had seen about their secret lakes. Mandoran, Mooncoin, and the Black Stair were these mountains' lovely names, and whatever was afar and unknown and remote unto themselves in the children, was joined and linked to the dispassionate ecstasy of these mountains.

Easter, at fourteen, was the queerest thing. In

love one moment with life, in despair the next. Wildly speechless when all she could not say burnt and deafened her whole being ; and again times when all the secrets of her days were poured out in easy luxuriant words. The divine talks she had with Patsy and with Fortune and with Basil and with Mary Josie too.

" I wonder you wouldn't get married, Josie," Easter would say, hitching herself on to the edge of her dressing-table while Mary Josie put away her clothes that lay in an abandonment of order round the room ; and Mary Josie would answer gravely : " Well, the way I'd look at it, Miss Easter, I wouldn't give a damn if I was married or single."

" Don't tell *me*, Josie ! An' all I heard about you and Jim Doyle."

" God, I wouldn't like him at all, Miss Easter. I'd never fancy a dark-skinned fella." Mary Josie was coyly appreciative of the badinage. " Did ye hear about Sunday going home from second Mass ? Well, he got up in the ass-car and sat down by me side, and the mother trottin' and beltin' th' ould pony down the hill behind us—wasn't that very remarkable ? *Oh !* " Impossible to reproduce the squirm of satisfied coquetry that accompanied the end of the tale.

" Do you love him, Josie ? " Easter asked very seriously, and Mary Josie would tell of his snug little farm and how only for the sour old mother she'd have him to-morrow—" a nice quiet decent boy "—

unlike the jockey fellows she had known in her
time, "and thim lads 'd take advantage of ye
while ye'd be lookin' at them."

"Well, you're a dinger after men," Easter would
assert, and add, as she strolled out of her room,
"I'll wear my blue velveteen to-night."

"Do, Miss Easter. I love ye in that little dress.
The cream silk collar suits ye grand."

And Easter would leave her room, leave Mary
Josie tidying up and banking the fire that had
been lit since before she got up this morning in the
high slender oval grate of an Adams's fireplace.
Such a room! Easter slept in a bed with four fluted,
soaring posts and a canopy of insanitary but divine
brocade. Max slept with her, his head on her pillow.
From the far mantel-shelf a Ming horse of untold
worth and beauty was flanked by photographs in
and out of their frames: of Daddy in uniform:
of Basil in very short trousers and of Evelyn in very
long trousers: of Aunt Brenda with white muslin
folded precariously above her bosom. But Easter
kept the Ming horse there because to look at it gave
her a curious shiver of delight. It was as remote as
Mandoran, Mooncoin and the Black Stair, and as
aged. But she also loved her picture of a lady
jumping a post and rails with a ruddy and beautiful
gentleman in a red coat beside her, and a hound just
about to be jumped upon in the fore-front of the
glowing scene. There were many books by Easter's
bed, shelves built into the alcoves in the wall held

them. Ah, rapturous moments she had known with Tennyson ! The unbearable sweet pallor of Rossetti. Tears and an aching throat and a heart that cried out with that Blessed Damozel. But to be more modern, there was that poet of all poets, who wrote of vague scarlet women and scarlet lamps and bright scarlet sins, rich rhythms drawing you to an ecstasy of emotions in which the Ming horse and the mountains had neither lot, part nor inheritance. And—still more modern—Rupert Brooke, who sang the beauty and the gallantry of war, glorifying the dust and ashes of bloody sacrifice and holding patriotism for an unblatant moment in his poet's hands. Curled in that vast bed, Easter would read and read with icy shoulders and a burning mind. She read but she never thought until one day she found and read a book of Aunt Brenda's that left her one crying discovery of this unknown forbidden magic—this so strange Love. Such an indecent book it was as to testify unkindly to the possibly vinaigrous virginity of the authoress, but *what* a woman Easter thought her as she gulped hot draughts from this bottled wine of life and dreamed on love only.

Easter was to go to school this year, next year, sometime—when the war should be over it was now because of the risk of submarines in the Channel; in the meantime there she was alive and natural, a dangerous, childish, waking person.

" Basil," she went calling down the passages. " Basil—Basil——"

Basil, who had been talking to Nanny as she sat in a patch of winter sunlight, the queer clear sun of a November afternoon, mending away at a heap of socks as many coloured as a globe, came lounging out of the nursery—Pidgie had her pups in the nursery, she was the fiercest mother and cherished her young most savagely.

"Come out, Basil," Easter said, and they went down through the afternoon house together. The straight light lay on the edges of tables, and the least dust looked heavy as pollard. Aunt Dicksie came out of the drawing-room with letters in her hand : " Post these like good children," she said. " I have five hundred bulbs to plant this afternoon. Easter, my darling, *did* you tell them to send up the eggs by three o'clock ? Not ? Then I simply can't face the cook. Go to the kitchen and see if I left my gardening gloves there—I may have."

" If they're going mad looking for eggs, there's a black hen that stole her nest up in the stable loft this minute. I saw six eggs in it yesterday." Basil pulled a short cane out of the medley of hunting whips and fox's brushes and field-glasses that cluttered a table near the hall door. " I'll send Fortune in with them," he promised, and he and Easter went out quickly while the charges that she wished to lay on them slipped like fish through the meshed net of Aunt Dicksie's mind.

Easter and Basil were going to ride. " Come on out," at Puppetstown only meant, " Come on out

and exercise a horse "; so when they had told
Fortune about the black pullet's eggs, and Fortune
had given his considered opinion as to their probable
age, and added that there was nothing you'd want
to be so exact about as eggs for a cake, he pulled
out Easter's horse and led it round the yard till
its back should go down. This was Happy Days,
a well-bred little chestnut mare, fired all round, and
with every known stable vice, so that she looked a
very poor thing indeed. She had no manners but was
an indefeatable jumper. Easter rode her in a plain
snaffle, and had almost less than no control of her
in a hunt, but she sat on her like a rock and smiled
pleasantly when she was taken charge of.

Easter's saddle had been a good saddle enough
when Aunt Brenda was a girl of eighteen. It was
now something of a curiosity. That Easter did not
give every horse she rode in it a sore back says
something for the straightness of her seat ; she did
not hang out of those sickling pummels.

Up the long straight avenue rode Basil and
Easter ; Basil on a beautifully made, iron grey
pony that napped horribly on the road and would
be sold one day to play polo. Basil had a nice,
easy-looking way of riding—a faint swing about the
shoulders and his heels well down. He wore a
brown check coat of which he was very proud ; it
had once belonged to his Uncle Dick and had been
cut down till it was quite good on Basil. The same
cannot be said for Aunt Brenda's olive-green habit

that nipped Easter's waist, spread its stiff fan round her hips and flowed amply to her feet. There was nothing attractive about it. Curious perhaps, a little like a faint engraving; Easter looked absurdly of no age in the grown-up habit and a shallow, curly bowler like a black halo for her wild, prim, child's face. Her hair was in two thick short plaits.

Out of the tall gates, they rode past an empty little wood, afar from the greater woods of Puppetstown; all its pale tree stems like lonely arms condemned to a passionless for ever. In the summer months Evelyn and Basil and Easter would tryst there on a Sunday afternoon to smoke rash cigarettes, their backs comforted against a sunny, hot wall. They clipped their cigarettes in half with a pair of nail scissors—thus you had two cigarettes instead of one. Here the dogs hunted through the bracken.

Now they talked, Easter and Basil, of hunts they had seen and hunts they had not seen and why; of horses and men and hounds and racing (they were both devout students of form). Basil told her a long complicated tip he had for next year's Derby. Once an ass-cart, rattling past, driven by a cloaked old woman, sent his grey pony soaring into the air and whipping round for home.

" I hate that Jesuit," Easter said, for Jesuit was the pony's name. " He'll come back with you one of these days, Basil. And he's a very moderate jumper. I know I didn't like him when I rode him."

This pleased Basil, who said : " Of course *he* liked

the horse, but it wasn't everybody's horse, for if he didn't actually fall, he never put a foot quite right any fence he jumped."

"Well, you saw the end of that good hunt from Lara hill on him," Easter interrupted with extreme tact, and Basil was pleased and told her what Fortune had said about the way she sat on Happy Days when Happy Days had bucked in rings round the yard last Thursday. All then was accord between the pair of them.

In the steep trough of a pale stony hill a young strong stream leapt out across the road. There was a little bridge for foot people to one side, hollowed and curling, and gorse with a faint scatter of gold flowers darkened the brief steep valley and the thimble-shaped hill behind. The sun was low now and the red lamps of a crooked thorn died in the evening. A bleak and lovely heron rose from his fishing on poetical strong wings and flew slowly down the valley.

Jesuit wanted to drink the cold mountainy water. Basil thought not ; and it was to Easter that the cry of hounds came, their thin striving, silver cry, from off that wine-dark little hill. Magically followed a tattered note on the horn, doubled raucously sweet against the evening.

Listen !

Easter flung up her head and her hand. The world for an instant was still, as quiet as might be in the hands of evening. And then again the wild notes

fluttered from the far, shrill horn and, in the open
now, came again the clustered, striving voices of
hounds hunting a fox, by distance enchanted,
glorious and romantical. . . .

That certain fever which is as a lust and a madness
of the body as well as of the mind, savagely alight
in them, the children dropped their hands and sent
their horses clattering up the rocky gully of the
road. At the hill's crest Basil stopped as if he'd been
shot, for, atop the lowest point of the bank that
dropped steeply to the road, a fox stole swiftly
down, delayed and listened one sliding, careful
second on the bank out of the road (his muzzle was
grey and his brush was nicked), before he crossed
the field, and over the next fence he seemed as
small as a cat in the evening.

Mighty and thunderous the children's hearts, hot
with that wild bravery the view of a fox inspires.
But Basil had a certain sense of venery that lent
him wits even at the hottest moment.

"Keep an eye down the road, Easter," he said. "He
may run the river bank and cross back at the bottom."
And Easter, swinging the mare about, was gone.

Five minutes, and they seemed five hours, while
the hounds hunted steadily towards them. A bit
of scent, with the chill taste of frost nipping the
air, there was, and Jer Donohughe's ten and a half
couples of half-bred foxhounds enjoyed every inch
of it. Each one must have it before the slowest
would get forrad a yard with their leaders. Not

much drive but they'd hunt a fox gone an hour in front of them. To Basil, turning the Jesuit round and round again in the road, and to Easter, her eyes screwed on the river crossing, their music was God's most glorious, their wisdom a sanctity and a corner-stone, their huntsman chosen among all men.

Basil could see him now a field behind his hounds ; he was always with them and never seemed to hurry. To-day he rode a gaunt shadow of a white mare. He had taken his hounds out because the humour for a hunt was on him. He knew he should not have drawn Kilooley Hill so late in the evening ; and young Bernard (his brother and whipper-in) likely enough lying quinched in a ditch below that Kilbrennan four-year-old. He'd stop them the first minute he could, but—be the Holy !—they were running on nicely now. A lifted hat on the Puppetstown road—who would that be ? If it wasn't the two Puppetstown children, drunk with excitement. Well, no two ways about it, they must have their hunt. And his cheer as they crossed the road was as much for his field as to his hounds.

Free from wire that country, and was it not well for them, Basil and Easter and Jer Donohughe ? Jer Donohughe's white mare was a milky beacon before the children in the grey light as he led them across bank and stone wall and bank again. His hounds were hunting at a faster pace now over this grand grass country. The solons of the pack were beat for pace, though still a string joined the head and the tail. In the lead a strange, copper-coloured harrier and a lemon-pie bitch . . . Danger, Racer, Daffodil, and three and a half couples more before the tail lengthened to old Diligent, a great authority for a fox and a wonder to take a line down a cold, frozen road, but she can run up no longer. Not such a cry now, nearly mute they race into the evening.

Crabbed and cunning, with quarters like a squat ark, Jer Donohughe's white mare deals with each fence as it comes. Long abandoned the pride which earlier in the chase compelled them to choose their own place in every fence and charge it unfaltering, the children follow. The Jesuit is going steadily now ; though, for the first mile, it was hit them and leave them and tip them and go with him, and only the luck being kind saved Basil the fall that was due at each fence.

Easter, though no longer a passenger, goes cracking on into the highest and narrowest banks with a loose rein and a heart two fences at least before her, a virgin votaress to the very sacrament of fox-hunting, effort hers and the wild fulfilment of an hour.

Down a glen of grey hazel the hounds ran the wet bank of a little river and turned short from it to strive and scramble up the rocky face of that steep glen. Jer Donohughe jumped off and plunged down towards them on his feet : " He's in the rocks, by God ! " he said. And the old mare stood with her lean, proud head up, like a faery horse on

the edge of the dark glen, while the last light was
a slow spear thrust behind Mandoran, Mooncoin
and the Black Stair.

" Leu wind 'im—there ! Leu wind 'im, wind
'im," and the winged stammer of notes on the
horn came again from where the hounds marked,
growling and shoving between the grey stone lips
of the fox's earth. A retreat and a harbour it was
for the Thief of the World, of most impregnable
safety. " Leu wind 'im there," and their voices
strove in the dusk.

Then up a twisting goats'-path Jer Donohughe
came stumbling back to his field of two, his hounds
round him and before him—Accurate, Wistful,
Acrobat, Sampler, and all the rest that had so meri-
toriously deserved their fox. With stars pricking
the sky and the last long notes on the horn a silence
at last, they jogged down the little roads that spun
their careful mesh about the country, adventuring
into the near dark hills to serve one small house
only and curling hopefully on towards the high road
to Dublin.

This was the time for great talking, for the
glorious reliving of those sixty-five brave minutes.
The recapturing of every dangerous second lent a
rapture of the gods to the homeward way. No
Nimrod of old ever had more of the blood and bones
of *Foxy-ness* in him that Jer Donohughe. He loved
his hounds and he loved a hunt, and there was not
a fence in that little triangle of country, which his

uncle (the great Jer Donohughe) had hunted before
him, that he did not know. Had he not jumped
them all many times and often on the young horses
that he bred on that limestone land of his, and made
into such good hunters as are not often found—
" Born with a horn in his hand," he was a natural
genius of a huntsman, a horseman and a liar. The
last trickle of gentle blood ran dimly in his veins ;
there was an affinity between his lean hawkish lines
and that old grey house where he lived, with its
lovely mantelpieces and leaking roof, filthy stable-
yard and rare shrubs fighting feebly for existence
between shooting thickets of sycamore and towering
Portugal laurels. He had no education and his
speech was the direct, illuminating speech of the
people. His uncle (the great Jer Donohughe) had
despised his ignorance and valued his cunning (his
trickle of the gentle blood ran a generation stronger
than his nephew's), and found him as a rough
rider, whipper-in and farm-hand too useful to be
spared for the lesser purposes of education. Now,
the great Jer Donohughe was almost a legend, and
Jer Donohughe had succeeded long ago to hounds
and estate with his young brother Bernard (who had
received some education and was slighty ashamed
of Jer) to turn hounds to him and be his heir, for
Jer would never marry now ; he was fifty-two, and
none of his dallyings had resulted in matrimony,
although they had at times a less creditable (if
less binding) conclusion.

"Now that's a right cut of a pony," said Jer
Donohughe to Basil, as one man to another. "I saw
him light clean in on the top of a fence with you, and
never a living twig shook on the face of it."

"And the first three banks he jumped he never
left an iron on them," shrilled Basil and Easter in
excited unison.

"And Happy Days never put a foot wrong all
the way——"

"And wasn't that an awful drop over the stone
wall—— ? "

"I saw you go out on his two ears ; I thought
you'd never meet the saddle again——"

"Did you see *me* jump the high devil with the
stones in it ? Did you, Mr. Donohughe ? "

"I saw you riding for it very wicked, Miss Easter,
and you had a right to jump it out of a stand."

And Easter's laugh shrilled out on the frosty air.
Jer Donohughe's coat was the colour of blackberries,
his hounds were slim ghosts and his horse a fanciful
white moth : Life was delight, and the stars rang
faintly in the skies. Now the hounds were lapping
as they splashed through a little stream, drinking
its waters noisily. Now it was : "Daffodil—Daffodil,
old lady ! " as a pale bitch loitered, fostering her
lameness. Jer Donohughe, who needed no whipper-in
in the field, whose hounds would instantly fly to
him when he wanted them, would have it that to
get them back to kennels without the help of the
children was a matter past hope of fulfilment. So

they rode home with the hounds to the propped and shattered gates, divinely proportioned, of Ballyluff (where the Donohughes lived) and there, the horn sounding their coming, his hounds broke away to their kennels. And Jer gave his hounds flesh, the children watching the grim, exact savagery of the rite before going in to eat a vast tea (eggs and sausages, soda bread, barm-brack and blackberry jelly) in a room where a good fire blazed and mouldering foxes' masks grinned from the gloom and dust of the walls, and hunt-fixture cards of years past were a frieze of memory along the mantel-shelf.

Night when they got on their horses in the kennel yard, and their cheeks bulged with the bulls'-eyes Jer Donohughe gave them to keep the cold out on the way home, they rode the dark avenue singing songs (through the bulls'-eyes) and congratulating themselves that their horses had pulled out sound after their half-hour in a stable. And the blinded windows of Ballyluff stared after them palely.

. . . .

" And in the great name o' God, what should keep yez out this time o' night ? " Fortune greeted them, a stable lantern in his hand which he clapped on the ground as he went to take Happy Days from Easter. " Be the Holy ! " he said, " me horses is gutthered to blazes—I'll bet ten bob to the sight o' me eyes ye were going mad through the country after Mister Donohughe's Harriers ? Well, would no time fit yez for a hunt only the dark of night ? "

" Oh, don't be vexed, Fortune——"

" *Dear* Fortune——"

" We've had *such* a hunt."

" From Kilooley Hill to Garrylofty."

" God be good to us ! How did the Jesuit go for ye, Master Basil ? Did he fall ? "

" The devil a fall—he went the best."

" Did he scutch with ye ? "

" The devil a scutch—he was mad to jump every fence he saw before him."

" Well, that bates the devil—he a great little hardy little beggar."

Bridles were off and saddles as well, and Fortune and two nondescript underlings fussed and chided to and fro about the horses, while Basil and Easter leaned against stable doors, boasting tireless and insatiable, and young horses stamped and whinneyed in near boxes, and Easter's hound pup came in to trifle with her fondly. They left Fortune at last and stormed into the house, told Patsy they had had a great hunt and they hoped the bath water was hot, and went on to the drawing-room. Here Aunt Brenda was playing cards with two soldiers from the Camp and the wife of one of them, and only said : " *Well*, I thought the pair of you must be lying under your horses in a wet ditch somewhere. And what are you going to ride when the hounds meet here on Thursday ? I bet Happy Days don't pull out sound for the next week. However, I know a hunt with Jer Donohughe is the breath of life to you——" And she laughed her lovely, indulgent laugh and returned to the bridge.

Aunt Dicksie was waiting for them on the curve of the stairs. "*Children!* Have you had your teas? What have you been doing—tell me—*what* a good hunt! And such a lovely bit of country. And you enjoyed it, darling Easter? *And* that horrid Jesuit went well. If I'd known you were riding him, darling Basil, I'd have been mad with anxiety—but I wouldn't have known you were having a hunt, would I? So after all—mind yourself, Easter! How dark it is—has Patsy forgotten to light the lamp, or did I forget to give him the key of the paraffin? Anyhow, he's busy now, he's carrying up buckets of boiling water to the bathroom for you, because it's not very hot in the taps. Now, I wonder if those people playing bridge are going to stay for dinner. I must go and see." And Aunt Dicksie went downstairs, her candle flame a prick of yellow in the damp well of darkness.

A fire blazed up the chimney in Easter's room, a leaping, dog-toothed frenzy of rose and blue turf and wood flame, and a faint curtain of its scent hung ravished about the Ming horse. A horse was Easter's song to-night. She swept the lesser gods away from this ancient idol, and a worship for the delight and the frenzy of the chase seized her mind like a prayer in the sacrificial light of that fire burning below the aged strange horse. "I love," her heart cried, "I love Mr. Donohughe—I love hunting and Fortune

and Patsy and Basil——" Delight seized her so
that she wept.

" Miss Easter "—there was a muffled knock at
the door—" Miss Easter, leave the water in the
bath for Master Basil, I'm not able to squeeze
another drop out o' that One Below—she tore the
face off me and every dirty little tinker's curse she
put on me I wouldn't choose to repeat."

" All right, Patsy—Patsy !—tell Master Basil I'll
be out in ten minutes."

On her way back from the bath Evelyn and Easter
met : Evelyn very tall like a young novice in his
long blue dressing-gown ; Easter wore its twin
(which Basil had outgrown at his preparatory
school), and in it she looked indescribably of no sex
or age. Her hair was twisted in a screw on the top
of her head. Nanny had embroidered rabbits' heads
on the toes of her flat flapping slippers. Her legs,
white streaks as straight and narrow as pencils,
were swallowed up in the dark bell-mouth of her
dressing-gown's skirt.

" Oh, Evelyn, did you hear about our hunt ?
Oh, *Evelyn*, I do wish you'd had it too. Have you
seen Basil ? Did he tell you ? "

Evelyn, who had heard for the preceding half-
hour of nothing but the hunt he had missed, was
still creditably full of enthusiasm and interest. He
went back with Easter to her room and sat down by
her fire to listen and question.

" And what did you do, Evelyn ? "

Ah, that was just it. Could Evelyn have so magnanimously enjoyed the relation of their great doings with nothing to show out of the ordinary for the hours of his own afternoon ? He could not.

" Oh, I went up the Red Bog after snipe," he replied with becoming carelessness, and he added thoughtfully : " They were pretty wild."

" And how many did you get ? " Evelyn's shooting was a bitter matter at times, so Easter rather dreaded to ask a question which might precipitate them in gloom.

Evelyn threw a sod of turf on the fire and a log after the sod of turf, and replied, with a hardly concealed smirk of complete satisfaction : " Three-and-a-half couples and a woodcock."

Seven snipe and a woodcock. It was almost unbelievable for Evelyn to have slain so many. Basil had never equalled that and he was better with his gun than Evelyn. Indeed this was a day to live for ever.

" *Evelyn*—how marvellous ! You must have been shooting terribly well."

" Oh, no. I missed a lot of quite easy shots."

" But if they were getting up wild ? "

" And there was one Peter couldn't find, I think it must have been stuck on a bush. I was awfully lucky about the cock, Easter. It was on the way home and the light was pretty bad when Peter put him up out of a thick bit of covert near the drain in the gate wood. I blazed away and hit him hard but he carried on into the field. We spent simply

ages looking for him. Peter found him on the edge
of the ditch where you were so sick cigaretting last
summer. Peter worked terribly well all day. He's
asleep now. He was too tired to eat his dinner. I
shall give him a lovely dinner later on. I only wish
it was liver and bacon. I would like him to have his
favourite food. Come in ! Who's that knocking,
Easter ? Come in ! "

It was Patsy who had been bidden to say that
there was only what cutlets would go around the
company and the children were to dine in the
schoolroom.

" Thank God ! We can stay in our dressing-
gowns then——" Easter tied her hair viciously
back with a piece of black ribbon. " Let Master
Basil know, Patsy. And—*Patsy* "—as the door
closed—" what about those snipe Master Evelyn
brought in ? Is she cooking them for dinner ? "

" Well, I'll take me oath she's not. Sure the
kitchen-maid's out and ye wouldn't see That One
sit down pluckin' snipes in a hurry."

" Well, whip three of them out of the larder,
Patsy, and bring them up to the schoolroom."

" And some butter——"

" Yes, and flour and a saucepan——"

" And bread for toast——"

That was the start of a wild night. In the schoolroom by the light of one lamp and an army of
candles in branching Sheffield candlesticks, they sat
in a solemn ring, plucking snipe with staccato

inaptitude and wiping their sticky, feathery fingers surreptitiously upon each other's dressing-gowns. Basil discovered Evelyn doing this, and mightily incensed, emptied the fish basket of feathers over his head. Everywhere were feathers. The boys fought and trod on one of the snipe and the dogs sneezed and fought too, so that Evelyn and Basil had to stop and separate them.

Easter squeezed the trodden snipe back into shape and put it into the saucepan with the other two, and nearly half a pound of butter, and sat her down to watch the brew and make toast.

Pidgie came in and Basil must cease from making war, and make love to her instead. He wanted to hear how her favourite child was to-night, and if she still enjoyed being a mother.

Patsy appeared to lay the table—they grew drunk on the news that Miss Dicksie had said he was to bring the port in to them after dinner. Evelyn sat down to play on the untuneful schoolroom piano. He had just mastered the honeyed hesitancies of Dvorak's *Humoresque* and thought it the loveliest thing in this world. Basil, who had taken the gramophone to pieces yesterday, now busily fitted its pieces together again because he preferred " John Peel "; but, though he clamoured for it, Evelyn, caught away in an ecstasy of his own, paid no attention. The delight of this day was in his pausing hands singing out the chastened, languishing melody.

Listening, Easter dropped tears upon her burning toast : Evelyn to her was wonderful, the person of all persons who was afar unto himself—like the Ming horse, like the mountains. Then he crashed a discord (which he said was like the smell of burnt toast) and came over to see how his snipe were cooking while " John Peel " twanged shakily on the air from the reconstructed gramophone, and Patsy came in with the soup.

" Soup, Patsy ? Why, our snipe aren't half cooked yet. Take it out. Keep it hot. Don't bring it yet."

" Easter, those snipe are very nearly cooked enough."

" They are not."

Basil came sniffing. " We can't eat raw flesh, we'll get as savage as Jer Donohughe's Harriers."

" Snipe only want to look at the fire."

" Well, these haven't even done that yet."

" You had your tea at Jer Donohughe's—I didn't have any."

" Well, that's a fact too. Start your soup, Evelyn, I'll shake the snipe-pot for a bit. They're oozing blood yet "—thus Basil, prodding with a fork. " Tell Patsy to bring up some more wood for this fire next time he comes, Easter."

Soup and snipe (burning hot and dripping butter and blood on their slabs of toast), roast mutton and red currant jelly, chocolate souffle and toasted cheese, the children ate ; and drank port with due ceremony after. They drank to fox-hunting and to Jer Donohughe's hounds and to the covert that held to-day's fox (might it never prove blank), and Evelyn (as was proper), proposed the fox-hounds, and said they should have come first among the toasts; however, it was now too late to think of that, so they made amends by drinking the toast with their feet on the table. Then they decanted two wine-glassfuls into a medicine bottle (for Fortune) and, collecting all dogs, went out, girding their dressing-gowns about them, to see how the horses were after their hunt, and to draw the stable lofts for a cat, for the stable-boys' lovers, or any game that might come handy for a hunt.

Fortune they found in his saddle-room. A stove burnt brightly. Long ranks of bridles hung in endless perspective upon the dark panelled walls, the lamp-light glancing from plain snaffle to gag, from half-moon pelham back to twisted snaffle. Every variety of bit, in fact, made to go in a horse's mouth, their clean steel shone out like evening stars from the dark wall. Saddles on their stands towered one above another, smelling darkly of saddle-soap and oil, and stirrup irons (in a glass-faced cupboard) caught curves and strokes of light. The bridles the children had ridden their horses in to-day hung from a wire hook in the middle of the room, and their saddles were turned up to dry.

Fortune was looking at the paper when they came in. This was his evening unalterable affectation, for he was quite unable to read. But he kept up the pretence so studiously that even the stable lads were deceived, until one unlucky day he was discovered reading the field for the National with the paper upside down. " Wouldn't any b—— fool be able to read it the right way up ? " was his lightning answer to the boy, who dared comment. The unfailing photographic memory of the illiterate served him well—he was a perfect record of the turf.

He stood up when the children and their dogs came in, and drank off the medicine bottle of port much as though he was taking the Sacrament. " Best respects, Miss Easter—Master Basil—Master Evelyn," and tipped it down with strange and various noises, for the bottle-neck was narrow.

" Horses all right, Fortune ? Did they eat up their feed ? "

" They did, Master Basil ; they took a hell of a delight in it. They didn't leave what a bird'd pick after them."

" What about Happy Days's back ? "

" Well, 'tis the least sign up, Miss Easter. But sure that wouldn't signi-one-bit-a-fy. She'll be right a-Thursday, God willing."

" Are you sure, Fortune ? "

" I am—certain sure, I gave it a great steeping with salt and water—that'll crown her, you'll see."

Evelyn said : " I wish Tom Jones had had that hunt this afternoon. He gave me a rough ride this morning round the Long Pasture. I went out on his neck once, and I was gone—only he waited for me to get back."

" Ah, 'twas the rain vexed him," Fortune spoke indulgently. Tom Jones was his favourite among the children's ponies, " above all ever I seen he hates the rain. Cripes Almighty ! that's the coldest little lad in the world. Now if he seen a bucket o' water coming in the stable door of a frosty morning he'd commence to shiver till he'd have every hair on him standing out from his body."

They stood round the stove scorching the tails of their dressing-gowns for some time longer. Basil picked up the paper and read out the racing news and Fortune's eyes snapped his derision for the wisdom of " our correspondent." Basil had a little book on form in his dressing-gown pocket. He read it especially in bed and in the lavatory ; and they took a dip into that and then had another go at the paper and proved themselves right without a doubt.

The dogs sniffed about for mice, and Peter (Evelyn's cocker and one of the day's heroes) snapped a mouse-trap on his nose or almost, which was a more than shattering incident, especially as in the general consternation Pidgie secured the cheese with which the trap had been baited. Then Evelyn said they must go and rattle the lovers out of the hay-loft, and they moved off to the night's draw, lifting the dogs one by one up the pigeon-hole ladder to the lofts.

Darkly the lofts towered and stretched, their

purplest blackness storied hay; their distances
hazardous floor space, riddled with holes to catch
the toe of the uncircumspect and send him crashing
to a fall. Many a dangerous hunt the children had
seen there with Joe Byrne and Tommy Norris (the
stable boys) for game. Never to be forgotten was
the evening when, unkennelled before the pack,
one Bridgie Foley, led them a stern chase through
the lofts, while her tardy and craven lover, Tommy
Norris, cycled furiously into the night madly estab-
lishing alibis for his innocency of the tryst he had so
luckily delayed to keep. Sometimes they hunted
rats. To-night a wild cat growling in a corner was
dangerous game. Her eyes spat greenly at the dark.
At last she broke covert and was gone, a darker
meteor in the darkness. Wild the children's voices;
wild the torn cape of starred sky, breached by a
curious round of window through which their
hunted cat shot like a rocket to land in the swaying
safety of a laurel tree. The dogs stopping themselves,
with their toe-nails on the utmost edge of the sill,
leaned out, vainly screaming into the night.

The horses then were visited and Happy Days
had her back pinched three separate times and
flinched three separate times before they pulled her
sheet back and gave her the sugar that Easter kept
in her dressing-gown pocket for distribution. The
Jesuit was lying down in the deep straw of his box,
and Basil said: " Ah, me poor fellow ! " with deep
satisfaction that he had won so much of his own

back to-day—for the Jesuit had given him many
unpleasant and unsatisfactory rides. But to-day
he had ridden him well and the Jesuit had carried
him the best.

The night air pinching through their dressing-
gowns at last they went back to the house, and
finding the decanter still on the schoolroom piano,
had another whack of port all round, then rang the
bell for Patsy.

" Have a drink, Patsy."

Patsy looked from Evelyn, pale and fiery, to
Basil, dark and foolishly smiling, and last to Easter
burning through with excitement. He observed
that there was no more than one glass left in the
decanter, and he said : " I will, Master Evelyn,
thank you," without hesitation.

" What tune would you like on the gramophone,
Patsy ? I'll play you your favourite tune. Any tune
you say, Patsy, my gramophone will play it."

" I'll put you and your gramophone out through
the window." Evelyn was very fierce and proud.
" If any one wants music I'll play music. If any one
wants a fight, I'll fight. If any one wants a hunt,
I'll go out and draw the laurels now."

" I want to play cards," said Easter.   Who will
play cards ? "

" Come on, we'll have a game of cards with Patsy."

" Oh, God, Master Evelyn ! Sure, I haven't the
half o' the dinner things washed up yet. The
One Below'll tear the face off me."

" Dammit, Patsy, are you a man or what are you to be frightened of an old woman ? " Evelyn, too, had been bitten with a sudden lust for cards. So they cut for partners and they played whist (a game much in vogue with them). Patsy played with the excitement and venom of the Irish. He licked his thumb and dealt the cards around for the second rubber, his washing-up forgotten, the vengeance of the morrow forgotten.

The lamp went out and the candles burnt low in their silver sockets, and still the young Chevingtons played cards. They played for stakes (Patsy's partner carrying his losses, that was understood), and in no gambling house of earlier days did ever a great-grandfather of Evelyn's lose more gracefully than he did, or prove a more gallant bettor. Easter, holding the end of her tongue between her teeth, played a thoughtful and painstaking game. She concentrated with all the emphasis born of the knowledge that it was not beyond possibility for her partner to mete out corporal punishment for her mistakes. Basil knew where the cards lay. He was cute as a dog in this and other games. Patsy was perhaps the best player of the lot of them, with an exact and unfaltering memory, but then he never, or hardly ever, held cards.

On into the night they played, the cards falling quietly between them, the candles dying two by two till only a branch of three set upon the table lighted the game and crooked their cowled shadows to the ceiling. The fire was hollow and the dogs were sniffing and fidgeting unhappily before Basil and Evelyn had wrangled out the last score, and Easter and Basil had divided one and eleven pence to the equal halfpenny between them. They stood up stiff and yawning and cold and wished that they had not been so free with the port, for a thimbleful now would prove most comforting.

The dogs sat and looked at them expectantly as they stood with their backs to what was left of the fire. Evelyn yawned again and snapped his fingers to Peter. "He had a canker in his ear," he said. "I was reading about a great cure for canker in the *Field*. This man says——"

A storm of barking from the assembled terriers effectively quenched Evelyn's relation of this man's sayings.

"Curs! Blast ye, curs! *Shoor-up!*" Basil's rate rang above their voices.

Patsy said: "'Tis nothing. 'Tis the wind"; he had heard a little knocking at the window. He picked up the empty decanter and the wine-glasses and was whisking out of the room when the knock came again and the dogs broke forth in furious accord.

"There's some one at the window." Easter pulled back the curtains and peered down, seeing at last a white patch that was a face outside the glass.

"I'll speak to him, miss. What a time he should choose to come, whoever he is." Patsy slapped up the window and leant out.

"A telegram." The children even detected the relief in his voice. "God save ye, Michael. Was it to walk out on yer two feet from Bunclody this unmerciful hour o' night ye done ? "

" I did begor' ! And I'm going around and around this half hour roaring and battering and ringing bells and there's not one o' yous, blast yous, could step out to the door."

" Well, here's two shillings for him anyway." Basil took the telegram from Patsy. "Who's it for ? Miss Dicksie. Well, she can't answer it till the morning so it may as well wait till then. *I* won't wake her up to read it, and I bet no one else will either. So there it may stay." He put it down among the spilt cards. " Don't forget it in the morning, Patsy. Good-night. Good-night, Michael." Basil was off to bed.

Evelyn followed.

Easter, with Max and Kit in attendance, found her way to her room and fell exhausted into bed and dreamless to sleep.

His head out of the window, Patsy listened still to whispered words in the darkness—" Nine o'clock Thursday night—by the Fall Rocks, 'tis an order from the Hills—the column to parade in full stren'th—there's to be an inspection o' the boys——"

" God save ye, Michael. Good-night."

" So long, now, Patsy."

Patsy came over to the table where the telegram was lying. He turned the envelope over and back again.

"God rest his soul—the poor Major," he murmured. "God grant him to see the Light o' the Glory o' Heaven. He was a good sort." He pinched out the last candles and slipped without a sound through the dark house he knew so well to his bed in the boot-room.

"Ah, God help them," he thought, as he dropped asleep. "They should have the day's fun out—the creatures——"

.   .   .   .

And so it was not till the next morning that they heard Easter's father had been killed in France.

III

THE moment that for four years had been a milestone in the world's mind had come—that mystic moment that should see the accomplishment of all dreams and all resolutions—"after the war." But so many poor plans were broken in that war, and so little resolve was left towards anything, that the moments and days and months wavered on into uncertainty of time and saw but pitiful accomplishment.

But there was a generation that had skipped the war by a few merciful years. The war had pulled their lives about strangely, it is true, more strangely than they could realise, but it had not put them out of focus with a life of peace time. They were too young to have suffered very much : too young

to remember very much. Kinder stars had crowned
the sky and ruled their begetting. Of this generation were Evelyn and Basil and Easter. The war
had been to them a matter of periodical great
excitements.

They had enormously enjoyed the beginning of it
—August, 1914, was a time of great cheer and excitement. After that Christmas Aunt Dicksie and
her war-maps and the blood-thirsty cartoons which
she fastened to her bedroom wall with pins, became
but an ordinary part of life, such as the dogs' dinners
or exercising your pony. Of course, they hated the
Germans—but that was a commonplace of religion.

Then there was the awful time when Easter's
father was killed—that did hurt them, and the bruise
of it took long to die out. They loved him. They
were proud of him. They missed him for a time,
increasingly. Then he grew into a kinder memory.
They remembered him riding at point-to-point
meetings and how they had all fought for the
possession of one pair of field-glasses (serious im-
pediment though they were to the vision of the proud
wearer), and had seen him take awful falls and had
seen him win races when the crowd had surged
and roared with excitement : " *Come* on, Chevington ! Chevington wins !—he wins ! B'God he have
it——" And he would take them into the ring to
see the horses saddled up for their race and teach
them to watch a race intelligently and use their
brains when they backed a horse. And once they

went to Punchestown—that was before Basil and
Evelyn had left their preparatory school—to see
him ride in the Connyngham Cup when the horses
start tails to the Double and came round to race
over it—that great solid green bank with its for-
midable ditches. And to see a horse meet the Big
Double really right, is so see the very divinity of
movement, of speed, of effort directed to the
fraction of a second.

That day, though, was fraught with other and
many excitements. In Patsy's charge and bound
by oaths not to leave the vantage point of the
Priests' hill (and the Priests' hill is some way away
from the bookies' stand upon the course), they
watched the first race, their devilry for the moment
paralysed by the excitement that for a week had
boiled within them, almost sickening in its intensity.

The sun of April shone, a warm wind charged the
air with a smell of earth and gorse and oranges and
excited humanity. Dim and raucous from the stands
came the clamour of the bookies betting on the race,
and out here on the course you were near to the
actual hot striving of the race itself. They swept up
to the Double, bright, dangerous horses, grim
jockeys, their faces harsh with the reality of the
moment. The going was good and they rode into the
bank at a wicked pace. They were up, five of them
abreast, and landing out in the next field, and gone
like a broken wave, the wind bulging in the backs
of their bright silk shirts ; their horses' thin racing

plates the shortest second's flash of silver in the abiding sunlight. Three more over and a fourth down. The crowd closed in on the prone jockey.

" Ah, God help him ! He's killed ! " " Ah, pity ! Ah, a nice young fella ; I knew his father well——" " Where is a Priest ? Send for a Priest——" " Docther ? Arrah what doctor—aren't his eyes closed ? " " Here's Father Rossiter ! Make way now, boys." " He's here, Father. I think he's dead."

" Well, you're a bigger fool even than I took you for, James Mahon. Go get Doctor Murphy, he's beyond at the stone wall, and don't delay telling him the boy's dead or he might see no great reason to come." Black, overbearing and efficient, the priest cleared the crowd back, and presently the boy staggered stupidly to his feet after the manner of the concussed.

All very exciting for the children : they strove in the crowd to gaze at their first dead man, and a groom they knew told them that Great Prospect was a good thing for the next race. That was enough for Basil. Regardless of Patsy's prayers and invective he was off to the bookies' stand like a shot to bet with Jerry Regan, selected because of his vast bulk which would be likely to make welshing a difficult matter for him. He marked the starters on his race card, watched the horses go out, subsequently collected the useful sum of fifteen shillings, backed his uncle for his race and returned to the Priests' hill to divide the bullion with Easter and

Evelyn, and to eat an enormous lunch of dismembered chicken and bread and butter.

A divine day indeed they spent on the Priests' hill. Pidgie was the only member of the party who did not enjoy life on the end of her lead. Neither, perhaps, did Patsy enjoy himself to the utmost. Nominally in charge of the party, the only part of it over which he had any control was the lunch basket, and this he had carried round most of the course since to abandon it for a moment was to make it a present to the tinkers. The children, tiring of the spectacle of the Double, stationed themselves at other fences, and Patsy, whose orders were not to let them out of his sight, must follow. The stone wall pleased them particularly ; since their ponies nearly always˙ jumped them off over smaller obstacles of the same variety, it was frightening but entrancing to see these gallant jockeys sit their horses as they swept down to it, took off as if to music, and soared over the wall to the height of themselves. One horse hit it hard, but made a most marvellous recovery, while that god among jockeys stayed with him as if by magic.

Uncle Dick's race was the Connyngham Cup— where the horses were started tails to the Double, and Uncle Dick on Sea Fog (by Scotch Mist out of Seagull), a little bit of a grey mare, came with the other jockeys, cantering and walking and jogging down to the start, their horses pulling and fidgeting, shaking their heads, and fighting their bits. How strange and small Sea Fog looked to the children. Tears were in Easter's eyes to see her there, and Daddy looking so cross about something and so distant from them, the children, among those horses and queer men. (Easter recognised many whom she had often seen at Puppetstown.) She wiped her nose on her white woollen gloves and her heart shouted : " *Good luck, Daddy ! Good luck, Daddy ! Please-God-let-Daddy-win,*" as the horses came under the starter's orders.

Down fell the flag at last, and " They're off," on the same beat of breath, came from the crowd. A tangled rainbow of colour, a medley of horses, and half a length in the lead (Uncle Dick nipped a sweet start), the grey mare—cerise jacket and black cap—jumped the first fence and then horses and jockeys were only a mist of colour. Easter continued to pray and Basil and Evelyn continued to fight for the possession of the glasses through which they viewed the race in alternate spasms. According to them, Sea Fog was always going well. Lying third. Now she's second. Jumping faultlessly. Down they came to the Double, thundering down ; Sea Fog was fourth, but, oh, she jumped it well, she gained every time over her fences. The third horse fell and she was going up to the leaders now.

" Daddy ! *Go on, Daddy !* " Easter screamed in her excitement this time, and the boys were so bitterly ashamed of her hysteria that they pushed her off the top of the wall they stood on, and pretended she did not belong to them. Then Easter ran, her brown stockinged legs and laced boots streaking over the bright grass, to the bookies' stands, determined that no second should delay her fever to know whether Sea Fog had won her race. Patsy, encumbered still by the lunch basket, and towing a furious Pidgie, hastened in her pursuit.

"What won ? What won ? " she asked the crowd. Her face was scarlet, her nose a bright blue button, and her eyes streamed in the wind which fluttered in the blue ribbons of that dreadful H.M.S. *Dreadnaught* cap.

"Sea Fog won it, miss," a young man, wearing pointed yellow boots and carrying a little switch in his hand, told her, and Easter thanked him and shook hands with him and indeed progressed so well that she was eating an orange at his expense when Patsy found her after ten minutes anxious searching in the crowd.

"Oh, God ! Miss Easter, I thought I'd never clap an eye on you again this day " ; crimson and perspiring, Patsy deposited Pidgie and the lunch basket and gratefully accepted an orange tendered by Easter's escort. "When I looked around from the horses ye were gone, and Master Evelyn and Master Basil legging it their best for those lads o' bookies, God knows when will we get to come near them again. I'm heart-scalded with this day's sport. I wish it was in the pantry I was, and the full o' the little trough o' dishes before me this minute."

"Ah, ye'd have no great comfort with childther on a day's pleasure," sympathised the provider of oranges. " Ta-ta now, miss. I'm delighted yer Da won."

" One pinny th' oranges ; One pinny th' oranges," shrilled the tawny woman who kept the stall above the voices of the bookies and the cries of those who ran roulette and the exponents of the three-card trick. A jockey came limping back down the course, his horse had fallen and was lame too, a friend led him slowly, the sweat was dry on him now. The jockey spat blood out of his mouth and talked cease-lessly. The afternoon sun turned his green shirt to gold—the day was frankly afternoon now, the sparkle that winks in the rim of morning's cup had died. Easter walked quietly back to the Priest's hill with Patsy and Pidgie. Her excitement had sub-sided to a feeling of quiet gladness. She would have liked to hold some one's hand. To tell the truth, she was rather tired.

They found Basil and Evelyn sitting under a gorse bush dividing the winnings. There were three more races on the card, but they had prudently decided not to have a bet on the last as it would mean keeping the party waiting while they collected their winnings. They had not the least doubt but after backing two winners in the day they could possibly fail to have a third and a fourth.

A man in a check tweed coat came walking over the field towards them. He raised his shooting stick in greeting and Easter ran to meet him—Daddy—

he had left the enclosure and come down to have a race with them.

" Daddy ! Wasn't it splendid ? "

" Oh, Uncle *Dick*, well done ! "

" Well *done*, Uncle Dick ! "

" Mind you, I was very lucky," said he, and told them about the race as circumspectly and with as much detail as though they had all been jockeys of experience. He took them away to see the horses over another fence, leaving Patsy free to disport himself among his friends for this race. They all three enjoyed it mightily, in spite of the fact that their horse was beaten and they went down two shillings each. But Uncle Dick said : " Well, I think I'd have backed him myself at the weight," so Basil and Evelyn lost nothing in self-esteem over the matter, however they might be out of pocket. Easter remembered that race and her father smoking a pipe, and the hushed, tired air of content about him, for a long time. She never afterwards went to Punchestown or saw primroses growing in a dry green April ditch, in the late afternoon, that she did not remember his coat and the rough tweed smell of it and his contented voice. She remembered that well when she had long forgotten how she was sick in the train on the way home and how angry the strange lady was whose feet she was sick over, although that, at the time, appeared the most disgraceful incident that had ever happened, or could happen in life, and quite spoilt the day's delight.

However, she revived in the air as they rattled the
pony and trap from Bunclody station back to
Puppetstown : Puppetstown awaiting them with
the flat, dignified calm that houses whose inmates
leave them for a day's jollying assume like a mood
or a garment, and discard only when they have with
due dignityremitted the unkindness of their children's
desertion. For houses can be as jealous as lovers
and mothers, and under provocation more bitter
than either. Nor do houses ever forget. What are
ghosts but the remembrances they shelter ?

Puppetstown did not forget Uncle Dick, although
soon all that the children remembered of him were
vague, momentous days like that outing to Punchestown which stuck so clearly in Easter's mind,
although indeed she had only been with him less
than one short half hour of it. Basil's chief memory
was of the first hunt he had really ridden like a man,
and Uncle Dick's delight in his prowess ; and Evelyn
remembered the glorious hour when he shot his
first woodcock.

All the servants at Puppetstown looked back on
the days of the Major as on a golden age—a splendid
time the like of which they were never to see equalled
again. They would tell tales of fox-hunting and
racing ; of days when all the quality would be
gathered from the country round to ride schools
over the fences at Puppetstown ; of the winners the
Major had bred and trained and ridden they would
tell ; of the wine in the cellars, the horses in the

stables, the foxes in the coverts, and the notable runs they provided. They had scores of stories wherewith by contrast to darken the leaner years that followed the Major's death and the Great War in Europe and the little bitter, forgotten war in Ireland.

Those were times when the fastness of Mandoran, Mooncoin and the Black Stair saw secrecy and striving and plottings, and blood was shed there quietly and wickedly, and one half of the young men of Ireland were held in a pitiless lust of cruelty, and the other half in a wanton spell of fear. Through all the land no man trusted even his brother. All was silence and covert looks. A word spoken and carried again could quite well mean death—a lone and unshriven death of which no man dare bear witness. In those days a little knowledge was indeed a dangerous thing. The faces of servants were turned from their masters, and the Church, trafficking with deceivers, lost her authority over them. The Church followed because she could no longer lead or drive. In those times men in authority would go and come from their houses always a different way, life was a little surer thus, not very much, or for very long, perhaps, but they took what small precautions as were in their power and charged the rest on Luck or Fate or God, as they pleased.

Meetings by night : oaths to their darkened land sworn, signed and forgotten : drillings and revolver practice and always the romantic cup of dizzy words, promises of land (that never-dying fever of the Irish), promises of office and of glory to crown their endeavours for this their beleaguered country, these things ran in a golden exciting vein through the years before the grim actual happenings took shape of horror in the land. Then it was too late for the young men to regret oaths that others remembered, oaths that a handful of leaders enforced with the mastery of a death-threat hold in their powerful remembrance. Oaths that to death they must keep and obey ; even to the shedding of their friends' blood, be such a friend, master or brother or dear companion. On a tide of sentiment and excitement they had been swept out to a sea from which there was no returning, and where strange undercurrents wreathed lines about them. A life was required and the casting of lots decided who should take it, a house for the burning and the firers were called and chosen. Not a young man in Ireland was there who did not belong to some secret society that compelled implicit obedience or a sinister disappearance. And no questions were asked in those days.

The Puppetstown branch of these moonlighters numbered Patsy among their ranks, and counted him with his indoor opportunities of espionage in a house frequented by the soldiers from the Camp, a not unuseful adherent.

They were strange days for the gentry of Ireland these, strange, silent, dangerous days. The morning's paper (and if the post was late it was because a bridge had been blown up the night before or the

mail raided on its way from Dublin) might tell of
the murder of a friend ; or the burning of a house
that had lately been like Puppetstown, careless in
its wide hospitality ; or, more rarely, of the capture
of rebels or a successful raiding for arms.

Curiously untouched by it, as by the greater war,
life at Puppetstown went on, as though no tide
could lick close enough ever to suck Puppetstown to
destruction.

The boys came back and forwards from school,
and Easter went for one term to a curious school in
a suburb of Dublin, to which she stoutly refused to
return, so her genius for mathematics was fostered
by the National schoolmaster, and her naturally
good ideas about literature fumbled out their dreams
alone ; at any rate her liking for poetry remained
undisturbed by having to learn verses by heart.

Aunt Dicksie was very grey now, and in her vague,
lost way, despotic ruler of Puppetstown. Even in
those days when servants indoor and outdoor were
notoriously difficult and insurgent, not one of them
ever dared show disrespect or disobedience towards
Miss Chevington. Her nephew's death had shaken
Aunt Dicksie pitifully. Life had wavered for her,
its balance weighted to despair, but the love of
Puppetstown and its children was greater than
sorrow and more abiding. Puppetstown had taken
the best of her in its service and gave her back now
a strength and an interest and a reason to be until
the last inch of her life. She gardened in a dim way

with the loveliest results. She had the luck to make her dreams of how flowers should grow come true, and strangely better than true at times. Her housekeeping was as vague and as much of a wandering success as ever. But there was nothing in the least vague about her scrutiny of the accounts of farm or estate. Then all the dreamy Celt in her nature melted like mist from a diamond point of commonsense. Uncle Dick had shown a streak almost of genius in making her Easter's chief trustee for Puppetstown. But Aunt Brenda was her guardian.

Aunt Brenda, at thirty-three, was almost more good-looking and attractive to children and to men than she had been at thirty or twenty-five or twenty, and that is to say a great deal. Her gold hair was as bright as her laugh, and as genuine. She adored life and admiration and her sons, and remained as lazy and as selfish as she had been born, one of the restful things about her being that she never tried to improve herself in any way. All her relations-in-law, with the *Morning Post* strongly supporting them, wrote letters explaining to her the wicked risks she was taking for her children and herself by continuing to live in Ireland. The great-uncle who paid for Evelyn's and Basil's schooling wrote a dignified letter of protest about it, and, which was more to the point, invited her to come over to England and inhabit the dower-house of Tattingham Park where he lived. But Aunt Brenda was much too easy-going to make any such definite move, although she sometimes pretended to contemplate it, when life at Puppetstown chanced to be exceptionally dull, not when Ireland chanced to be exceptionally dangerous.

But Puppetstown was not often dull. It was one of the houses where Sunday Afternoon is an institution, and these are seldom dull houses, because on Sunday afternoons people feel that they have been enough bored for one day, and try to go where they will be enlivened of their depression. In summer people came to play tennis at Puppetstown and looked at the garden, or at Aunt Brenda or at the young horses, as their age or mood took them; and in the winter they would sit by an enormous fire in the drawing-room and discuss the week's hunting and the intimate affairs of any neighbours who did not happen to be present.

When lunch was over Aunt Brenda always had the comfortable premonition that some one pleasant would shortly arrive, and as nobody ever bored her and everybody adored her, she waited the arrival with expectant satisfaction. Nearly every one who lived within six miles of Puppetstown came, and, of course, soldiers came too, as they had done before the war and during the war and ever since Aunt Brenda first radiantly grew up and promptly married the nicest of them all, whose faint memory she still cherished with the one groove of any depth in the nature of her being, although quite realising that it was very stupid of her not to have married again. On days that were not Sunday at Puppetstown she went out hunting and played bridge and attended dinner-parties and danced, and made plans about her clothes and wrote to the boys and did the flowers. She wondered if Easter would ever be attractive to men, and had the sound idea of dressing her in the most unbecoming clothes, so that she was indeed depressing to look upon, because by force of contrast she would then look so much more handsome when she finally grew up and came out.

But Easter did not care at all what impression she might make on young men. She fled before their arrival if she could, saying she hated them, but that was largely shyness; what she really fled from was the terrific bogey of silence that seized on her in their company. They would see her in the distance fishing down the sally stream attended by two white dots which were Max and Pidgie; or they would see her out hunting and sometimes overhear with awe the conversations she held with grooms; or exercising her pony when, if she saw any of Aunt Brenda's friends on the horizon, she would slip her heel into whatever horse she was riding, and make him fairly tip it till they were at a safe distance from society.

There came a time, however, when matters in Ireland were at such a pass that for the first time in remembrance life was positively dull; a time when almost no one could come to Puppetstown on Sunday afternoon because they had no cars to

come in. Cars had either been commandeered by
the Sinn Fein forces or else their owners had laid
them up and buried some integral portion of their
works in their gardens, in the same way that they
buried boxes of silver in case their houses should
be burnt down in the night. However, Aunt Brenda's
soldiers still came out to see her, though it was a
long and risky drive from the camp, and they had to
pass through some dangerously lonely localities
before they got to Puppetstown. Aunt Dicksie
protested with them for coming and Aunt Brenda
pretended to be very firm in her expressions of fear
on their accounts, but she would have been dis-
gusted with them had they failed to appear. At
the moment she was having an affair that interested
her exceedingly with an attractive Captain Falloden-
Grey, who had wit enough to enjoy even his own
love affairs. This made a flirtation with him so
much more amusing for a widow of Aunt Brenda's
experience.

"But really, Aunt Dicksie," she would say, a
faint rose triangle of excitement in her cheeks, and
eyes that did not wait to see Aunt Dicksie because
they belonged to a further secret. "I don't a bit
see why they shouldn't come here if they like. It's
no farther than going to Coolgarrow, and they aren't
bored by those frightful Copely girls (all looking for
marriage, poor dears) when they get here."

Aunt Dicksie was arranging double violets in a
silver sugar bowl—the tips of her fingers were wet

and cold and her finely cut nose was a little blue.
She had been out after tea to gather the violets.
February, she thought, was the best month of all
in the garden, when that faint, perishable quality
of excitement, unendurably, impossibly unen-
durable, was a garment over the earth. And the
moonless evening sky was like a green bell above
the world, silent with dreams of its own music.

Aunt Dicksie arranged the last leaf, curling its
heart against the smooth heavy silver of the little
bowl ; and Aunt Brenda arranged her hair, pulling
it out against her cheek. She had warm, amusing
thoughts of her own.

" All the same," said Aunt Dicksie, " they should
not come out here—don't forget the road to Coolgarrow is the main Dublin road and their way here
goes over the shoulder of Mooncoin. It's a lonely
road, Brenda, and when you think of that frightful
ambush in Cork last week "—Aunt Dicksie put the
violets down on her writing-table beside a photograph of Easter's father—" those men were going
to a bridge party."

" I don't know why Patsy hasn't taken away the
tea things." Aunt Brenda rang the bell fretfully,
and when Mary Josie answered it, demanded as
fretfully where Patsy was.

" He's out, ma'am."

" But this is not Patsy's Sunday," Aunt Dicksie
observed, with the memory that served her startlingly
when some one relied on her forgetfulness.

" 'Twas what he said he should go see his father, his father is sick, miss, and I said I'd carry out the tea for him." Mary Josie departed with a heaped tray.

" Well, that's a bad lie," said Aunt Brenda. " Easter and the old man were ferreting rats in the long ditch at five o'clock ; Ronnie Grey and I saw them, and Patsy wasn't with them then. It must have been him that was pedalling his bicycle like blazes down the back avenue. I expect he had an assignation with a girl. Don't be unkind to him, Aunt Dicksie. Do you remember my assignments when I was Easter's age ? "

" Do I not ? At all points of the compass and all hours of the day and night."

" It must have been so exciting for you, Aunt Dicksie. I do wish Easter was like that. Easter is so quiet. You know, Aunt Dicksie, we must send her abroad or something soon. She's becoming nearly impossible. The only people she wants to talk to are Fortune and Patsy. And she'd rather go out hunting with Jer Donohughe and his harriers any day than come out with the fox-hounds. I don't think it's a bit good for her being the queen of the harriers with ten awful buckeens cheering her over every fence she jumps and giving her quite a wrong idea of her own importance, do you ? "

" Perhaps not. But I think she gets quite a good idea of hunting a fox from Donohughe. Anyhow, she may as well finish this season. After Easter I know we must really think of a school for her."

" Yes. It'll be awkward for the boys if she grows up too hopeless." Aunt Brenda lit a cigarette and leant her bright head against a cushion.

" The boys "—Aunt Dicksie always stiffened at any vulgarity of mind—" don't want Easter one bit different from what she is. They adore Easter."

" Oh, yes, they're quite fond of her, poor little thing ! " Aunt Brenda crossed her ankles before her and let the subject drop. She was thinking of nothing now—which meant she was thinking of Ronnie Grey. But she would not tell Aunt Dicksie that he had said he was coming over again on Thursday. It would only fuss the dear old thing.

Thus they still came, the soldiers, to Puppetstown, although strongly discouraged in so doing by their senior officers. Aunt Dicksie looked grave and white when she said good-bye to them, but Aunt Brenda was all the sweeter to them because they had dared something to see her. And because she was sweeter they dared again. There was quite an air of excitement to it all through the delicious dim spring months.

And all this time the tyres of Patsy's bicycle wore thin with the miles they covered by night when he delivered his reports of who had come to Puppetstown and when they had left and by what road and at what time.

Once there had been excitement and a burning flame of romance in these dark journeyings to the mountains. There were nights when Patsy would slip out of the pantry window (as he had done when Evelyn was a little boy lost in the woods) with his heart on fire for Ireland, when his bicycle beat through the night on wings to set her free, and there was no thought of lesser treachery in this great loyalty of his to Ireland. This was loyalty that would have smote his own mother with a sword if need came for Ireland—a loyalty that was almost as much lust of the flesh as it was an intoxication of the spirit. Now these days were cold ashes and sour. Only fear of that which would befall him should he dare fail in his trust kept Patsy constant now to the cause. For Ireland was sick of the blood and tears on her own hands and driven by fears and craven with horrid secrets. Patsy had seen death in the hills. It was a haunting and dreadful memory and it was always with him now. When he pedalled his bicycle back through the night to Puppetstown, and the fir trees were blotted sinister against the sky, stars in the gulfs between their dark branches, chill stars with the breath of to-morrow pale in them already, he would think : " God, deliver me from thim crowd ! " for he was only a young lad, Patsy, and very frightened. He would leave his bicycle in the laurels and climb through his window and into bed. There were no ferrets now in the sedan chair. Patsy had no heart for rearing them and had brought them all up to his father's house. Only a faint fog of past generations of ferret hung about the boot-room now, a memory of happier days—

days past when Patsy would cod the cook and slip off
to the young gentlemen on the river, no thought but
pleasure in his mind and the desire to stick a gaff in a
salmon, the only desire that burnt in him. And when
they caught and killed the kelts that grew every
moment eelier as they lay on the bank, Patsy would
button the murdered things inside his coat and so
convey them through the woods to his father's
house. But now there were messengers waiting for
him in the silent woods and his heart was not at one
with anything that he did.

Master Basil and Master Evelyn (their tweed coats
and fly-stuck hats moving up and down the river
bank) found Patsy sulky and despondent. They said
to each other, " I wonder if Patsy has turned
Shinner ? " and laughed at the thought ; it did not
trouble them at all. The sun shone ; the dogs ex-
plored a mouse-hole with ridiculous exactitude,
their noses were black with river mud ; Basil had
risen a fish and was changing his fly to fish the
stream down again, faint fleets of willow catkins
came drifting down the river. The water swirled
behind a silver saddle of grey rock and went on a
faster arrow-shape. The almond and honey of gorse
came distantly on the air, an occasional warmth
above the stranger, colder smell of the river bank.
" And God help me," again thought Patsy, " the
great life I had one time when I'd be cutting jokes
with Miss Easter and the young gentlemen, or playing
a hand o' cards, or fighting the cooks. It's little

I'd care now if they best me, they may best away—
God knows I'll never make a soldier—I haven't the
element for it. I'd lay down Ireland's Cross this
minute for it's nothing only a torment and a great
curse o' God——"

.   .   .   .

On a day in August Easter and Basil and Evelyn
would go fishing. To a lake high on Mandoran they
would go where trout might be caught, granted the
day and the hour and the weather and that you had
the fly they were taking at the moment. All of which
things made The Man more desirable and attractive
than the river. Besides it was eight miles from
Puppetstown at the least. Four of them could be
bicycled, but the other four were a long and weary
climb up the mountain-side till you came to the
dark cup of water that was The Man.

At ten o'clock they started, their cased rods tied
along the bars of their bicycles, Basil and Evelyn
sharing the burden of the lunch between them and
very exact in its fair division. Patsy came out at
the last moment with six tomatoes on a plate which
Miss Dicksie had sent as an afterthought. Their
disposal in secure nooks took some further time.
Patsy was silent and fidgety.

" It'll not stop fine," he said at last. " I'd know
it be the crows."

" How would you ? " Easter took a piece of string
out of her mouth to inquire. Natural phenomena
continually intrigued her.

" When ye'll see thim lads tossin' in the sky and roarin' ye may know it'll rain ere night." Patsy shook his head in gloomy presage. " If ye'd be said by me, Miss Easter, ye'd stop on the river in place o' goin' mad over the mountains afther trouts that'll not be cot with rain to fall. Indeed they're not very easy to be cot," added Patsy, " at any time."

" Rot. Glass is up. I don't know where I'll put this tomato, Basil, unless I eat it." Evelyn was the instigator and in a way the leader of to-day's expedition. " Are you right now, Easter ? Come on, then——"

Patsy watched them depart down the long slope of avenue. Easter between the two boys had an arm twisted in each of theirs, no hand on the handle bars of her bicycle. Thus they got up a terrific and frightening speed, their treble weight carrying them onwards. Patsy watched them for a moment, but long before they were out of sight, he turned and went into the house again, smoothing his dark quiff of hair away from his forehead. " And the mountains stiff with lads on the run," he meditated as he cleared away the breakfast things, " but sure they knows that as well as I do meself." He gave Pidgie a pat of butter, stooping to stroke her head in miserable silence. Pidgie looked at him for a fraction of time sufficient to allow her to see there was no more butter coming, then she walked with stiff dignity to a square of sunlight where she sat herself down, fanning out her person to the warmth. Patsy was a servant and uninteresting to her.

On through the bright morning the children pedalled towards distant Mandoran. White dust was thick on the bramble-laden hedges along the road and on the flowers—pink mallows and honeysuckle and late wild roses, blown flat as stars, that grew on the uneven stone faces of the banks. Just below them as they rode along, the river coiled and uncoiled its shining way, beech trees, darker than purple, glooming beside the water in the heat of the day, and willow trees were a dark strange silver, like foreign coin when the least wind turned their leaves. There was a long hill in front of them, then they came to the village of Clohamon. A lovely dusky woman was sitting on her doorstep holding a sick baby in the sunlight. From here a smaller road seemed very long to them, as they pushed up its gradually steepening slope with the wind contrary. The fences on either side grew stonier and the turf more clipped to the bone of the poor land. A thin air from high spaces spun the faint tang of excitement that nipped their unthinking beings. Presently they saw by the road an encampment of tinkers—their caravan was like a round-topped ark on wheels to hold their all safe from the floods and tempests of the world. A man was sitting in the ditch doing nothing. He watched them as they passed. A thin little girl of about thirteen, with sunburned hair, was cutting bread from a loaf so busily that she did not even look up, and two sprites of boys were playing with a white greyhound puppy.

" Give us a copper, miss, God may save ye, miss, give us a copper, will ye, miss ? " One of the little boys came pattering behind them down the road ; after Basil had given him one, he turned and besieged Easter again.

" Be off with you, now ! " Easter commanded sternly. " I have not got one single penny."

" God may save ye, miss, God may save ye." The child repeated his little chanting prayer and skipped back to his sunny ditch.

" Those are Lyons," Basil said. " Not one of them ever did a stroke of work in his life."

" I'll tell you what, though, all the same, those Lyons are beggars to catch rabbits with their hands, and Joe Lyons is the best shot with a stick in the country." They were friends of Easter's, it seemed, so the boys said no more against them, poachers and idlers they might be.

" I wonder where they got that greyhound puppy," Easter continued. " It's very like one that Fortune's sister had stolen from her. And I had just given her a tonic for it. Such a waste ! "

" You may depend it wasn't wasted," Basil grinned. " Fortune told me she took it herself. He said it played puck with her altogether. He said, ' that one's as mean she'd build a wran's nist in yer ear.' "

They had come now to a place where the deep

mouth of a lane led away from the main climbing road and down to the foot of the mountain. Here at a grey narrow-faced farmhouse they left their bicycles. A mountainy man, his dark face incongruously surmounted by a pair of gold-rimmed spectacles, knew them well. He accepted the charge of their bicycles and wished them good luck to their fishing as they set off down the lane. Then he turned back into his house and said quietly in the shadowed kitchen : " It's all right, Jim ; ye may come out now."

A young man came out from an inner room and stood for a minute in the tall sunlight of the doorway. He was dark-faced like his father but wanted the air of aristocracy to which the simple are heirs in mountainy places. There was instead a look of cruel fugitiveness about him—a look of outlawry.

" Who in hell was it ? " he asked, with the roughness of one who has been frightened and is ashamed of it.

" Nothing, only the young Chevingtons of Puppetstown going up to fish the lake."

" Going up to spy could they clap an eye on some of our chaps. If they cot them and held them in the lake water till they drownded thim in it, wouldn't it be the price o' thim ? Yes, and bruk up the fishing rods to float them with their bodies," he added, with a gleam of real savagery. " The dirty little Saxons."

" Jim," said the old man sternly, " I'm a father

to you and I'd give my body for your life, this
minute, or I'd give a shelter to any poor boy on
the run in the mountains, but—be the Holy Seaman
(and he swore a good oath) " if harm should come
to those poor children this day or any other day—
there's deeds known to me and places known to me,
yes, and names I could tell when they are wanted ;
yes, and would, too, if yous should crucify me (and
yez are well able) on that door afther——" He
smote his fist upon the palm of his open hand. He
was as steadfast and wild as his own mountainy
places, although like Mandoran, Mooncoin and the
Black Stair, he too was a retreat and a harbour
for the fugitive and the evildoer. Yet he too was afar
unto himself. And he was a protection to the children
for that very quality of steadfastness in him which
was known to his son too well to be set aside.

The children walked slowly down the lane which
held sunlight without its depth of green. The secret
sweet lamps of wild strawberries hung low in the
banks, and these they must find and eat. Above the
lane little stony fields hung, the sun yellow as butter
on their thin grass. The fields dropped to their
netting walls and dropped again, little field by little
field, to a river beyond which, defeated by the heather
and the rocks, they ceased. And this was where
Mandoran's lonely roots gripped into the land.
Stepping stones, set to balance exactly a man's
stride, led the lane across a young river, its waters
like brown clear wine this day, and curling out round

the stones with small and gentle patience. A wind as young as the river ran its fingers through a thin wood of hazel, where water dripped from tall rocks darkly to rusty pools and the bracken was all sword-run with foxgloves. The lane, leading upwards now, skirted round this strange little wood as though it felt it unfriendly, and having brought the feet of its travellers safely to the kinder wildness of the mountain, it fainted to a thread at last and the heather reeled in its end.

The children sat them down by the river for a short rest and watched its leisurely small progress from pool to pool.

" I can remember," said Evelyn, " this time two years, Easter, you and me and Patsy murdered trout here when there was a flood in it, do you remember ? On a worm."

" I do," said Easter. There were low frochaun bushes near her and she was rapidly purpling her mouth with their fruit. Basil, silent on his stomach, followed her example. The mountain leaned away from them and the day breathed its life close to their hands on the earth and to their faces in its wind and sun.

" Come on," said Evelyn, " we must start or we'll never get up there."

Resolute at last they faced the heather and climbed their changing way up the mountain side. The country below them dropped and spread its distances to new proportions, its sunny fields fat and

sleek compared to this raw airy world where only
their own striving bodies should avail them, and
thoughts were for idler moments. Grouse rose at
their feet thunderously and were gone, the curve
of their wings and the curve of their flight as one.
Basil and Evelyn had flung up imaginary guns, now
they grinned at each other and continued on their
way.

For five short minutes, counted by Evelyn's
watch, they sat against a small rick of turf, a very
luxury of repose, until Basil, spying afar off a white
goat, would have them capture her that he might
extract hairs from her beard for the dressing of
salmon flies.

The last mile was very long to them—exhausted
and out-manœuvred as they were after their fruitless
contest with the goat. Easter, her blue serge skirt
fastening round her toiling legs, the sun hot on the
back of her neck, wished that wish which through
life fastens itself on every effort, a very leech to
suck endeavour : " I *wish*—I *wish* I hadn't come."

But at length and at last round the jealous
shoulder of Mandoran they saw it there before them,
the little lake, keeping its waters and its secret
so dark unto itself—high in the hands of the
mountain. On one side the heather met the firm
mountain turf and the turf met the pale stones
and few paler reeds and rushes that frilled the lake
water like lace on a black sleeve, and on the other
side the mountain stooped low and darkly as

though it would hood its lake for ever unto itself.
(This side was very difficult to fish.) There was a
tree of mountain-ash — its berries still as green
as china apples—and who can tell what bird had
dropped that seed ? Now its two stems were as
twisted as an old woman's wrists and its branches
tilted affectedly backwards. And the colour of
heather was in the air. When you shut your eyes
it was still there. Only in the lake waters the
bracken met its reflection, green as foreign birds.

" Beer, dear ? " said Basil.

Easter shook her head.

" What ? Not beer, dear ? Oh, *Easter*, after all
that ? Well, don't say I didn't ask you to join me
in my bottle." Basil sunk his head back. " That,"
he announced after a long minute, " was worth
every inch of the agony I endured carrying it up
this highest of all mountains."

" Well, nobody forced you to burden yourself
with it." Evelyn was sucking a tomato in rather
sour silence. " And I bet it's pulped the two tomatoes
I gave you to look after."

" I know nobody forced me. It was my own chosen
burden." Basil assumed a little air of patience.
" And it *has* mashed the tomatoes," he said, " but
really I don't mind. I'm not such a hog about
tomatoes as you are. In fact, I simply hate tomatoes.
Where are the eggs, Easter ? Where *are* the eggs ?
This is simply awful. Is there to be no food for me
to-day ?—oh, thanks. If you were a really womanly

and lovely woman, dear, you'd have known at once
where those eggs were."

" I will never be a lovely or womanly woman."
Easter was lying on her back eating a hard-boiled
egg towards the sky. " I will always be shy and
rather dirty and I will always have hot hands. And
I heard Aunt Brenda telling Aunt Dicksie that I will
never be attractive to men."

" *We* like you," said Evelyn and Basil in instant
unison, and Evelyn, who found the discussion of
personalities at all times discomfiting and of doubtful
form, changed the subject at once to the nearer
matter of their fishing.

" There's a rise close in," said he ; and sure enough
a fish was cruising round in the shallows at the lee
side of the lake, imbibing nourishment every ten
yards or so. Farther out in the inaccessible middle
waters, potentially monster trout betrayed their
presence by occasional torpedo-waves, rings or
plops, according as they were clean or messy feeders.
But these trout were not practical politics unless
and until they went a-cruising round the tiny bays
and islands of rock which marked the shores of the
lake. When the wind blew out of the west, as it
nearly always did, it swept into the bays at the
shallow side all the heather moths, beetles, bracken-
clocks and daddy-longlegs which God had set aside
for the fattening of fish.

But, though there were more fish there, the east
side had its objection—a head wind which made

casting quite impossible at times, except from the two or three small promontories which thrust out inquiring noses into the blackness of the lake.

The difficulty could have been removed by the use of a boat but for the still greater difficulties of carrying one over the miles of trackless heather. Besides, though they often talked of doing it, they would none of them have dared to insult the waters of The Man by launching a boat upon it. An occasional pair of nesting teal were the only boats that ever used there.

Without rising from their sheltered corners in the heather they proceeded to assemble rods and thread reel-lines from ring to ring. Evelyn was the first to finish. He got up, stretched himself, and walked over to where the gut-casts and flies had been soaking during lunch.

" What are you going to put up, Basil ? "

" Oh, I don't know, I suppose a Wood-fly on the tail, fuzzy March Brown at point and an Orange Grouse in the middle."

" You would," said Evelyn ; " just what I was going to try myself. I'll put up one of those new Black Rat flies we tried the other day. What about you, Easter ? "

" I don't care, so long as you only put up two flies, so I shan't get muddled up ; and I want to start at the other side the way I'll have the wind behind me."

" All right, but mind you don't crack off the tail

fly, we've only got three spare Wood-fly between
the whole of us."

Their trout flies were very much their own. They
had all the contempt of the amateur fly-dresser for
what they called the " new-beginners' flies " turned
out by the tackle dealers. For trout fishing, their
materials were chiefly the duns and drabs of snipe,
partridge, grouse or hare, in fact, whatever came
their way in the shooting season. The so-called
Wood-fly consisted of a tiny pinch of fur from the
dark part of a hare's mask, hackled with a soft
grey-brown feather from the neck of an old cock
partridge. The " Black Rat " owed its virtue to the
shiny black whisker of the old black rat, now almost
exterminated by the brown variety. For this reason
it had acquired a value not altogether justified by
its success as a killing pattern.

It was nearly two o'clock by the time they had
started fishing, and the breeze which had been
good during lunch showed signs of dying away.

Easter took herself off to the far side of the lake,
where she balanced over a fifteen-foot drop into
deep water, a perch which she well knew was
favourable to casting, though the sheltering cliff
left the surface of the lake scarcely ruffled. The boys
started at either end of the lake and worked towards
the middle, flogging the water hopefully when they
could see no fish to cast at. It required nice judgment
to measure the position of a cruising fish, some move
faster than others and there is nothing so maddening

as finding oneself continually behind a rising fish
until at length he passes out of reach.

Basil was the first to move a fish. A sudden boil
as the fish made a grab at the tail fly and turning,
spat it out. Basil felt the weight of him for a tiny
moment, then the rod was light again in his hand.
" Pricked him," he sighed, and wondered whether
he had been too quick or two slow in his strike.
He never could quite fathom the ways of these
mountainy trout.

Just then Easter appeared, having flicked off her
tail fly as usual.

" Did you count three before making your
forward cast ? " inquired Basil sternly.

" Yes, I'm sure I did."

" Well, then, count *six* in future, and if you lose
this Wood-fly you can't have any more."

Basil walked up in time to see his brother slip the
net under a fish at the other end of the lake.

" What did he take ? " he called.

" Good old Wood-fly," came the answer.

The trout in The Man ran about eight ounces,
rather long-shaped fish and definitely blackish. Their
orange and gold markings, though deep in colour,
were dirty with the same peat that coloured the
waters of the lake.

They seldom made much of a bag on these expedi-
tions but this day there seemed to be an exceptional
" take " on them. As a rule the fish came short and
three were pricked for every one that went into the

basket. Whether the light was better than usual or whether the Wood-flies were tied more convincingly than of yore, it is hard to say. At any rate the boys had collected a good number of fish when suddenly Easter's reel began to yell as it had never yelled in its life. As they watched in amazement, far out in the lake what seemed at least a fifteen-pounder jumped once, twice, three times, lashing with its tail at the casting-line as it fell. They left their rods and ran to where Easter stood silent and pale, her knees almost giving way with excitement as she slowly recovered line after the first mad rush.

" Let him go when he wants, and drop your point when he jumps or he can't help breaking you," Evelyn reminded her breathlessly.

" Oh, chaps, I'm *sure* to lose him." She moaned in an agony of excitement, her eyes were glued to where the line cut patterns and curves on the water as the fish turned this way and that, now shaking his head, now diving deep in search of snags. Slowly, slowly they reeled him in, until, just as they were beginning to think he was a slug after all, he caught sight of them and was off " like a thrain," into deeper water, where the jumping performance began again worse than ever.

The backing was almost spent before the fish changed his tactics and came to the surface where he stayed threshing and humping himself against the cast for what seemed like hours, and must therefore have been at least three seconds. But this time he was definitely weaker. His rushes grew each time more controllable, till at length she had him swashing about within ten yards of the shore, eyeing his enemies savagely but still not able to escape. Another minute and he lay played out on the top of the water, the sun gleaming on his golden belly as Easter drew him towards the net, ready sunk to receive him. But still too soon. He recovered himself and gave a roll away. To their sick horror they could see the fly just holding by a torn piece of skin in the corner of his mouth. However, Easter, by the gods inspired, kept her head and led rather than drew her fish over the net once more.

Swoosh, and he lay motionless and gasping in the dripping meshes. Tenderly Evelyn carried him, far, far away from the water's edge and laid him in the heather where they gazed upon his sooty and shark-like splendour with ravished and incredulous eyes. Over three pounds they guessed him to be, a record that should stand for many a long day.

And while they talked it all over and compared him with the other trout (the total bag was eleven), the shadows lengthened with the suddenness that is only seen in the hills, the lake grew cold and the trout stopped rising. A cock grouse said " go back " somewhere round the shoulder of the mountain. An old heron stood on one leg in the stream that ran from the lake, eyeing them in the distance and wondering would they be going soon now.

" Come on, now, we'll fairly have to tip it if we're to get down before dark." Evelyn buckled the straps of a little canvas bag with pleased carefulness. Basil tied the bottom tape of his rod casing very exactly and called out to Easter as she came scrambling round the lake side. A gentle, wild little creature in the evening, she sat on a stone to take down her rod. Her feet seemed too large for her snipe-like legs, but her small head and quick hands were balanced as fine as any etching.

" Come on, Easter," they said. " You caught the great trout. You're a grand girl, Easter. Now we must go home."

The little lake was a dark thumb-shape behind them, its bracken a deadly green, its one tree leaning backwardly from the cold still water, as the lake waited for their going. And the children did not turn again to look at it.

There was a hymn in the evening. It carried their feet on down the mountain-side to the happiness of its rhythm. We have endeavoured : we have wrought skilfully : we have killed eleven trout : our day is crowned. The evening sang it for them, setting these words to the music of a green sky and the carefulness of a little path, to a river's evening gentleness and to the lonely height they put behind them.

Down the dark lane and upwards again to the coarser world of fields fenced and houses builded they went together, tired a little and untalkative, but more content than tired in this day's ending.

Harmonious one with another, their hands smelling
of fish and their minds faint with the unrealised
happiness of their lives, they reached the thin grey
house where in the distant morning their bicycles
had been left for shelter.

" We'll have a cup of tea," they suggested to each
other, " with Jimmy Mahon. Mrs. Mahon makes
great bread. And duck eggs." They remembered
with a sudden rising of appetite, former teas at
the thin grey house, and waited expectantly after
they had told the dark-faced Jimmy Mahon of the
day's conquests. But he did not ask them in to tea
as was his accustomed pleasure to do. He brought
their bicycles, helped them to tie on their rods and
other things, and watched them go almost in silence.
His house door was shut and even the sheep dogs
were inside.

It was a strange disappointment to them, a dis-
jointedness in the right procedure of their day, but
bicycling ever faster down the steepness of the
mountain road, so fast that at last they seemed to go
like bullets before the wind, they forgot their
unkind surprise and delight was with them for a
farther stage even till, from a lonely cross where
the four roads were peeled level with the rock of
the land, Patsy stepped out in their way.

" *Patsy !* " they exclaimed, jumping from their
bicycles which nearly ran them off their legs, they
had been going so fast. They turned and came back
to him.

" Patsy, who are you courting up here ? "

" But, Patsy, what's up ? " Basil had seen the three-cornered white look of his face and realised that there was more than a girl in this trysting.

" There's nothing, Master Basil ; only see here " —there was a break of urgency in his voice—" go the hilly road home. Don't go the Clohamon road at all. Hurry now in God's name, and don't say you were talking with me if one should ask. Say, ' A dark man showed me my road.' Can ye recall that ? " He looked up each of the four crosses, then mounting his bicycle, took the road from the mountains they had just come down and went away without ever a backward look.

The children stared at each other. Their faces looked green and pointed in the dusk. There was a little creeping tide of fearfulness in each of their hearts. No excitement. Only a faint small feeling of sickness and a consciousness that they must deny this fear.

" Patsy's mad, I think. I think he's cracked." Evelyn looked at the other two uncertainly, and Easter, her heart hurrying her, agreed and glanced at Basil to know if he too was afraid.

" Look here¸" Basil put his toe on the step of his bicycle, " we'll go the road home Patsy said and we'll hurry. If any one stops us I'll talk to him."

It was the greatest relief that one of them should admit to a possibility of danger. It warmed that cold feeling from their spines and lifted the sick constriction off their stomachs. A storm had fallen, shattering the mirror of their bright day ; the mountains were strange behind them and the way home beleaguered against their return. The bag of eleven trout seemed nothing to them now. Stiff little darts they lay dead in a handful of pulled grass, forgotten memorials to the lovely day. The bag that held them slapped on Evelyn's back as they hurried, pedalling their way through the evening.

On the way Patsy had bidden them take the hills were against them as the road led back in a shallow circle towards the foothills of Mandoran before turning and coming out again within a mile of Puppetstown. It was when they were on the homeward falling miles that they knew without any least doubt that they were followed. If they rode fast some one just out of sight rode fast behind them, and if they slowed down their follower slowed softly down too. They knew that when they reached the edge of the first wood he would overtake them and not till then, for, in the hanging dark of the trees they could never recognise his face again.

Evelyn went ahead, Easter next and Basil came behind her. They plunged into the mouth of the woods and, in the darkness that took the road, heard the heavy, circling windiness of bicycle wheels closer behind them. A twig cracked sharply, and :

" Good-evening," said Basil politely.

A stooped figure, with a black slouch hat pulled
well down over the eyes, shot past them, slowed and
turned to face Evelyn.

" I have ordthers to inquire stric'ly into your
movements," he began. " What are yez goin' the
roads for at all this time o' night, in any case ? "

" Well, we happen to have been on the mountain
all day," said Basil.

" On the mountain ? "

" Yes. Fishing."

" Fishing ? Did ye see any one on the mountain ? "

" We did. A dark man showed us our road home."

" Very good so." The young man, for his voice
sounded young, turned towards them before he rode
away : " I'd advise yous," he said, " to leg it now
for home like the wheels o' hell," and he, too, like
Patsy, rode back towards the mountains.

" A dark man showed me my road home——"
The words fluttered ghostly in their minds like eight
cold fingers. There was no fun about this adventure
at all. Awful thoughts took them : Puppetstown
had been burnt—Aunt Brenda had been murdered—
all the Protestants in Ireland were to be massacred.
What was Patsy doing up in the hills ? It was not
his day out. What was this strange password ?
What might happen to them before they got home ?
If the house had been burnt, had the dogs been
saved ? Or had they perished dreadfully ? Basil
trod so heavily on the pedals of his bicycle at the
awful thought that he shot yards ahead of the others.

" The sky would be red, wouldn't it, if that had happened ? " Easter said in a small voice, although no one had voiced this idea, or spoken at all, indeed.

The boys said : " Yes, they supposed so," silencing her crossly and adding that they did not know what she meant.

Another dark half mile they rode by the demesne wall and turned in at the wood avenue gate and along the way where, on a night long ago, Evelyn had known a lion was loose in the woods : " Where would he go ? Maybe to the fox's burra' would he go." He could hear again O'Regan's voice in the crowded circus tent and could remember the leaping inspiration that had prompted the obvious sacrifice of Basil for Her safety. Evelyn was very much that little boy still. To-night he cared not for Basil nor for Easter nor for Puppetstown, so She was unhurt and unfrightened and safe for him.

Walking towards them down the avenue came Aunt Dicksie. The dogs were safe with her and ran on to meet them. In the half light they saw her stumble weakly and recovering hurry uncertainly forwards.

" Aunt Dicksie," they said, " what is it ? What has happened ? "

She said : " Captain Grey was murdered by the Sinn Feiners on the Mandoran road this afternoon. Your mother was with him. No, she's quite all right. But she's taking you all over to England to-night."

.   .   .   .

It had happened at lunch time, when Patsy was handing round the raspberry cream, that Aunt Brenda had said to her Captain Falloden-Grey:

"How d'you go back, Reggie? By Mandoran, don't you? My dear, you can drop me at the Charters. I simply must see poor May. She's been most dreadfully bad."

And Reggie Grey had answered: "But I'm *not* going by the Mandoran road, I'm going back by Mooncoin. I'm awfully sorry but I have to pick up young Fawcett from Grange Fort." And when Patsy had gone to fetch the coffee he said, as he lit her cigarette: "Of course I'll take you to Chatterstown. You see, I didn't want to say which road I was going while your man was in the room. It may sound awfully silly to you but it's one of the things we are meant to be careful about. That was how poor Tim Connol was copped, you know. Like an ass he told some fellow gillying for him that he was going such a road and the fellow nipped off to his pals—and they waited for him."

"Reggie," said Aunt Brenda, suddenly shaken. "I don't think you ought to be coming over here. Look here, you must stop it. You must promise me that this is definitely the last time. I don't know what I shall do without you, but still it's not right. It mustn't go on. I shall be 'out' to you if you come again." She nodded at him forbiddingly, but as her eyes never forbade anything, he was not so very discouraged.

" My dear," he said, " don't take it so seriously. Here to-day and gone to-morrow." He was very bright and soldierly.

Aunt Dicksie was late for lunch. They drank their coffee slowly and went out to follow a sleepy path down to the river, to a little wood by the river where all the warmth of an August afternoon was folded windlessly.

. . . .

In the pantry Patsy was washing up the luncheon silver. Flies buzzed on the dusty window pane and wasps growled about a jam-pot. Like the flies they ignored the ingenious trap of beer and treacle which Patsy had set to take them. Mary Josie had removed the dry dish cloth which he had left folded and warm in the sun ready for his silver. It was the last stroke of injustice on a day when things had gone bitterly for him. " You couldn't leave a thing down out o' yer hand but Mary'd have it whipped," he reflected miserably. " Ye'd have no comfort in the house along with that one—only roguery and trickeries and strong annoyance. God knows I get torment enough the way I am——" He wiped the silver with a damp cloth and put it away in its green lined basket, and when he encountered Mary Josie a little later, angrily demanded the where- abouts of his property.

" 'Tis in the laundry," Mary Josie admitted, after a faint protest of complete innocence. " Sure, 'twas in me hand going back to the pantry with it when

a big lad of a wops come for me like a bull, and didn't
I take a drive at him with the cloth——"

" Did ye get him ? " Despite himself, Patsy's
interest in the drama of the chase knew a sudden
flicker.

" I did not. He wheeled out the window and
'twas then I should leave the cloth down out o' me
hand."

" Well, it's all I wish," said Patsy, with gloomy
forbearance ; " ye were in the pantry. The wopses
in it is passin' in an' out in hundthereds through me
hair."

" Ah, go to God ! " exclaimed Mary Josie, with
sympathetic appreciation that did not for a moment
question the picturesqueness of this statement.
" Is that a fact ? "

" Stand out now from undther me feet the lot o'
yous," commanded the voice of Mrs. Kelly from the
fastnesses of the scullery, " and I'd be obliged to you
Patsy Roche to take up the dogs' dinners is waiting
on your convenience this half-hour, and when ye
have that down go out and see could ye gother
what eggs'd wet a sponge cake. Whatever's on those
hens, when ye wouldn't want an egg at all ye couldn't
keep thim drew in from laying, and if an egg was
all was betwix you and death, that's the time ye'll
get nothing from them."

" I will, ma'am," Patsy murmured obediently,
as he picked up the dogs' dishes to fulfil the first
of his missions.

Miss Dicksie was in the dining-room when he opened the door to look for Pidgie, Max and Kit. She was standing by the window, and so thin and still she was, one almost had the impression of seeing light through her cheeks and shoulders as she stood there against the afternoon sun, and the little dropped look of sadness always withheld troubled her mouth. Patsy thought: Miss Dicksie looks bet up altogether, and snapped his fingers quietly to the dogs, but she turned to ask whether that was Captain Grey's car at the door.

"It is, miss. Himself and Mrs. Curtis went down the river walk afther their lunch."

"Yes. I see. Miss Easter and the two young gentlemen won't be back till late, I suppose?"

"They'll surely fish late, miss."

"Yes. I wish rather you had gone with them, Patsy. However——"

"I'll go meet them if you wish, miss."

"Yes, do that, Patsy. I would be happier if you were with them." Miss Dicksie moved away from the window, having laid her charge so quietly on him.

Patsy thought: "I'll gather the eggs for That One and I'll leave in the tea and I'll go then if I get no great delay." But in the dusty gloom of the farmyard loft one waited for him to hear his report of who had come to lunch at Puppetstown. Never was there any escape from the shadow of Ireland's cross.

"Captain Grey is in it." Patsy spoke surlily, for

indeed he hated his part of spy. Suddenly, seeing the look across the eyes of his questioner, he hated it overwhelmingly. There was a near wickedness, a whiff of savagery present for a little monstrous moment. The man leaned forward quickly. " Have ye any idea what road Grey is going back ? " he asked, and there was a false carelessness about the question that gave Patsy a quickened knowledge of himself as spy and underling. His own trusted him not, only those he spied upon. " I'd be happier about them if you were with them——" he heard Miss Dicksie say. He did not at the moment re-member the many half-crowns and few and pleasant words vouchsafed him by Captain Grey and his like. It was a strange loyalty to the hospitality of Puppetstown that caused him to say, as he stood there in the choking gloom, with the black hen's egg in his hand: "Well, Mrs. Curtis asked him at lunch would he take her the Mooncoin road, and he allowed he should be going the Mandoran road."

"You'll swear that was the way of it?" There was more urgency than met the case in this question, and Patsy knew now without any doubt why the truth was required. While the sun slanted hotly on the slates above their heads and all the bright peaceful life of Puppets-town moved without in its slow eventfulness, he held a life in his hands as surely as he was holding the black hen's little egg.

" I will," he said. " I'll swear that was the way
of it. Didn't she tell Miss Chevington after she'd be
in to her tea."

" Well, if that's the way it was," said the man,
" I must be going on now. Good-bye." He stepped
back from the bright circle of a window to hand
Patsy a slip of folded paper. " Yer ordthers for
to-night," he said, and then he was gone.

An order signed romantically " Rory of the Hills,"
bade Patsy attend at eight-thirty that evening,
when a detachment of the I.R.A. should assemble at
the Dark Man's House.

Patsy read his summons through and stood for a
moment, his arms hanging down by his sides, his
head tilted strangely like an animal's at the presage
of danger. " Jesus, Mary and Joseph," he prayed
blindly, and his eyes by fear were holden. He did
not see a man's head rising slowly in the hay beside
him, he did not know of the long dark look that was
fixed on him for that brief revealing space. He folded
the paper and slipped it carefully into his greasy
breast-pocket and continued then his search for
eggs, the custom of long obedience to the monarchy
of the kitchen stronger in him and more prevailing
than any further danger.

. . . .

" Aunt Dicksie ! Aunt Dicksie ! My God, where
is Aunt Dicksie ? Patsy !—Aunt *Dicksie !* "

" Steady now, Mrs. Curtis ; you been marvellous
—*marvellous*. Don't let go now, please."

That was how they talked to poor Aunt Brenda,
the soldiers who had brought her back to Puppetstown. And she was not being marvellous at all and
knew it and did not care. She was mad and out of
her mind, not because Reggie Grey had been shot
in the car beside her, but because her Evelyn was
fishing on Mandoran (Basil, too, of course, and poor
little Easter), and God only knew what might happen
to him—to them all three—before ever she saw him
again. That was what they could not understand,
these soldiers. She had not time to think of Reggie
now.

The shadowed hall of Puppetstown was strange
against her and unforgiving as she ran in and stood
there calling, while the dark, heavy lorry waited
outside in the lovely evening, armed by watchful,
angry men. The peace of Puppetstown was shut too,
and watchful against her. It was as if she had brought
this destruction, she and none other—but it all sank
from her mind, lost in the conscious agony and terror
of her anxiety for Evelyn, her handsome young son,
the little boy.

Reggie Grey's friend followed her across the hall
and into the long graceful drawing-room where, in
the low evening light, the room seemed drowning
in a vapour of past elegance. The thin, reeded legs
of card tables barely tipped the dark floor, the
mirrors were panels of quiet green light and the
scent of lacquer boxes lifted itself sharply against
the scent of certain thick white roses.

" She's not here," said Aunt Brenda, despairingly. Her voice and her terror cleft through the room in waves that must shake its serenity for ever, and when she fled down it and out through the great open window, its silence closed like a malignant wake behind her.

Down the terraces Reggie's friend followed her and across the tennis court, and ran behind her down the narrow shrubbery paths that led to Aunt Dicksie's far garden. Here, where larkspurs burned their blue against the evening, and white mallows flowered like veined, thin shells, they found Aunt Dicksie, with earthy hands and distant eyes.

" My dear," Aunt Dicksie said. " What ? Tell me." She walked out to the little sunken lawn where the sundial was, holding Aunt Brenda's hand, for she knew that they had news which would disquieten her garden so that, should she hear it there, some gentleness of the place would be for ever lost to her.

" Miss Chevington," said Reggie's friend, " I'm afraid Mrs. Curtis has had an awful shock. She was driving Reggie Grey's car and between Knocklanden and Bruffney on the Mandoran road, the shinners waited for him and shot him there—yes, with her. In the car. They drove cattle across the road to stop them. She got through somehow and brought him back to the mess, but they'd done for him. It's so frightful for Mrs. Curtis——" He stood there looking apologetic and helpless though indeed all he was feeling was : " That blasted, blasted woman.

If he hadn't come out here to see her, if only he hadn't been half off his head about her. And he knew he was for it." Reggie had been his friend, and there was no fairness or softness in his heart for his friend's love. He condemned her as she stood there twisting her gloves in her hands like an hysterical housemaid, and with her eyes on that grave old lady.

" Aunt Dicksie," she was saying, " what are we to do about the children ? Can you think—I can't. If they would only leave the brutes alone till the children get home safe, but they're sending the soldiers up the mountain now, to round up some of these fellows on the run. And supposing they keep the children hidden away up there for—reprisals ! " Her voice fell to a little whisper. " Aunt Dicksie, what are we going to *do* about it ? Quick, think of something. Aren't they late already ? If they were only here we could catch the boat-train to-night and be in London to-morrow morning. Just think of it—the *safety* of it ! But do think of something for us to do *now*."

" The best possible thing *you* can do, my dear," said Aunt Dicksie firmly, " is to go back to the house at once, and see that Nannie and Mary Josie start packing their clothes. I don't for a moment think they're in the smallest danger, and in any case there is no use fussing about them yet, as they are never back from the lake till at least nine o'clock. Besides which, I sent Patsy up to meet them, and, as you know, he is hand in glove with every shinner and poacher in the country. I imagine they will be fairly safe with him."

But as they walked after Brenda through the slow turning evening light, there seemed to Aunt Dicksie a falseness in the evening peace of Puppetstown, a leaning, listening quality, as though Puppetstown had lost her honour and stood now betrayed and forsaken and most desolately in sin and shame before the world. A lonely, wicked old woman of a house. Through her this had come to pass—of that very quality of warmth and of fun and of golden careless laughter that was in Aunt Brenda and the house alike had this come. And now Puppetstown was to be left desolately, a sad grey house leaning blind-eyed down her valley, her beauty gone and her gladness withered and shrunken from her.

" Will you tell me, Major Holt," said Aunt Dicksie, " will you tell me quite frankly if you consider it necessary and advisable that Mrs. Curtis should leave for England ? "

" Well, I do think so, yes. You see, she could quite well be supposed to be able to identify the fellows who got poor Reggie, if we ever catch them. And that being so "—he jerked his head decidedly— " she is just as well out of the country—for a bit anyhow."

" And the children ? "

" Oh, I don't see the least chance of danger for them—unless——" He hesitated.

" Yes, unless ? "

" I was going to say, unless they should happen to run into any of these swine on the run in the hills to-day. In that case their evidence might be supposed to fit in too nicely with their mother's for it to be very healthy for them here."

" Ah, yes," said Aunt Dicksie. They had reached the house now and she leaned the palm of her hand against the day's stored warmth in a granite window-sill. " But as I know nothing," she said, " I am perfectly all right, I imagine ? "

" If there were no loyalists in Ireland," the little English Major said with sudden nervous anger, " there'd be a great deal less trouble for us in the country."

" Yes. Yes, indeed," Aunt Dicksie agreed mildly. " Loyalists are never very popular or very fortunate people. Do come in," she said, " and have a drink, and what shall I send out for the men ? "

But no servants answered when she called, and the kitchen when she went there was empty as a forsaken ship. The great echoing passages of Puppetstown took up her voice and cast it about, and Aunt Dicksie felt a little dismayed, a little shaken, but more than ever sure of her determina-tion to abide by Puppetstown. She brought the men out beer and cake and took two of them back with her to boil a kettle of tea for the rest.

It was eight o'clock, and for the first time in Puppetstown's life as a house, no table was set for dinner. Fled were Mary Josie and her satellite, fled the cook and the kitchenmaid. What word of disaster had been carried to them, or how, would pass the wit of man to tell. They were gone, lifted on the wings of fear. So Puppetstown had lost her ministers, and the early summer darkness settled in on her empty rooms, while upstairs Aunt Brenda packed trunk after trunk, as one possessed by a very frenzy. She would stop and look out of the greying window away towards Mandoran, and stoop to an open trunk again, her eyes changing terribly. Aunt Dicksie did not go up, because to say : " No, they have not come back yet," was really beyond her.

Blank of its flowers and its silver, the dining-room table stared emptily, and Aunt Dicksie, setting glasses and spoons and plates and the branched candlesticks on it, felt strangely void of sensation to meet this occasion. It was as one of the two things she had not known—marriage and death. And she wondered if the one might not have proved and the other would prove as matter-of-fact a business as this unimagined tragedy.

Reggie Grey's friend was sitting with his drink in the hall, the door open to the evening, and the lorry of soldiers was silhouetted blackly against the mountains and the sky. From their several baskets the dogs regarded him with bright, unsympathising eyes. They were uneasy and every now and then walked out on the steps and stiffly round the lorry, that it might be clearly understood this was their house and theirs to keep.

The Major twisted his wrist up sharply to look at his watch as Aunt Dicksie came into the hall.

" I think," he said, and it sounded as kind as a doctor's worst verdict, " if they aren't back in the next half-hour, Miss Chevington, we must be off and find them for you. What do you think ? No need to say anything to Mrs. Curtis, of course—of course not."

" Thank you so much, Major Holt. You are so kind. The thing is I have sent a man after them."

" Your pantry boy, didn't you say ? "

" Yes." How utterly futile and inadequate it sounded. Too absurd. Aunt Dicksie laughed a little, but immediately realising how deeply she was shocking Major Holt, she grew grave again and asked him to come into the dining-room and have some cold food. She did not tell him that the servants had all gone, nor did she talk of the day's disasters, nor yet of what the night might bring forth. Aunt Dicksie did not see any reason to discuss unpleasant realities at meal-times. Polite conversation could quite well be sustained without touching on un-necessary topics.

Major Holt was to remember that dinner hour as one of the most unreal yet actual experiences of his life. He remembered the long, bare table with their two places laid nearest to the window that was open to the dangerous summer night ; the plumey depths of the shrubbery to the left of the house and the decisive steps of the terraces with their grey stone vases cornering them squarely. Death and tumult seemed so preposterously impossible as he sat on the old lady's right hand, listening to her expert talk of dry-fly fishing and of music— two of the things in life he cared most about—and wishing that he could see what that picture was behind her that faded so greenly into the dark wall.

Aunt Dicksie had put on a plum-coloured velvet coat over her tweed skirt and, he thought, all the jewellery she possessed. Diamonds flamed and smoked at her neck and rings slipped and turned on her thin hands. A pocket of her velvet coat looked as though it were bulged with pebbles, but an ear-ring had caught its little hook through the stuff at one corner and hung there, a pearl with two diamond grape leaves, lending a strange, exciting clue to what might be within the pocket. There were blue flowers on the table and the curling branching candlesticks. They drank coffee that had boiled in a silver pot above a little flame during their meal, and a very delightful liqueur brandy before they went out to the hall again, where the dogs suddenly stirred and rose from their baskets and were off towards the wood avenue like three white bullets.

" That's the children." A blade Aunt Dicksie was, haftless and scabbardless, a wind seemed to sing through her and turn on the finest edge of determination when she said : " You'll be able to take them to the boat to-night ? How kind—thank you so much." And then she went to meet them.

Up to the last minute they all thought Aunt Dicksie was coming with them, and there were not many minutes between their return and their long departure.

Evelyn went to his mother's room and sat on her bed. She was all that mattered to him and he was not going to let her out of his sight now. A surge and mist of excitement lay between all their minds and the realisation of this flight and what it must mean. Everything was exaggerated and out of perspective. They had no time to think of Puppetstown. Puppetstown was but a shell now, and without were danger and tribulation and within the hurrying of feet and shiftings of luggage, and Major Holt looking at his watch and saying, " ten more minutes."

Basil tied labels to the dogs, putting on their collars and attaching their chains—Evelyn's spaniel and Max and Kit and Pidgie—and he did not realise that Aunt Dicksie was staying behind till she said, noting his preparations : " Darling, leave Max and Kit with me."

" What ? Aren't you coming ? Well, then, I'm not either."

" Don't make it difficult, Basil. It's quite all right for me. But if you were here I'd go out of my mind with worry."

" Why must you stay, Aunt Dicksie ? "

" There's no ' must,' darling. Only because I'm an obstinate old woman."

" I'll stay too—really I want to."

" You can come back. But you must go with your mother now. It would be so cruel to her if you didn't."

" Come on, Basil," they called him. " Come *on*." He had Pidgie in his arms ready to go, but now he gave her back to Aunt Dicksie. " You take care of her," he said. " She's too old for journeys and it won't make much difference. I'll be back so soon anyway."

" No," Aunt Dicksie said decisively, and tipped her in after him ; " she'll enjoy the change." And the lorry had started and was gone before any one except Major Holt and Basil knew that Aunt Dicksie was going to stay at Puppetstown.

But how unkind a Puppetstown it was. Not so empty as it was vacant ; not so desolate as it was sulky. Rain wrapped the house suddenly about, driving in through the windows in vicious slants. Aunt Dicksie opened the door of the kitchen passage calling for Patsy, who perhaps had returned by now, but no Patsy answered. The kitchen fire was out and those soldiers had left a basketful of dirty tea-cups on the corner of the kitchen table. In the scullery a half-plucked fowl glimmered whitely through its stripped feathers, and a forgotten hound puppy nosed forlornly at the grating of the drain outside.

" Out in the rain and *very* empty—you'll have
yellows, my fellow ! " Aunt Dicksie let him in
and dried him and walked across the yard to put
him to bed with a dish of food in her hand. She
looked in at the three occupied boxes to make
certain that the horses had been fed and then,
a thought suddenly striking her, she led them out
one by one to the field and turned them loose.

" You may kick each other to pieces if you like ; "
she watched them galloping giddily into the distance. " I won't run the risk of having you burnt
in your boxes." She let the hound puppy loose
again outside the stable yard, to sleep in the hay
barn or to contract yellows as seemed best to it,
and bolted the slow, creaking wooden doors before
returning to the heavy indoor coldness of the
house.

There were those who watched Puppetstown that
night. They had seen the soldiers come and go, but
they did not know how many had stayed behind.
They did not know that only Aunt Dicksie was left
at Puppetstown. The house crouched into the night
like a toothless grey wolf, and only Aunt Dicksie
went from room to room with a wandering light,
but twice she whistled a sharp signal into the night.
Her clothes felt heavy on her body, she was very
weary and very lonely and nowhere could she
fortify her sorrowing spirit. Everything she did
was a helpless triviality and her staying at Puppetstown only the idiotic obstinacy of a silly old woman,

availing so much less than nothing against the strong men armed without. How long the marches of that night were in passing by! Afterwards Aunt Dicksie thought how easily she might have gone to bed. Yet at the time it seemed all important to sit up and keep good watch; to creep with attentive busyness from room to room; to listen for feet on the gravel without and brace herself to hear the clamour of men's voices, horridly insistent on admittance.

And little as she was ever to know it, Aunt Dicksie's faint presence it was that saved Puppetstown from fire that night. Some little signs of life they heard—a whistle faintly carried, a dog's barking silenced, a light here and there through the house— convinced the column of soldiers detailed for Puppetstown's burning that the house was not alone nor unguarded, and they waited listening through the night, and before the dawn they went back to the mountains.

That morning came on grey slow feet to Puppetstown. The first sign to Aunt Dicksie that the night had gone was the sight of bats pressing home in their blind thousands; wheeling endlessly and sickeningly in the grim first light, while a legion of all-devouring rabbits moved upon the face of the grass before the windows, and like small creaking wheels the birds' late August singing strained out against the morning. It was the morning at last.

Aunt Dicksie went out on the wet granite steps

with one of Uncle Dick's long tweed coats round her shoulders. Whistling to the dogs, she started out across the soaking grass to see if the horses she had loosed last night had kicked each other lame. But though she tried for half-an-hour, she could not get near them, so, with her long tweed skirt sticking wetly round her legs, and the shakings of laurel bushes crowning her head, she went back to the house and hurried in to open the windows that last night she had blinded and shuttered against she did not know what perils. But in the hall she paused. For, from the kitchen, there came the unmistakable and cheering sounds of a fire being lighted, and when she went down to look in at the door she saw that the efficient maker of the fire was Patsy.

Aunt Dicksie did not ask him why his clothes were so wet or his face so white and sleepless. Never had the sight of any being so pleased her as that of Patsy did at the moment, engaged on this most distasteful piece of domestic servitude.

" Bring the tea up to my room when it's ready, Patsy," she told him, " and pull out the damper for the bath water."

And Patsy, strangely delivered from the perils of the spoken word, and in Puppetstown's present circumstances of no more use to Ireland's cause as spy or discoverer of enemy movements, watched the kettle boil with a freer mind and heart than he had ever carried under the shadow of Ireland's cross.

   •   •   •   •   •   •   •

That was how it started—the absolute reign of
Aunt Dicksie and her able prime minister, Patsy.
For Aunt Brenda did not come back and she kept
the children with her.

" It is the most delightful house," she wrote to
Aunt Dicksie. " Anne—simply too perfect. And
the old gentleman (this was the boys' great-uncle,
Colonel Tattingham) simply adores me. I have
always been just IT to old men. Don't ask me to
let the children go back. It was all just the most
awful nightmare. I can't believe it ever happened,
but it has been a lesson to me about taking risks
for their young lives. My own doesn't matter one
bit, but I do think, Aunt Dicksie, it would be
kinder to all of us if you would only do as all the
other trustees want you to do, and let the Land
Commission have Puppetstown, and come over here
and join us. We can't bear to think of you alone
there where anything might happen, which reminds
me, don't you think the Sèvres ought to be packed
up and sent over here ? It's frightfully valuable, I
know, and the small silver tea-pot, also the Anne
chest that is in my room would look awfully good
in the little hall here. So you see for every reason
you ought to come over. There is the sweetest
cottage with pink hollyhocks in the garden, and the
old gentleman would put a bathroom into it to-
morrow if he thought I wanted it for you. That is if
you didn't want to be with us, which we would
like best, of course. . . ."

At this point in the letter Aunt Dicksie looked up and out through the wide windows, away towards Mandoran, Mooncoin and the Black Stair.

" My niece Brenda," she reflected, " is a vulgar and a selfish woman—and *hard*." Her eyes came back into the dim, lonely room, her spirit seemed to be outside herself and to hover almost greedily about the house she loved and served. She was fanatical in her devotion. " And if she teaches my children not to need Puppetstown "—Aunt Dicksie leaned herself together in her chair—" for whom shall I keep it ? For whom and why ? " And from every side the house whereon she had spent herself whispered and answered : " For yourself. Forever."

So Puppetstown possessed Aunt Dicksie and as the weeks and months and dim hours slipped and shuffled into seasons and into years, more and more she grew at one and at peace with this Puppetstown that was hers alone.

But money was scarce in those days. An obstinate and naughty old woman, the other trustees considered Aunt Dicksie to be, and indeed she was very trying to them. Out of Puppetstown they could not make her go if she did not wish it, there had been provision for that contingency in Uncle Dick's will. There she might live and there she might die, and they could not but regret the fact that she looked like living for very many years yet. The land was let and so was the fishing and shooting, but of the house and the gardens Aunt Dicksie was absolute mistress, and pinch allowances as they would, they failed to embarrass her, straitened though she might be, admit it she would not.

No more did the lavish hospitality of Puppetstown flourish before the countryside. An empty house and blinded, Puppetstown leaned down her river valley. Grass grew in faint tapes of green on her avenues and the rides in her woods closed and met together. Foxes—the woods were full of them, and they would sit on the uncut lawns and bark round the house on a moonlight night. Still there were young horses in the fields, for Aunt Dicksie sent the mares to the stallion in their due season and paid the fees herself. Yearlings, two-year-olds, three-year-olds, and four-year-olds unbroken and unridden. " Sure, they're as throng in it," said one, " as pins in a bottle. There's horses in it now ye'd get up out o' yer bed in the night to be lookin' at them. There's horses in it would win in any show, and there's more ye wouldn't take them in a present if they were throwing after ye." But there they were at Puppetstown, perpetually beautiful, perpetually interesting, and those who thought that Aunt Dicksie did not know them separately and intimately were very much mistaken. She occasionally stuck one of the worser sort into a neighbour with a vague misleading insistence on some minor defect and a glorious ignoring of any major fault in conformation. But nothing of any real value left Puppetstown. She would stand in the humming sweetness of the lime trees on a summer's day enjoying them, and soon even the thought that such a one would not be up to Evelyn's weight or such another must be ridden soon ceased to vex her. They were part of Puppetstown, and Puppetstown was only hers.

In vain Fortune mourned his empty stables and lamented his servitude to the garden. For although the shrubberies might grow until they closed in against the windows of the house, and the daffodils in the grass each April flower smaller and more rarely, in the gardens, and above all in her own garden, Aunt Dicksie's energies were herculean and unflagging.

How lovely Aunt Dicksie's garden was. The ordering of her flowers was conceived in genius and by happy accident. Or was it accident ? It was instead the essential beauty that was undefiled in her and unused, and by herself unrealised, finding here its right and only medium of expression. Was it February ?—that faint, esctatic month—violets were there to fill the cold, quiet rooms of Puppets-town, set about everywhere in the silver violet bowls and in the children's christening mugs. As fires were rare in those rooms the violets would last for days and days, slowly losing their own sweetness to absorb the faint murk of sandal wood and lacquer and old materials that was laid on Puppets-town like a canopy of sprigged brocade. And later, growing on a bank in the garden, there were iris'—

iris' like droves of doves, so silver-breasted and
winged, and purple widowed doves, and Spanish
gentlemen—blue Toledo blades. Those were the
days when a rich wet yellow, and a rich cobalt
blue would have painted you a May-day. And little
sweet plants Aunt Dicksie had that she cherished
in their favourite scattered corners, more loved by
her than were her fine successes. Although the blue
of larkspurs would put her heart across in her body
sometimes, the frozen chastity of Christmas roses
held her in a tearless gratitude.

Inch by inch and little by little, the stirring and
unequal campaign in the garden absorbed more of
Aunt Dicksie's every energy and all her time and
mind. She had at last in her life leisure to make
gardening into a vice—a strange and lovely vice,
a passionate ecstasy. And another strange ridge of
character developed to companion Aunt Dicksie in
her happy loneliness—she grew economical. Partly
because she did not care what she ate, and partly
because she really did not know quite how poor she
was, and had the fixed determination not to outstep
by one shilling the money allowed to her, she
spent less and less on food, nothing whatever on
clothes and as little as she could help on servants'
wages. And what began as a virtue of denial developed into a secret pleasure.

The last of an untrained series of sluts who had,
under Patsy's harsh ruling, formed the female staff
of Puppetstown was dismissed and never replaced.

" Aren't we well enough the way we are ? " said
Patsy, and settled down to his reign undisputed.
He shot rabbits and skinned them and cooked them
(and he trapped them and sold them, too). He
gathered wood and lit fires to air the rooms and their
beds when he saw the paper peeling by the yard
from their walls. The idea of collecting all the
beds in one room and lighting one fire to air the
lot was Miss Dicksie's economical amendment. If
her fishing tenants gave her a salmon, Miss Dicksie
promptly sent it up to Dublin and sold it, and spent
the money on roses for the garden. Her clothes wore
out, but a darksome cupboard full of strange bell-
shaped skirts, and coats with hour-glass middles
and stuffed shoulders, that had belonged to an almost
forgotten Aunt Fanny, filled up the deficiencies of
her wardrobe to her own entire satisfaction. She
saw very few people, for the longer she lived alone
the better she liked her own company and that
of her garden, and her rare visitors, easily perceiving
that they were not wanted, stayed away entirely
or only went to Puppetstown to gather some fresh
tale of Miss Chevington's growing eccentricity and
meanness, with which to divert the countryside.

And if Aunt Dicksie had known she would not
have cared. That extreme and unaffected uninterest
in what her neighbours might think of her actions,
which is one of the few unassailable prerogatives
left to the aristocracy, Aunt Dicksie possessed in
a marked degree. If she chose to eat boiled rabbit

and drink tea at the same meal, what was that to any one ? Certainly she asked nobody to share it with her. If people stayed to a meal it was afternoon tea, when they had red currant jam always. It was sour and fozey because Aunt Dicksie did not allow more than half a pound of sugar to a pound of fruit, and she always picked the currants green to save the ones the birds would eat if she waited for them to ripen. Forgotten indeed were the dinner-parties and all the fun that used to go on at Puppetstown for so many years. Forgotten by Aunt Dicksie too. She had never been so happy in all her years at Puppetstown as she was now, with nothing left to her but the house itself. She had always worked to keep Puppetstown for others, now for herself she made beautiful the things she cared about and neglected what seemed to her of no account. Always before her was the dim thought that the children would be coming back, that this was for them. But they did not come for so long ; they would be strange to her and to the house both if they should come now. There grew in her mind, like some strange little plant that she had put in her garden and forgotten, the thin and shadowy hope, never denied because never admitted, that perhaps, *perhaps*, they would not come at all.

PART II

I

EASTER was twenty-one. She was of age. The outward sign of this exciting circumstance faced her across the empty railway carriage in which she was travelling to Oxford. This was a large crocodile leather dressing-case complete with gold fittings, and of such stupendous weight that three men and a boy would scarcely have proved adequate for its porterage. Easter had bought it only yesterday from Asprey, and had not yet come to regret her rash act. She gazed at it now almost with reverence. It was the tangible and outward sign that now the spending of both her life and her money was her own undivided concern. As the carriage was empty and there were, she knew, nearly ten minutes before they came to the next stop, she decided on the pleasant pastime of squeezing the contents of a tube of vanishing cream into one of the legion gold-topped boxes in her case. A pleasant sport it was too. After which she ate a banana and thought about Life, especially her own life. A good deal of it, she could not help feeling, had slipped past her already. Ridiculous that at the advanced age of twenty-one she should be as she was now, on edge

with excitement over her first Commem. week ;
although Evelyn was now in his last year at Oxford,
and had asked each year if Easter might not come
up for the Commem. balls. But until last year
Easter had been away at her school in Paris,
where Uncle Vivian had insisted with Aunt Brenda
that she was to stay. There they had tried to teach
her, among other useful things, how to use her eyes
and a lipstick, instructions which she absorbed
eagerly, but had not yet learned to put to any really
devastating effect. Last year Easter had wound up
her education by a tour of the Chateaux on the Loire
and had set about Life in earnest and in the right
way by being presented at one of the first courts
of the season. Alas, this excellent beginning was all
that she accomplished before a childish plague of
chicken-pox fell upon her to devastate and desolate
of their bright doings the first months of her grown-
up estate.

Last winter had been all right. She had hunted
two days a week and attended most of the more
pompously excellent of the hunt balls and county
balls. The end of the season she had wound up with
a fall on her head so severe that she had scarcely
protested when they packed her off to an elderly
cousin, who had a villa on Lake Como, for the rest
that the doctors ordered. But now she had recovered
and while acutely unable to realise this new emanci-
pation, was more than ready to have another go at
Life. The only question was—had she not left it

rather late ? Twenty-one was a vast age at which to start what should, properly speaking, have been begun quite three years earlier.

The boys were very sweet with her, but she wondered if they didn't (especially Evelyn) find her somehow wanting. How, she was not sure ; certainly not in sophistication, for after Madame Liènard's (and all the amazing things the girls there knew) she felt that there was very little left in the world of which she would not have a working knowledge when the time came to put it to the test. Besides she had told Basil a story last Christmas which he had even advised her not to repeat ! That was like Basil. Of course she had told Evelyn afterwards, but had chosen an unfortunate moment to do so, for all he said was :

" 'Ware Riot, Easter. Muck, my girl."

She might have known it would not come off. So few of the things she did with Evelyn were completely successful, although she had known moments of vivid excitement with him. His mind never slurred back to discuss such times ; perhaps that was what lent them a sort of freak preciousness. He never tried, Evelyn, about anything. But when you were with him you were keyed up to an intense point of effort. In streaks you knew supreme enjoyment in his company. Yet, on the whole, for solid slumping comfort, Basil's companionship was difficult to better.

Both the boys were to be in Oxford for these three

days. Basil, who was a pupil at a stud-farm, Easter suspected was definitely interested in some girl (her name was Sarah Middleton) who was in the party. Easter and Basil and Evelyn would all stay at Luddington Court where Sarah lived with her mother, Lady Anna Middleton.

Easter thought furiously about her clothes. That new pink dress which she had been convinced was so immensely fetching, now only reminded her of pink blotting paper. On the whole she decided that the black satin which fitted like a second black skin, and which Aunt Brenda had vainly implored her not to buy, would perhaps be the most attractive to men. She had never seen herself approach so nearly to her own ideal of seductive womanhood as when, having strained it about her skimpy form, she practised undulations and pinched up her new ten guinea permanent wave in front of the big glass in her hotel bedroom. Simply she felt that it was very good. Evelyn even, who was devastatingly unobservant, could scarcely fail her in excited approval.

Easter burrowed in her dressing-case for Evelyn's last letter.

" MY DEAR EASTER,—So glad they will let you come. (Didn't he realise that she could come and go now as she pleased—but of course he did, for had he not joined with Basil in a twenty-first birthday present of an inordinately expensive gramophone,

together with a record of each of his own six
favourite tunes.) So glad they will let you come.
Come by the 3.20. Basil and I will meet you at
Oxford. Could you bring a box of Charbonel's
chocolates—chiefly No. 9's. Put it down to Mother.
I'll pay her.

" Yours ever,
" EVELYN."

Horror ! She had forgotten all about them.
Easter raised her eyes from the letter, to stare
despairingly at the coloured photograph of Torquay
on the opposite side of the compartment.

Well, what was to be done ? A thousand times
over would she have exchanged her new dressing-
case for a brown papered parcel of chocolates.
That was one of the worst things about Evelyn.
One felt as though one had committed an atrocity
of national importance did one so much as forget
to bring him the tube of tooth paste he had asked
for. Not that he fussed. It wasn't that. But he
asked one so seldom to do even the smallest thing,
that the mind counted forgetfulness of his wish as
a betrayal. " If I wire for them," Easter thought,
" they'd be here in the morning. I can say they
hadn't got No. 9 ready." The rocks in the picture
of Torquay relaxed their sternness. She sank back
to renewed contemplation of her dressing-case.
Really it was almost bridal in its magnificence.

She was regally conscious of the independence it typified. The dressing-case was hers. Puppetstown—far off, beleaguered, and forgotten—was hers. What of Puppetstown ? Nothing, simply nothing.

Evelyn and Basil and Easter, old Colonel Tattingham's nephews and niece (it was never remembered that Easter was no relation), who lived at the dower house of Tattingham Park with their bridge-playing mother and aunt (who rode to hounds with such nice judgment and was so excellent a hostess)—that's what they had become, Evelyn and Basil and Easter. Colonel Tattingham liked to have them there—they came up to dinner on Sunday night (that was a permanent institution). He liked to see the children riding in the park. They were as incident to it as were the deer. He liked to pay for the twins' schooling ; he had put their names down for Eton when his nephew was killed, that gay young Harry who had made so little of a business about being his heir. He liked to go with Brenda and that funny little cousin to see the boys on the 4th of June, but not on St. Andrew's day now. (Shocking cold he caught last time he watched the game.) He was so fond of Easter too. Sometimes he gave her a throat lozenge and sometimes a sovereign. Alas, that vulgar paper money ! He would slip his forefinger and thumb into his waistcoat pocket before he remembered that sovereigns belonged to the older, more gentlemanly days, and dislike of the nasty fuss incident upon the extraction

of a note from his case was responsible sometimes
for the more easily produced cough lozenge. Easter
could never quite tell which it was to be but was
equally polite in her thanks for either.

The boys rode so nicely. He liked that in them
and dared say Evelyn would make a polo player
one day. And when, as he had done ever since
he remembered, he removed himself and many of
his servants and rod cases and gun cases and much
more impedimenta of sport to the north in August,
it was an interest and delight to him to take the
boys and Easter as well. They were all fishers and
so keen—knew a great deal about the thing too.

Smooth and pleasant were the children's days at
Tattingham—unadventured and orderly. Even Basil
produced no more brogue in his holidays now.
Easter asked her girl friends to stay. Uncle Vivian
gave a dance for the very young at Christmas time,
and there was a lawn-meet at Tattingham the
following day. Uncle Vivian wore brightly-coloured
worsted gloves and walked out to see the hounds,
stepping precisely down the long grey *perron* from
the door. His black silk stock was polka dotted in
white, his tidy white side-whiskers crisp in the
winter cold. Everybody must have a drink. And
he followed the hounds in his car (careful to do no
mischief) and saw a good fox found in his coverts ;
and saw Evelyn having a real go and (more unusual
in the very young) bring it off too : and saw Easter,
who had been left, doing—by Jove—the cleverest bit

of skirting he'd ever seen. He was very contented
in his riches and his benevolence. He delighted to
see them so happy.

Easter remembered that day's hunting after the
dance so well. Silver Flare had one of her real
going days (rather a spasmodic event with her) and
between having her heart in the matter and never
putting a foot wrong she earned the praise that
fell to her name as Easter (Easter and Evelyn) rode
home in the evening.

What a day it had been indeed. From Waterloo,
the last of Tattingham's woodlands, Evelyn had
viewed their fox away : a dark grey-hound of a
fox, no heavy-bellied, chicken-stealer this. He
slipped over a corner of the fence and along the
ditch, stopping and listening, before he upped with
his glorious full-tagged brush and set his mask for
the open.

Evelyn watched him over the first field from the
covert. He was savage with excitement. But no
cracked schoolboy holloa from him. He slipped the
spurs into that blood-like weed (bred, Evelyn
thought, well enough to win the National, and a
certainty for point-to-points in the spring) and up
the ride with him to where Jim Tucker, first
whipper-in (a bad man to view a fox, but rather a
pal of Evelyn's) sat on his horse, quiet and alert—
a perfect tailor's-dummy of a servant, all beauty
and uselessness.

A good boy, Evelyn. He fairly had that bridle-

gate off its hinges when the huntsmen came galloping to the shrilling ecstasy of Jim's holloa. And,
not three minutes behind their fox, sterns down and
heads up, hounds fairly raced over the wide demesne
fields. Out of the woodlands in good earnest they
were, and with such a start the field may gallop
to catch them.

All very nice for a sweet short space, but the stain
of sheep brings hounds to their noses. Charles
is over the main road now, reeking yet with the
traffic of horse-boxes and cars innumerable which
have come that way to the meet, and Jim, galloping
on for a view, is only just in time to hold up the
cursed crowd of following motors, while his horse
skates across the tarmac.

As the huntsman holds his hounds on over the
road, the richest gentleman in the country steps out
of the leading offence in the way of cars : " Remember I'm shooting Hendaby on *Thursday*,
Master." (To-day is Friday, he says.) " W'ere's
Vi ? " he says to his wife. His daughter Vi, having
let her 600 guinea hunter full out in the wake of a
young Lancer soldier, is here all right. And so by
now are most of the field. A trim young thing, Vi.
A bit free with her tongue :

" *As* usual, Papa—*the* unforgivable sin—you and
your old cab bang in the wrong place. What a
God-damned old fool you are ! " She smiled on her
soldier pilot. " Well, we've caught them, anyhow,"
said she.

"*And* considering the sub. I pay, the least he could do was wait for you——"

"Oh, *shut-up*, Papa!—Christ, they're on." said Vi. "Now stay where you are, damn you, Papa," said Vi.

Jim's holloa half a mile down the road put matters right indeed; he has viewed their fox crossing back over the tarmac. Hounds are lifted on and a couple of rough Welsh hounds do rather more than their share of it over a forty-acre field of wheat, round which the field gallop jealousy, lest they be given the slip once more.

"Gallop and jump—blast ye! *Blast* ye!" thinks the huntsman. But his hounds are on grass again. Luckily it proves a holding sort of scent to-day, for they are some way behind their fox now. However, on grass they can do what they're good for, which is galloping. However, though Jim, on for a view, holloas again at a lucky moment and, catching hold of his hounds once more, their huntsman lifts them across half a mile of country, their fox beats them to the sanctuary of Hendaby Wood, short of which point hounds are stopped, since the richest gentleman of all hopes to shoot his pheasants there next week.

Did daughter Vi ever know whether hounds were hunting a fox or merely scratching themselves, whether they were at fault or whether they had been stopped, she might have said: "Oh, damn Papa! *Please* carry on, Master." But as she has not even the remotest idea that these are the woods of her home she leaves Papa alone for once and occupies herself with cursing the groom who fails to put in an appearance with her second horse.

After a tedious, badgering forty minutes with a home-lover in another big woodlands, they jog on to the next draw—Little Barkington Spinneys. Here the terriers are run through the artificial earth. Out comes Charles James over a sack neatly laid like a doormat at the mouth of the earth. And the way hounds bust him, through cars, over tarred roads and across a railway line, as if tied to him, is indeed surprising. Then—who-whoop !—fair and square in the open. Very sensational reading it made in the next account for the sporting press when, curiously enough, no mention was made of the fact that hounds hardly attempted to break up their fox. Well, a fashionable field must gallop and jump, and a professional huntsman must kill foxes for his great name's sake—scarcely for the sake of his hounds.

Evelyn and Easter enjoyed themselves thoroughly. Even their young stomachs had had enough of galloping and jumping—and most certainly their horses had—as, in the evening of the day they rode home together.

Motor-buses passed them on the main road, looming by like great lighted liners, putting their horses into the ditch, filling their hearts with fear. In Perpingham they gave their horses a drink and bought themselves a packet of ginger biscuits before they

rode on. A shower had turned the tarmac to black
ice. Twice Easter's horse nearly slipped up and once
Evelyn's sat down fair and square. The headlights
of cars came ravening out of the growing dark.
It was lucky that their horses had the day behind
instead of in front of them. Four horrible miles of
it and they turned to their left along one of those
narrow, deep roads that are left in England yet.
Before them were bare dark woods, solid and purple
in the body, and pencilled with grave strokes against
the sky. Rooks tossed over them; innumerable,
their thin black profiles against the red sun.

Easter and Evelyn rode side by side then, eating
biscuits, their joint memory warmed to the same
chord. Evelyn, the aloof, Evelyn, the inaccessible,
in his present mood was close and garrulous as a
little boy. How I viewed the fox. How I won the
hunt, the true burden of his cry but little concealed.
Effort had been his and fulfilment. Easter was there
to hear his boast, and Easter, listening and saying
nothing, as was her part to do, smiled to herself,
her first conscious smile of womanly indulgence,
and held her tongue about her own successful nick
in, and how she had pounded Vi Rayner, whose
horse had stopped with her at a stiffish stake-and-
bound fence. Of more consequence to her than
this telling was Evelyn's confidence.

Along a wide, pale ride they went through the
wood, the red sky straightly before them, the
woods closing darkly behind. Their thoughts were

together close and untroubled. They were content together in a faint, delightful exhaustion—exquisitely content. Their horses went placidly home, their minds flung forward to their feed, and the deep rustle of straw and the kindness of hot bandages. The shrill excitement of the morning was as if it had never been, for now it was past. That was one of the moments with Evelyn that Easter remembered with a burning secrecy and lonely shyness. A day to echo clear in the better remembrances of years.

Basil, who had gone home early with a lame horse, was playing bridge with his mother and two other ladies when Evelyn and Easter came in to fall on their tea like hawks, and swagger after with arrogant stomachs full-fed. Basil had missed the fun, to be sure, but was that a reason good enough for him to say at the conclusion of the high tale of their doings :

" Well !—hunting here *is* a bit vulgar——"

They stared at him. What indeed he could have meant they did not care to guess. Poor Basil ! He was soured by his bad luck that day. They pitied him and raced for the boot-jack and the first hot bath.

Basil, having collected six shillings at the conclusion of the rubber (he was a terror to play cards), had betaken himself to the study where he would write one of his short, infrequent letters to Aunt Dicksie. He felt impelled thereto by the vulgarity of English hunting. Aunt Dicksie never answered his letters.

" My dear Aunt Dicksie,—How are you ?
We are having good sport here. A great scenting
season. Easter and Evelyn had a good hunt to-day.
I missed it. My young horse was lame so I had to
take him home early. Very sore on splints. I am
using a blister I got from a fellow who trains near
here. It is such a pity, he was coming on so well,
and that hunt to-day would have done him a world
of good. Pidgie's pup is brave and true to a
fox-scent. Mummy is very well and playing bridge
a lot.

" With love from
" Basil."

Over the writing-table there hung a picture. A
picture of an Irish point-to-point. In this picture
rain fell with a south wind strong behind it, driving
it into the faces of the young lads whose horses
were landing (all of them as it chanced right-side-
up) over a bank and ditch of uncleaned and vast
proportion. A wave caught at the turning this
picture, speed and effort and the wild romance of
a moment. Almost the curse of the man who was
bumped sobbed out savagely, snatching against
the pace and the rain. Oh, intricate and observing
artist ! He had not forgotten so much as the tube
in that blood-like bay. " And the wind," Basil
pondered, " will be in the tube. He'll not win it."
An old priest reared his vast umbrella with practised
exactitude against the rain. In rapt satisfaction

he saw the horses well over that fence. More than likely he had backed a useful winner. All the humour and discomfort and light gallantry and great roguery and enormous sincerity of sport in that country so near and so very far away, it was all captured there and set down with a brief and laughing sympathy by one who knew.

The pulse of it beat through Basil for the many hundredth time. He would return, yes, he would go back to Puppetstown. But not as a visitor, it must be to live there. And how should that be done when Puppetstown was Easter's and Easter asked no more of life than this, to live here in the exquisite carefulness of England : to hunt with the fashionable fraud that here took the place of the blood and bones of sport she had known and forgotten. The prospect of her next London season, a stable and pleasant prospect before her. Her many nice girl-friends. So many anchors to the busy placidity of life. Easter would never want to return to Puppetstown. When Aunt Dicksie died (before, perhaps) Puppetstown would be sold, and Basil would not have the money to buy it. His visions of blood-stock on the limestone land, and himself thinking and planning about the mares and the young horses ; and himself fishing the Sally stream and the Phuca's pool and Lennon's stand ; and himself shooting cock in the thick woods with their wet, soaking springs : and himself walking the little roads home after a day up the Red Bogs after snipe,

with a small bundle of a cocker tired behind him,
they were fated poorly, those dreams. Uncle Vivian
had a low opinion of Ireland—a savage and distant
land. Never would he provide the money for Basil
to set up a stud farm there—whatever he might
do for him in England. And it was now that Basil
wanted to be back in Ireland. Now—now—not
when he was old and had given up longing. The
wishing of the very young is a hard and a bitter
matter.

. . . . . .

But now long, long meadows brazen with butter-
cups and strident with advertisements of pills,
warned Easter that Oxford was near. She prepared
feverishly to make the best of her appearance,
excoriating her nose with a new and untamed powder
puff and wrenching furiously at her clothes and hat.
The train did not wait to allow her to complete the
work by a smear of lip-stick. It slowed mercilessly
down to where a multitude of hatless young men
in flannel trousers and pale tweed coats swarmed
on the platform, each saying : " Hallo ! Here you
are ! Splendid ! " to some peerless and only girl
as she stepped out of her carriage.

" Hallo ! Here you are ! Splendid ! " said Evelyn's
voice as Easter vainly tried to descry a porter
among the throng of young men. He loomed towards
her through the crowd like a bright star caught
down suddenly from the sphere where it belongs—
that was always one's first impression of Evelyn—

wherever he was or whatever he was doing he could not possibly belong there because he did not care enough about it—one could not tell about him at all.

He picked up Easter's dressing-case and put it down quietly and immediately. " What is it, my dear ? The body ? I quite see. Porter ! P'raps this porter won't give us away."

" Easter ! Hallo, Easter ! " It was Basil. You didn't see Basil coming in a crowd like you did Evelyn, but there he was, solid and dark and friendly in the bright crowd ; a very worn brown coat that he'd ridden in a lot, flannel trousers and a blue shirt and a battered Old Etonian tie, and his three-cornered blue eyes screwed up in a doggish dark face—Basil.

Easter, feeling a little shy of them both, talked at once not very intelligently : " I nearly lost this train, you know. What are these people like ? Shall I like them ? I know I will if you do, but tell me. Oh, Evelyn ! Those chocolates "—she dashed on, forgetting her well-prepared lie—" I *am* sorry, I forgot about them. Do forgive me. We can wire, can't we ? "

" Oh, it's quite all right, Easter. It was a stupid thing to ask you to do. You must have been awfully busy yesterday, too."

" I was. Evelyn, I must tell you about the lawyer—never can I describe to you what he was like."

" Here's my car——" They had talked their

way through the subway and now stood in the gold-beaten afternoon light outside the station. The hot light seemed to be burning fumes of petrol and tar.

Far beyond the present drab squalor of the station, the spires of churches pierced through a thick blue blanket of haze. Easter recognised with the little shock of surprise that familiar things seen suddenly give us, Evelyn's rather down-at-heel Morris car. Then, with an inward gasp as though there was a step missing from the orderly stairway of her mind, she was saying, " How do you do " to Sarah Middleton. And Sarah Middleton was the loveliest girl Easter had ever seen. She had the beauty of absolute quality and she was so well-made that one did not realise her height, yet when she got out of the car and stood beside Evelyn, as they packed Easter's suitcases in, she was nearly as tall as he was. She was wearing a very thin, yellow straw hat that bent and flopped exquisitely almost to her shoulders. Her unbelievable grey eyes were set, it seemed, almost inches apart in her head and her hair, which was red (a dark colour like wood), waved squarely. There was about her an immortal moment of beauty, and an unawareness of its power on others that only reminded Easter of—suddenly she knew—of Evelyn.

They drove through Oxford ; past bright shops and past the grey, breathless beauty of colleges, with burning glimpses of gardens seen through their deep, safe gateways ; and cars full of young men in flannels with sleek, dark heads and astonishing fair heads, and exquisitely dressed, cool girls spun by in the heat.

Evelyn stopped outside a yellow hotel with window boxes and a black gulf of hall full of deep-blue chairs set about in tactful corners. He wanted to speak to a man. Basil ordered four cocktails and a packet of Goldflake cigarettes.

Here there were girls with their mothers pouring out tea for young men, and girls without their mothers drinking cocktails with young men. A little dull these last seemed, finding each other's company a trifle difficult as the very young sometimes do. The groups with a leaven of elders were the gayest.

Easter drank her cocktail when the waiter brought it because she thought this was the correct thing to do, but Sarah would not : " I don't like them," she said, " you'll have to be kind to it, Basil." She had a laughing, hurrying voice, not very distinct, and she had carried a large white paper bag into the room with complete unconcern. Now she said to Easter :

" Have you met Sinclair ? Oh, you must—how very careless of me ! " and opening the bag, in which she had poked round air-holes with the top of a pencil, she picked out a young tortoise not much bigger than a crab. She did it very quietly, showing it to Easter behind her chair, obviously not wishing to create a sensation. " He's for my little brother," Sarah explained, packing him up again. " It's his birthday to-morrow. Basil, do you think you could ask the waiter for a little bit of lettuce ? He might eat it on the way home."

" Oh, he *is* attractive." Easter peered into the bag. " How old is your little brother ? I *would* like to buy him a birthday present too."

" Oh, no, you mustn't, Easter. Really, you must *not*. Please ! Well, if you really do mean to, what he would like best would be a film for his camera— No. 2 Brownie." She called after Easter, who was shooting out of the lounge in immediate quest of a chemist's shop where photographic material might be found. They saw her encounter Evelyn and the pair went out together, Evelyn stooping politely to hear what she had to say.

" Your cousin is nice," Sarah said to Basil. " How sweet of her to want to buy a present for Benjy ! I like her tweed. It's awfully good, and her dressing-case. Have you and Evelyn finished paying for that gramophone you bought her ? Really, Basil, you should, I think. It is terrible to be in debt. You lived in Ireland with her—you and Evelyn——"

" Yes, at Puppetstown, we all lived there. It belongs to Easter now." Basil looked round the hotel lounge with level eyes. Puppetstown was such a funny place to name there. He usually kept the word Puppetstown to himself and said : " Oh, yes, we used to live in Westcommon," when he was asked about Ireland.

" How lovely to have a house of your very own, wouldn't it be—such fun ? Think of all the people you could ask to stay ! How old is Easter, Basil ? "

" Oh, she is just twenty-one."

" Well, I'm very nearly, almost, twenty-one. I'm sure she's clever ; she looks clever."

" No. No, not a bit," Basil reassured her. " She plays tennis well, though, and she's easy to dance with." He got out of his chair as Evelyn and Easter came towards them.

" Sorry we were so long," they explained. " We bought a camera—yes, for Benjy—you know that Brownie lets the light in, Sarah."

" Oh, how awful of you ! Evelyn, why did you let her ? " Sarah was embarrassed with her thanks. " Thank you so very much indeed," she said. " Thank you ever so much."

" It's from us all three." Evelyn finished his cocktail and looked dreamily at Sarah's for an instant. " *Sure* you don't want to drink this ? But you hate them, don't you ? Would you like a lemon squash ? Would you, Easter ? No. Well, do you mind paying for it all, Basil. I have no money."

" I spent most of mine on Sinclair." Sarah peered into a very small green purse. " Almost none," she reported sadly.

" I have only two bob. Basil extracted it solemnly.

" And I suppose Easter has nothing but a dressing-case full of solid gold ? "

" Well, I have about six pounds," Easter said,
" and I can always cash a cheque."

" So can I if I walk to my tailor's, but he was rather
grim with me this morning. I think I'll take ten
shillings off you, Easter, if I may. Thanks very
much."

" Perhaps we had better go home now." Sarah
swung to her feet like a poem suddenly set to music.
" As it is, I'm afraid we'll be rather late for tea.
Mother is expecting us back or we could have it
here "—she smiled at Easter—" out of your six
pounds," she added quaintly. " Perhaps we'd
better go, though. What do you think ? "

" Yes, I think we'd better if Lady Anna is expecting us."

" Oh, yes, better go home," the two boys chorused
at once, and they went out into the afternoon heat
once more. The cushions of Evelyn's Morris blazed
with heat as they packed themselves in—Sarah and
Easter in front with Evelyn, and Basil blocked into
a corner of the back by Easter's suitcases. Sinclair
took the air on his knee.

Luddington Court where Sarah lived was ten
miles from Oxford. After eight miles of main road,
strident with cars, a small bye-lane turned down
to the Court. Dark green woods embowered plump,
sunny meadows. Air-blown poppies floated out on
a field of corn as if on clear trembling green water.
The road wound downhill all the way, till it bridged
a little river, and all at once a high wall of very old,

very small dark bricks sprang up on the left-hand side, and over the top of it you could see the wavering sinking roof of a house and its tall needling chimneys like elegant grey lace. Evelyn turned in beneath an archway in the long wall and stopped the car in the hot blue shadow that was flung down like a cloak at one side of the courtyard. It had been the kennel-yard really, and the windows of one end of the house (wide uneven windows glazed with dimpled greenish panes of glass) looked out into the yard. A pear tree of great age with a thick stem and branches like the gouty fingers of an old man's hand slept against the hot brick wall, and in one corner a high and narrow iron gate with two grey stone herons (their feathers carved very distinctly), standing on its tall, stone posts led into the garden.

Basil shut the gate of the garden and walked behind the others along the narrow flagged path that faithfully pursued every curious corner and angle of the house, stepping aside politely for the buttress of a chimney and turning close again for the worn shallow step of a door. There were several small, friendly-looking doors leading out into the garden. A border of flowers grew along the house like a ribband below the windows, and on the other side of the path the garden dropped slowly down in measured flights to the woods and the river below.

Basil was afraid of Luddington. He was curious to see how the place would affect Easter. The re-action of persons to places always interested him.

He was fond of Easter. He liked her tidy, little brown face and shy green eyes and her thin eager body. He liked the surprising things she sometimes said (which always embarrassed Evelyn, who could not understand Basil's idea that Easter would be marvellous when she was twenty-eight). He was as interested in her as one can be in a girl one has known very intimately for all her life. He cherished her with a grain of possessiveness. She was their female representative, his and Evelyn's, and he liked her to do them credit. He watched her covertly when Evelyn introduced her to Lady Anna. He always liked Easter's manners with her elders—there was something very unaffected and exact in their politeness—something rather fine and delicate.

Lady Anna had been as beautiful as Sarah once and it was a lovely forgetfulness of that past time which was so wonderful in her now. She was entirely unaffected and sensible ; thanked God night and morning for a daughter so beautiful and so satisfactory as Sarah ; looked after her house with exquisite and loving competence, and her garden with unenterprising skill ; and was a very efficient mistress of her young son's property.

She was sitting under the layering shadow of a cedar tree when they found her, bright silver tea things beside her, and a big useful basket of mauve sweet peas that she had been cutting exactly matched her mauve linen dress. She was very tall like her

daughter and her manner was neither motherly
nor yet contemporary. Easter felt a little afraid
of her at once—always to herself a sign that she
would like a person.

After tea a small boy in grey flannel shorts and a
blue silk shirt came labouring up the flights of steps
from the bottom of the garden. He was hot and
crumpled and rather dirty, and so was the tired
little governess who hurried away into the house,
leaving him with his mother.

"Mummy, mummy, *look*!" he shrilled rapidly.
"I cort three fleas on Spider. Look!" He pulled
an envelope folded in dirty, careful creases out of
his pocket, breathing hard as he unfastened it
with inapt but careful fingers.

"Are they *quite* dead, Benjy?"

"Yes, Miss Smiff killed them. *Look*!"

Basil took his cigarette out of his mouth.

"*That's* what we should have had for Edward,"
he said, "an envelope. What mugs we were!"

"Edward——" Evelyn repeated. "Edward?"

But Easter remembered their worm, Edward, and
a reflection of past concern for his fate flashed dimly
through her mind.

Basil was gravely telling over the three corpses.

"Nail their noses to the kennel door," he murmured.

"No. I keep them on stamp paper in Spider's
book." Benjy dropped them carefully back into the
same corner of the envelope.

" You shall have three minutes in the strawberry bed," Lady Anna told her son. " Basil shall go with you. No, we've finished all the tea-time ones. You must get your own—and go to the dairy for your cream. Easter, will you come with me? I'll show you your room. Would you like to play tennis after that, or are you tired? "

" No, I would love to."

" Well——" Lady Anna picked up her basket.

" You'll play too, Mummy, please! " Sarah begged.

" No. I'd like to see you play against Easter. She's good, I know." Lady Anna walked briskly over the lawn—Easter beside her, her hat and small bag crushed under her arm, her short hair a little damp from shyness. Afternoon tree shadows skipped over it and across her eyes, deepening their colour.

" This way——" Lady Anna's footsteps sounded brightly on the almost bare boards of the hall, its walls were washed a warm uneven white and a wide blunt staircase led up from it to an oak gallery with a worn, wavy floor from which little dark flights of steps, twos and threes and sometimes a whole running flight of them, disappeared towards wings and passages and unknown parts of the house. Lady Anna opened one of the doors, it had a very bright brass knocker shining in its dark panels, and showed Easter her room. It was a wide shallow room full of light. A narrow bed with thin fluted pillars stood

at one end, a piece of deep bright blue brocade
spread over its blankets. There were cheerful books
on a table near—Edgar Wallace, a set of blue
Kiplings, and *Peacock Pie* to entrance fantastic
moments. A very long window, built in the deep wall
so that its sill was broad and as high as your elbows,
looked into the garden and down its depths but not
along, you could not see the whole of the garden
and what you saw was as though through sea water,
the bright colour of the flowers corrected by the
outbent, greenish panes of the glass. There was a
blue carpet on the floor and the walls again were of
the same warm white as those of the hall, and
indeed of all the rooms in the house. There were
dark beams of wood in the ceilings as if in the cabin
of an old ship, and cupboards flattened into the wall
with doors like the dark doors of little churches.

" This is your room," Lady Anna said. " I hope
you'll be happy in it. You know we have no *unkind*
people here—all our people are kind, though they're
not always happy, poor things." (Easter could not
think what she meant.) " Here you are—biscuits—
bath salts—cigarettes——" She opened lovely
boxes and queer, foreign jars that Easter would never
have guessed had been put to such useful purposes.
" Will you change now for tennis, and may I see
your dress for to-night ? I expect Huggott has
unpacked your things."

She had indeed. Easter experienced a thrill of
satisfied pride as her eye caught the perfect regiment

of gold bottles and brushes marshalled on the shining dressing-table.

" I thought I would wear my black dress to-night," Easter said boldly. " It's new."

" It is quite charming." Lady Anna swung the slender sophisticated wisp of a dress near the light. " Quite lovely," she repeated, " but almost too smart ; rather a fashionable restaurant sort of dress, isn't it ? Look, what's this ? " She picked up the soft blur of pink from the back of the cupboard. " Perfect, my dear—with a string of pearls—do you mind my telling you ? It's just right. I'll send Huggott to help you. I like dressing Sarah myself. I know Huggott will try to make you wear that lovely black, but don't let her—it's wrong for to-night."

" Oh, but," Easter protested faintly, " there are, there are so many different fastenings on that pink dress. . . . I hate putting it on."

" You shall have Huggott, my dear," Lady Anna promised brightly, " and now I must fly away and leave you. . . ."

.   .   .   .

" No, Sarah," she said just before dinner, " I couldn't allow the child to wear it. She nearly cried, poor lamb ! but in time she'll be grateful."

Sarah was standing before the glass in her bedroom, in a long, white dress like a bright cloud, like a bright swan, her body as disciplined to beauty, her mind as subdued. " Powder my back, Mummy," she said, " before you go. Thank you. She plays tennis well, doesn't she ? We had such a good game."

" Sit quietly here till dinner time," her mother said. " I don't want you to look tired."

" Very well, I can polish my nails. Would you turn out the centre light as you go, Mummy. Thank you."

Easter knocked at the door : " *Oh !* " She stopped —Sarah was so beautiful, so still with beauty, as she sat there looking up from her quiet hands, it was almost embarrassing. Such a fussy little vulgarity she made you feel. Easter came over towards her, her prettily tilted little body was insignificant. She was very sweet. She was nothing to look at. There she stood, twisting the lids of the boxes on Sarah's dressing-table, twisting her face at her own funny reflection in the looking-glass, while Sarah sat, bent divinely like half the moon, over her hands.

" What lovely scent ! May I ? " Easter poised the long glass stopper, oily with scent, over her wrist. Now it was Sarah's own scent. She was wearing it to-night. " Of course "—she hesitated— " but it's meant for auburn hair, you know—' scent for an auburn personality '—the bottle says."

" H'm." Easter put back the stopper with a faint click. " Essence of vixen, I presume."

Sarah stared up from her nails for a fleeting second. She saw no point whatever in the remark. Only Basil would have liked it. " It must be almost dinner time ; shall we go down ? " she suggested.

In the hall Evelyn was standing talking to Benjy's governess. The evening light streamed in, dyeing the white walls with queer, prismatic colours. Without, the garden was invested with a hushed, almost feline security that breathed and flowed up from it. And Sarah, standing with her back to the wide open window, seemed as though caught about in the same evening stupor. She was apart from the others and a part of the quiet garden.

Evelyn introduced Easter to Miss Smith and went over to stand beside Sarah. They went out into the garden together, and Easter saw them walking slowly down the shallow terrace steps, gravely distant. Evelyn, so young and prim and handsome in the almost princely elegance of his green Bullingdon coat, and Sarah with her white dress flowing down the terraces a yard behind her slow slender feet—they turned to their right past two urns of grey embroidered stone.

Easter was guilty of slight rudeness to Miss Smith. She picked up an evening paper and turned to the day's winners with concentrated emphasis.

Basil came in.

"Easter, darling," he said. "What won the 2.30. Tell me gently, will you? Was it Quick Return?"

"No," said Easter. "The weight beat him."

She and Basil sat in the window where Sarah had been sitting and talked of racing with keen and logical interest, while the radiance of the garden withdrew into itself in a still and secret spell of quietness. Only because the sun was setting.

Lady Anna came down as the gong rang. She was sufficiently painted to embolden her beauty, and diamonds shone in her silver hair and banded her graceful wrists.

" Oh, children. Dinner-time. Miss Smith, I don't think Benjy had his orange for supper, did he ? "

A faint blush ran down Miss Smith's neck to die under the modest *décolletage* of her blue taffetas dress.

" Oh, Lady Anna, I forgot his orange but he *did* have a great many strawberries."

" Yes, I think that orange is rather important." Lady Anna dwelt on the thought for a moment while little Miss Smith shrank into the blue taffetas dress that was too big for her. " However, we can't wake him up now, can we ? " said Lady Anna. " Ah, children," she said again, seeing that Sarah and Evelyn had come in from the garden, " shall we go in to dinner ? "

They sat round the lovely gradual oval of a polished table. Pictures of Sarah's beautiful ancestresses simpered down at them out of the thickening dusk. Basil sat between Lady Anna and Miss Smith, and Easter between Sarah and Evelyn. They ate bright unsophisticated food, starting with grape fruit, untampered with by alcohol, and ending with strawberries and cream. Sarah and Easter drank water, but there was cider cup for the boys.

" Not for me," said Easter. " I should go all

giggly," and Basil, who had seen her drink a whisky and soda without turning a hair, perceived and enjoyed her reaction to atmosphere. Basil talked to Lady Anna about the stud farm where he worked. She was interested in the horses and knew their breeding and all about the mares sent to them.

" But, Basil," she said, " I don't see a future for you in it. Who will make you manager of a stud farm ? Or not for years, anyhow."

Basil smiled his dark, doggish smile. " Something will turn up," he said. " I might get a job in Ireland."

"Ireland ? Would you go back to Ireland ? Would you care to ? Such a hopeless country, and every one one knows has had to leave. Easter, you have a house in Ireland. How did it escape being burnt down by the rebels, I wonder ? "

" Puppetstown," Easter said. " My aunt is living there. No, it was never burnt. It's there——" She spoke vaguely almost without interest.

Evelyn said : " It's a great pity it *wasn't* burnt. Then you'd have had some compensation from the government instead of a house you can't live in and can't sell."

Basil's eyes blazed out suddenly from across the table. They said : " *Cad,*" then turned questioningly towards Easter.

" Sell Puppetstown ? " she said quite coolly. " Where would Aunt Dicksie go, I should like to know."

" Well, *does* an old lady want an enormous house like Puppetstown to live in ? "

" It's *not* the house," Easter said. What was it, then ? Her eyes met Basil's and she saw that he knew what she meant though she herself did not.

" I should have thought it was rather dangerous, an old lady among all those dreadful ' gun men ' and things the *Morning Post* talks about," Lady Anna protested.

" Yes, but she's always lived there ; she'd rather be shot there by accident than live here on purpose ; that's what she said when Aunt Brenda tried to make her come away."

" Is it her house ? "

" No, it's—well, it's *my* house," Easter said. " I used to live there."

" So did I——"

" And so did I——"

" Mummy lived there——"

" My father lived there——"

" And Aunt Dicksie——"

" Really ! Quite a large family party." So was the wraith of Puppetstown hushed from that quiet English room. But when Easter remembered she was going to ask Basil what the question was that she had asked and he had answered. But now other things were more vivid—Evelyn was talking to her.

" Mummy was with you in town ? Is her ankle quite all right again ? It was rather a bad sprain, wasn't it ? Did you go to see ' Lady Love ' ? Oh,

Easter, we'll do that together, shall we ? On the way home next week."

" Port, miss," murmured the butler, and Easter, forgetting all atmosphere, nodded. A thin gold hoop of happiness had fallen unreasonably about her, circling the minutes preciously. Sarah had talked to Miss Smith all through dinner—about birds—Miss Smith it seemed was a keen birds-nester. Easter was in one of those lighted level moods when her words were easy. Soon she would say something at which Basil would laugh and Evelyn frown, but Lady Anna saved her (on the edge, too, of telling Evelyn that the lawyer yesterday had looked like a cross between Oliver Cromwell and a Nancy-boy). She rose from the table and they all followed her out of the room to drink coffee in the hall—coffee in little saucerless, painted mugs, and the trouble about them was to know what to do with your spoon. Afterwards the girls ran upstairs for coats and bags, and they all packed into an enormous old Daimler car for the drive into Oxford. Lady Anna talked most. The boys were quite gay with her. Easter, on the edge still of a wild eagerness for happiness said, as the car suddenly slowed and turned in the streets of Oxford : " Oo, I *do* hope I enjoy myself——"

Sarah and Lady Anna looked a little scandalised, then turned to each other with a simultaneous remark about the beauty of the evening, and Evelyn only just avoided a pained silence. Basil pinched her little finger in sudden fellowship. "*Silly*," he said, "you always *do*."

"Yes, but I do so hate being an unsuccess."

"Well"—Lady Anna spoke with friendly bene-volence—"you will be quite all right *to-night*. We can introduce lots of men to you to-night, though we can't make them dance with you to-morrow night."

"That's simply splendid," Basil sniggered, "and now you know the worst, Easter. I'll pretend you are my young girl friend if you like. Evelyn belongs here. We can eat bananas and shame him publicly."

The car stopped. Grey walls smoked up into the evening. A little door within a great door let them through from the world without to the strange outdoor dimness of a marquee, starred with lights and broken by further music.

In the hushed reserve that attends these moments, Sarah and Easter followed Lady Anna down the canvas-roofed aisle leading to the dressing-room, where in a sudden unkind glare of light their coats were laid in the reverent keeping of an attendant.

Girls with tense, unaffected effort stared at them-selves in the wide looking-glasses, dead and unseeing of anything but the reflection that stared back, solemn, grave-eyed. Each one of them was strung to the uttermost point of concentration on herself. It is in cloak rooms that a strange streak of the savage comes uppermost in the female. Here is revealed her deepest buried, most primitive resolve

—the resolve towards beauty. A woman's beloved friend may sink dying and ignored in the queue for a cloak-room mirror, while in any other place she would be mourned with every fantastic circumstance of grief.

To-night the cloak room was a crowd of colours, pale and burning; of pale backs and arms, and neat heads; of vacant, solemn faces set apart to themselves alone; they came in groups and singly and all unsmiling, and passed out again down the dim aisle, as Easter and Sarah, and Lady Anna were doing now. And there they were in the ballroom, the boys waiting on the edge of the floor, and all the night before them.

Canvas overhead and the dancing floor laid across the quad—sofas and chair round the edges where chaperones and dowagers sat stoically, brocade cloaks slipping from their solid powdered shoulders. Girded in jewels and pomp and fortified by proper pride in their young, they prepared to sit out the horrid night. The remote savage girls of the cloak room were warm living things again, and lovelier far than flowers. Their blank eyes fainted with meaning and laughter, they carried their heads like wild fauns, so proud and shy. They danced with their friends and their half known loves, and their brothers, with equal careless ecstasy and competence, for the band *is* good and the floor *is* good, and the whole show is *marvellous*.

Easter was dancing with Evelyn. He had asked

her to dance with him at once. " Come on, Easter."
The band played a sulky, hesitant tune and they
danced so well together, it was an equal pleasure
to them both. Evelyn was a studious and well-
mannered dancer. Above all, good form, his dancing
seemed to say ; like his riding, like his talking, and
probably like his love-making. Easter danced as
accurately as she played tennis. No one ever caught
her out ; she gave her mind to it.

" Nice dress, Easter," Evelyn said, and spoilt
that by adding : " Do you like Sarah's ? "

" Oh, very good indeed," said Easter. One spoke
like that to Evelyn—to Basil one would describe a
girl's dress cheaply, as " just a bit of forgetfulness "
or " quite prudent," but to Evelyn one said " just
extra," or " very good " or " a bit vulgar," as the
case might be. He did not understand excessive
cheap wit.

They walked down the stately faery splendour of
a great cloister, the night sky hanging stars in the
long perspective of its high open arches. Across the
wide square of the quad without dim figures postured
and grouped, laughed and moved off in couples,
the silver gravity of the walls that Wolsey built a
background still for the almost pious beauty of the
very young. And down and up the cloisters and
back and forth, exquisite and most cherished, the
loveliest girls with superb and childish dignity
walked in their beauty. They were still young
enough to play at being grown-up and hardly old

enough to play at being young. They mounted grey stairs continuously beautiful. And to see them round and climb the lovely climbing curve that flighted upwards in such assured austerity was to catch a breathless moment before its passing by.

"We'll go to my rooms afterwards," Evelyn said. "There's a man I know you'd like." He introduced Easter to several young men who asked her for dances with polite uninterest, and he timed their progression so well that they were back with Lady Anna just before the band started to play. Sarah sitting near her mother had as polite a fund of conversation for Basil as though she had met him not five minutes ago for the first time. But when she stood up to dance with Evelyn she had no words. She leaned away from him dancing; she was like a white flower dancing; swayed in the wind, heavy-headed.

Easter and Basil danced together with peculiar understanding and almost vulgar intricacy. "How Plebeian we are," said Basil as the music stopped. "Let's walk about, Easter darling, and you can be catty about these lovely girls; and I want to tell you about this young horse I've bought——"

"Oh, look!" said Easter (and a little wind hurrying down the cloisters set all the dresses blowing), "there are Evelyn and Sarah going up to his rooms. . . . Shall we?"

"*Let's.* . . . Wait! Here's a man I *know* you'll like."

It took time, that introduction which Basil accomplished, loitering longer than necessary in the cloister, some words of Evelyn's to him peculiarly insistant in his funny mind. Outside his rooms he had met an urgent Evelyn—that was the day before when he had just arrived in Oxford.

" Come in here, Basil," Evelyn had said. " Shut the door. Just sit in that chair, will you ? Basil, you see the thing is, I'm very much in—dash it, I mean I've spent a lot of money on this girl and *now* I think I'm going to kiss her. Well, you see, to-morrow night we'll be going upstairs to sit here after a dance and she'll come in and sit down— where you are now, you see—and I'll say, ' Will you have a cigarette,' and she'll say, ' No, thank you,' and I'll get up to find one for myself and go behind her chair like this, and—SIT STILL, Basil——" Other things Evelyn had said : " I think of her all the time, you know. No, it's rather nice—I like it. How long does love last ? You know, she's marvellous, Basil, isn't she ? Wonderful——" And now Basil looked at Easter, and named her troubled impatience to himself, and he thought of Sarah with whom she could never compete, and of how polite Evelyn would be, should they come to his rooms now when, perhaps, if they had escaped invasion by some other party, he had Sarah there in that strategically placed chair. So he led her instead to the rooms of a man he knew well enough to invade, and when they left the party (nicely in wine and caviare) Easter had made a distinct success in a game of Happy Families played with a uniform edition of different photographs of the man's unattractive school friends which friezed the mantelshelf in symmetrical regularity.

" May I have Lord Londsdale ? " said Easter. " *Thank you.* And Our Dentist ? *Thank you.*" They were late (as the game was good) for the next dance, and hurried laughing down the stairs and swept down the echoing aisle of cloisters to the ballroom. Easter was almost late for her dance with a new and strange young man.

" What did you think of Bill ? " Evelyn asked her as he met her punctually at the conclusion of her dance with Bill.

" Oh, a nice shy youth—he sweats and smiles."

" He's about the best fast bowler Eton's had for years," Evelyn told her a little stiffly. It spoilt their intimacy, that, so that they were both pleased when Sarah and her partner—an extravagant youth wearing a monocle and a splendid air of detachment—joined them on their way up to Evelyn's rooms.

Easter knew Evelyn's rooms with their windows looking down into the square, green jewel of grass in the quad below. She had covered many of the diversity of cushions that upholstered the chairs and sofa. Basil had given him the parchment lamp shade with a fox-hunting scene circling it in the glory of the chase. There were photographs of all their horses and a splendid one of Basil taking the world's most awful fall over the last fence in a point-to-point. Another graceful likeness of Evelyn winning his race in a distance. Easter laughing on her Welsh pony, her feet almost on the ground. Easter and his mother at a meet of the Duke's— cars and led horses in the near distance. A clever likeness of Aunt Brenda was on his writing table and, wandering over to look at it more closely, Easter saw too, framed in narrow bright green leather, a tiny photograph of Sarah—Sarah in a white dress sitting in a punt on the river and her head turned away. So Evelyn had stolen that photograph of Sarah.

Basil came in then, darkly smiling, with a dull, tidy girl.

" Lady Anna's talking scandal to Mrs. Hotham and Colonel Dickket," Basil explained, " we didn't think it would be good for us, so we came away. Vi—have some strawberries. Have something to drink. Have some *foie-gras*. Hallo, Miles ! " The eye-glass and Basil made conversational fools of themselves with some success for a space until the party dispersed to dance again.

" *Ours*," Basil said to Easter as they watched the others go. Evelyn and Sarah stood a moment in the doorway. The light splashed on his green shoulders and on her still white ones. Their faces were very quiet and withdrawn into an immense reserve which, said their eyes, is for ourselves alone. Evelyn followed Sarah down the long stairs, and Easter whirled round to Basil with a rain of words.

" Great show this, Basil—I'm simply loving it. Let's eat some food, Basil. What a frightfully dull girl you picked up last time; what's she like? Nice ? "

" Oh, all right. Doesn't see much life, poor Vi. . . . She's the sort of girl that goes to Lords with a girl friend and half a Rover, and then says it's overrated. Oh, yes, I'm fond of poor old Vi——"

" Poor old Vi! She seems nice. Basil, you are an idle brute. Come down and dance with me or Lady Anna will think I'm an unsuccess. Imagine how awful if she had to make young men dance with me to-night! "

" She needn't worry." Basil lit a cigarette lazily. " Don't fidget, Easter. Can't you eat and talk for a bit ? Vi has taken it out of me. A girl you have to pretend to enjoy yourself with is so tiring. Tell me, Easter, now you're a woman of independent means, what are you going to do about it ? "

Easter looked round Evelyn's room with wide, almost frightened eyes. " I don't know," she said at last, her voice was sulky, " and I don't care—I don't *want* the money." She looked round Evelyn's things again carefully. " Oh, *come* on, Basil," she said, " or I'll go down by myself and pick up somebody——"

Through the rest of that night Easter danced and laughed. Everywhere Basil saw that pink dress and those burning, wide eyes in her small brown face. Her success verged on the vulgar. She cut dances

with him and dances with Evelyn with shameless
regularity. Going into some one else's rooms with
Sarah, there was Easter, every nerve excited, the
centre of some splendid and (he did not doubt)
indecorous joke. He guessed she had made it for
she was the only grave one in the room. At seven
o'clock she could have given a couple of stone to
any of the marvellously fresh girls grouped for their
photograph in the yellow morning light, their
dresses new strange colours. He saw her again from
the cloisters, running on fast, tireless feet round the
big fountain in the centre of the quad. The morning
lit her and her laugh lit even that dreadful hour of
morning. Every possible inch to be had she was
going to have out of that night. At seven-thirty,
wrapped in the eiderdown of some man unknown, she
was going down the river to breakfast, and breakfast
itself did not defeat her. . . . Yet when they drove
home past the smoky morning woods and back to
Luddington, she sulked at Basil—who would have
maintained the spirit of carnival—and fled up the
stairs to her bright bedroom with tears soaking
narrowly down to the corners of her mouth.

And her room was waiting for her, very quiet
and ready. Her night-dress straightly folded on the
turned down bed seemed faintly ridiculous in the
bright morning. Those gold backed brushes—at
the remembrance of the happy, happy Easter who
had bought them a day ago (forever ago) the tears
of this unhappy one grew to an anguish of smothered

sobbing. It hurt her to cry, it bruised and wounded and tore her to a reality of suffering. Easter wept bitterly, but tears took nothing from her sad young secret. She could not abide this need and this emptiness. The thought of the endless future seized on her mind. It was terrifying. It was sickening. She gasped and she was sick—then, strangely bettered and comforted, hid her unwanted body away from this unkind to-morrow and slept. But slept entranced and without dreams.

II

THERE was a pond lying at the foot of the garden at Luddington. Its waters emptied in a sleek fall down into the woods below. There were scented scarlet water-lilies on the pond, and flaming masses of scarlet rock roses grew down to the water. Here were dragon flies darting in their bright armour, and an interesting party of ducks—Mandarins, Rosybills, Teal and Shovellers, all pinioned so that they might never give away to any foolish fancy for the wild—they swam and squatted flat on the grass with their bills tucked into their backs. They had little boxes neatly painted green, and comic ladders up which they waddled contentedly to bed. Green turf billowed smoothly down to the edge of the pond, and here the children sat watching the duck one sunny afternoon, the garden drowsing above them and the woods pondering deeply below.

" *Look!* " said Easter as a bosomy black and white lady took to the water with enormous pomp. " Doesn't she remind you of a rich Jewess sailing into the Berkeley ? "

Basil, cocking an eye, nodded lazy appreciation and Sarah stared up from sewing at green silk. Evelyn whose head was buried in his arms remained lost in meditation or sleepiness.

" Mummy said we might take tea and go on the river," Sarah said, folding the green silk into a neat square. For herself she wished no further happiness than to sit and watch Evelyn's bright head sleeping in the sunlight, but her sense of duty towards Basil and Easter forbade such an effortless entertainment.

" This is good enough, isn't it ? " said Evelyn, wakening up, his eyes meeting Sarah's in fore-ordained quietness before he turned to flick a lazy accurate pebble at a duck upon the pond.

Easter's thin, eager body was laid against the grass, drinking in the sun. She lay a little flatter to the ground now, the short, shaven grass pricked up between her stretched fingers.

" Would you like to go on the river, Easter ? " Sarah asked.

" No, Sarah, not a bit. Think of last night and the night before that and let us sleep," said Easter. But a moment later. " Basil," she said, " I'll play a game of tennis with you and I'll beat you. All right, we'll have a match—five bob a side."

They climbed the slow flights of steps up to the tennis court ; geraniums blazed back at the sun ; a peppery fragrance of purple catmint breathed up from the hot flagstones. Easter rolled the pricking sweet of a verbena leaf in her fingers and threw it away. Its scent was of stinging tears. And she passed quickly by the bed of red roses darkly sleeping, for theirs is a very anguish of sweetness. There are no kind flowers—all flowers are unmerciful. Now they were under the house again, its blue shadows had already begun to lick down towards the bright garden. There was no stir or movement about the house. Many of its strange unexpected windows stood open. One, set high up under the leaded stoop of the roof, was shaped like a wide horse-shoe with a green sense of space behind it. Little windows winked as they should say : " *We* know a thing or two," and others dreamed on the garden only.

Easter pointed to the shallow half-circle high under the leaden eaves.

" That's the music room. Have you never been there ? "

Easter shook her head.

" Well, don't," Basil advised her with ungrammatic and cryptic finality.

Easter went upstairs to put on her tennis shoes. Near to her own a door stood partly open. She had

always thought it was the door of a bedroom, but
saw now that beyond it a flight of pale oak steps
led upwards, and the light from an unseen window
made a green wedge of afternoon brightness across
the steps. Easter went through the door and up
the steps, a faint feeling of trespass in her mind as
she did so. The stairs led straight to a room, no door
dividing them from it. The room was as long as a
passage and not much wider. It was panelled in
white painted wood and the window like a long
fanlight was stayed open, and through it a light
air came washing over the floor.

Easter stood at the stair head. The pale, elaborate
banisters on either side rounded into the walls of
the room. No one was there at all, yet Easter felt
as though her coming had made a sudden hush in
a room full of people talking on matters which could
not concern her. She went slowly down the room
to the end where a tall, incredibly narrow window
opened almost into the dark, slender pyramid of an
Irish yew-tree. Obviously the window was not often
opened, for a twig of yew was worn and elbowed
from tapping on the glass.

A glass-fronted cabinet held a collection of faded
shells, each labelled in exquisite and clear hand-
writing, the ink faded to faintest sepia. The most
precious specimens were wrapped away in tiny
parcels of paper, browned like the ink with age.
Easter read, " Mauritius, 1865." There was a
spinette of lovely, deep-grained wood, its frail,

twisted candle stands held half-burnt wax candles
that had once been pink ; a round stool on a twirling
stem was covered in *petit-point* worked in a design
of green tulips. Easter wandered on to where a
modern upright piano stood, bundles of Czerny's
pianoforte studies lying on its lid. A harmonium,
complete with appropriate hymnal squatted
hideously against the wall. Easter espied a swathed
and dusty 'cello—and then it dawned upon her
that she was in the music room.

Why had Basil said : " Well—*don't*," like that ?
A peaceful, quiet place. Easter who seldom wished
to be alone enjoyed for a moment steeping
herself in a luxury of solitude. She wandered
and touched, read a hymn, " New every morning
is the love," at the harmonium, and studied a series
of framed samplers—the oldest of these depicted the
least felicitous scene enacted in the Garden of
Eden (but, after all, decency demanded that it
should be subsequent to the termination of man's
state of innocency). The last and least intricate of
the samplers was the work of Sarah Annastia
Middleton, 1912. It reminded Easter that Basil
was waiting for her to play tennis, but when she
craned out of the window she saw the tennis court
was empty. Its clean white lines lay very rigid
and sane, and its turf was the only browned turf
in the garden at Luddington.

Easter sat down on the window-sill which was
built wide and low to the floor. An old *Punch* lay

near her hand. She read a rather dreary joke about
a Mrs. Newlywed and a butcher. There was a
picture of a lady on a superb bicycle. Easter read
on—then with a feeling of satiety that was almost
nausea she looked up, and on the moment all her
mind and all the room were flooded with sadness so
unspeakable as to terrify her. It came in a tide
beating quietly between the narrow walls, flooding
gently in like sea water between rocks. The room
was filled with lonely, voiceless voices and sad
hands unseen. They pressed round Easter in a
gentle, silent stir ; and Easter rising to her strong
young feet ran from them headlong down the stairs,
her arms crossed before her face, while the room
she left behind stooped close about those lonely ones,
stilling them again to uneasy quietness.

Basil was waiting in the hall, an eye cocked up
the stairs, his brown face puckered up in curiosity.
As Easter came down he relapsed into complete
indolence and the study of a dancer's legs depicted
in the pages of the *Tatler*.

" Hallo, Easter ! " lazily. Then : " My dear, you
look as if you needed a drink. Come on." In the
coldness of the dining-room he measured her out a
deep one. " Tip it down. And now we'll drive about
in Evelyn's car till you've sobered up."

The friendly, common sound of the Morris engine
comforted Easter's mind as Basil turned out of the
hot violet shadows of the court-yard. They dipped
through the woods and up again to the vulgar

highway. Easter drew a deep, satisfying breath of petrol fumes and hot tarmac. The whisky Basil had given her revelled satisfyingly through her body. She felt expansive and affectionate. But deep in her there stood still a gap that hurt.

In Oxford they ate strawberry ices in a tea shop.

" Basil," Easter said, " *what* was in that room ? "

" The ghosts of Luddington." Basil licked his spoon reflectively. " It's full of them. But I must say they generally have the decency to keep to themselves. Middletons have *such* good manners. Look at Benjy."

Easter's mouth shook. " So many of them. . . . So *unhappy*, Basil, darling."

" What d'you expect, Easter ? England's full up, crowded out. No room for ghosts. Well, it's natural there should be a few old Middletons at Luddington, isn't it ? But there are lots more there too. It's a harbour and a sanctuary for half the ghosts of Oxfordshire *I* think—so quiet, you know, isn't it ? And Sarah and Lady Anna are so sensible about them ; they take no notice. They aren't curious."

" Does Sarah know ? "

That sleek and placid swan, Easter thought, how should she know fear of them ?

" Sarah ! My dear, of course. Ask her about the Spanish lady ? Or don't—she only told me that by accident. Have a cigarette," Basil flapped his case open. " Not ? Oh, my *dear* ! "

" Does Evelyn know ? "

" Oh, Evelyn wouldn't notice. He has more—
other interests. You and I know, Easter, there's
room in our minds for them, poor things. We aren't
in love, we haven't the blind minds of lovers. So
places and things matter awfully to us. And people
and horses and china and mountains, and lots of
fun and room to do things, darling, and the things
we want to do, Easter——"

What a Basil! Almost improper, Easter thought
it, to talk like that sitting in a tea-shop with the
cheap little waitress fluttering round, silk stockings
and trimmed up, and outside expensive cars and
chaps pedalling about on push bikes. And yellow,
dark clouds in the sky and in your mind too. Easter
wished he'd stop and wildly hoped he would not.
He stirred excitement in her and in excitement you
forgot—things.

" England," Basil said (such an awful word, and
his eyes were narrow flames) ; " she's too *crowded*.
We want a littler, wilder sort of place. We're half-
English, both of us, Easter, but we haven't got the
settled, stable drop of blood that goes down with
the English. Easter, the thing is we don't see quite
the same *jokes*. Isn't this a mad way to talk ? My
dear, don't think me an ass, but you do laugh in
the wrong places for them. You'll never be a
success here—why you're even conscious of their
ghosts. Easter, dear, let's run away from them all."

" Where ? " said Easter. The flame in Basil
smote her eyes too, there was a sudden spear thrust

of light through all her unacknowledged dark. " I
know," she said. " Basil, *listen*, we'll go back to
Puppetstown. It's everything that England's not.
And Aunt Dicksie's there. And I've all my money.
No one can stop us." She hovered, disappointed
here. " All the same—they'll try. They'll talk.
We'll have to slip off, Basil. Never tell a soul."

Basil said slowly : " Easter—could we ? " It
was as if he caught her hand and ran beside her,
their thoughts matching excitedly. " To-morrow
morning," he said, " we'll go up to town and buy a
present for Aunt Dicksie and instead of going down
to Tattingham we'll take the mail."

" And single tickets——" There was a crown of
hope in Easter's eyes. Already the world was full
of outsiders who knew nothing of this secret plan—
their secret to keep, their adventure. She thought
of Evelyn and to her wonder he had almost become
no more than Evelyn again. His vesture of change-
able romance falling—that love of his and Sarah's
an acceptable commonplace, or nearly.

Filled with a perfect arrogance of importance
Basil and Easter swaggered out of the tea-shop.
The cloud lay low on the spires of Oxford—as it
might for all they cared—they knew of another
country. They had their hidden plans. Conceit
and conspiracy were theirs—theirs the secrecy and
delight thereof.

Within a mile of Luddington Evelyn's Morris
unexplainably faltered and failed. Basil, who was

hopeless about cars, said that when she had stopped she might stay, and home they would walk. Over the fields and through the New Park. He knew a way.

They skirted a field of green corn, its poppies still laid upon the air like bright flowers on bright water, and found a ride through the woods and then a cross-ride to lead them astray. The woods were very dark and bold, and their unknown ways lowered unwelcoming. A cock pheasant crossed the ride like a jewelled Indian prince before them. The yellow green of the wild garlic carpeted every open glade. All at once Easter was afraid again—afraid of her past fear—they had mocked the ghosts of England, she and Basil. If only Basil had not admitted to her that such things *were*, if she had not told him of her fear, they might pretend to a sanctuary of unbelief each in the other. But they both knew. There is no false escape from knowledge.

Basil was lost. Now he admitted it. The New Park (it had been new in the days when Charles made Oxfordshire his stronghold) was a great wood, its many rides, some cut some closed, crossed and re-led through every section. The cloud that had darkened Oxford was low here too above the trees. A fever of rain delayed laid a threatening trance upon the silence. The green, dark air swarmed with innumerable small flies.

Nothing more than a wood, a quiet, dark wood out of which they could not find their way ; yet, as the children hurried down the long rides, fear was with them, very near. They would not panic, they walked sedately, measuring their steps lest they should hurry unseemly. Their feet sank in the soft stuff of the rides. They did not care now if they never found Luddington again. All they sought was the blessed edge of that lush wood——

What they found was Benjy and Miss Smith on their return to tea, following a pleasant afternoon's study of the nesting habits of a water-dipper. The quick flash of Benjy's blue blouse and the sound of his high, particular child's voice brought them an intense shame-fast relief. It was like the divine relaxation that follows after pain to walk beside Miss Smith and to hear how the day had proved too dark to take photographs with Benjy's lovely new camera, and to hear that one of the fleas Benjy had caught on Spider had escaped Miss Smith's dexterous thumb-nail, and had so bitten poor Miss Smith that she had been obliged——

" Hush, Benjy——" blushed Miss Smith.

"Nobody came." Benjy wagged his head. "Spider and me guarded the tree——"

Miss Smith and Benjy led them out of the wood by more used and friendly ways, up the steep slope to the pond of ducks sitting on their green lawn in placid self-assurance, as commonplace as bread and butter cut for tea. All omen had dropped from the garden. It was as blank now as it was beautiful— the whole face of the house was changed. It told nothing, nor hid anything at all. Four people were playing on the tennis court—Lady Anna and Sarah, and Evelyn and the curate (who played a magnificent game). Those two hystericals, Basil and Easter, slunk in to nursery tea with Benjy and Miss Smith.

III

BASIL came in to Easter's room and sat on her bed that evening. She thought how nice he looked with his black hair and his blue dressing-gown, and would have liked to look at him, but found it advisable to turn her light off in case Lady Anna should see it under the door and wonder what they were talking about at this hour of the night.

They were talking about Puppetstown.

" Wait a minute ; the blankets are unbearably tight."

" Sorry. Better ? "

" Yes, that's all right. Have some eiderdown."

" Thanks. *Easter*. You haven't changed your mind, have you ? I couldn't wait to talk about it, could you ? "

" No. Basil, is it going to be marvellous—do you promise ? "

" My dear, don't you remember ? "

" Oh, but I was so young, I didn't notice things —such a silly. I do remember Daddy and going to

Punchestown, but I can't even think what it feels like to jump a bank now. And what do you think Aunt Dicksie will look like ? Do you remember, she was very thin and she always forgot things. Do you think we ought to send her a wire to say we're coming ? "

" A wire ? " Basil scoffed at the notion. " And spoil everything. The great idea is just to arrive. It's not as if there wouldn't be room for us at Puppetstown."

" Patsy ? Will he be there ? I think he is still. And Fortune. Do you remember Jer Donohughe and his harriers ? Do you remember Teacher and Truthful and Tutor ? And Venus and Acrobat ? Desperate slow they must have been, Basil. We used to see hunts with them on our ponies."

" Our ponies weren't so awfully slow, though. And we used to quite set them alight when we were young and brave. I don't feel so brave about that country now, though—do you ? "

" No. I don't know. Do I ? Oh, I suppose so. I'm terribly excited. I'd like to break things. I'd like to run. *Could* you move off my feet, Basil ? "

" Not if you're going to run about and start breaking things. I'm not going to budge. Wait. Is that better ? "

" *Much* better. What else will it be like ? "

" It's July. There might be a run of peal in the river."

" We'll have to wire to Tattingham for our rods.

Do you remember Patsy's father ? He used to tie a wonderful claret. He dyed his own hackles."

" And he always asked for a little assistance to buy himself new milk that the doctor had ordered."

" He used to dye his hair as well as the hackles. Basil, we haven't thought about Puppetstown for ages, have we ? "

" Yes ; I have. I always meant to get back some day."

" What were you waiting for ? "

" I was waiting till I was old enough not to be ordered back to England, and then I was waiting for you to grow up, and then I was waiting for you to want to go. Now I can be agent or steward, or anything you like to call me."

" The extraordinary thing is, Basil, that now we can do what we like. We aren't really being beastly to Aunt Brenda by going, are we ? "

" Not a bit. She adores us to behave badly really."

" Basil, have you any money ? Bar your allowance from Uncle Vivian."

" No, my dear, not a penny. I intend to live on you for the future. As a matter of fact I'll be worth a lot more than my keep. Now I must go to bed. Don't think about ghosts and ghostesses, will you ? They can't come near you if you promise never to be unhappy."

" I'm not unhappy." Easter denied the thought.

" No. Well, you're lucky, darling. Cross your

thumbs." Basil got off the edge of the bed and gently in the darkness went out of the room.

When he had gone Easter lay apart from sleep, yet contented. Her mind was full of idle, indulgent hands, that built for her a bridge between hope and remembrance, that crossed safely over the black and bitter water where she had seen a dream drowning. But nobody knew. Nobody at all had known anything about it. And there was a way now bridged and open to forgetfulness, Easter set her feet gallantly on the bridge. Before she slept she raised herself, her two sharp elbows pricking into her pillows, and looked out at the deep, silent garden and the woods beyond, gathered heavily under the warm stoop of the sky. " England," she thought with the point of divinity that the night may sometimes lend to imagination, " would be marvellous if you were very old or very happy." And as she lay back into the smaller world of bed, there came to her a thought of mountains—mountains of a clearest violet, and a cold, thin wind blowing, and in the clear air a flock of Philippines were wheeling, their white bodies gleaming like fish in a net. What were the names of those mountains ? Their names ? If she had their names she was charmed for ever. Why should she think of a horse now ? She saw it from her bed—an ancient, strange horse of a wild, apocalyptic beauty. If he should speak it would be to praise their names— Mandoran, Mooncoin and the Black Stair. . . . The

charming spell was hers now. Never would she
escape it and so in delight she slept.

.   .   .   .   .   .

It was at lunch time on the following day that
the question once more arose between Basil and
Easter as to what they should bring Aunt Dicksie
in the shape of a present. For a present she must
have.

" Caviare," said Basil, without much originality
since he was eating it at the moment. They were
lunching expensively as befitted the greatness of
the occasion, for this very evening they would leave
London, taking not the three-fifty to Tattingham
Traceries, but the mail to Fishguard.

Easter, very slight and green, it was the sort of
hot day when she was as pleasing to the eye as a
little wood, disagreed at once. " You'd better send
her a Christmas hamper from Fortnum and Mason,
and be done with it," she suggested.

" Well, we might give her a couple of records for
your gramophone."

" Yes, or five hundred of your favourite cigarettes.
You are so helpful, Basil."

" Well, dear, as you will have to pay for it, the
same as I hope you will for this delicious lunch,
thank you, I don't see why you shouldn't have *all*
the fun of choosing it. What shall we eat next,
Easter ? I *do* love food. I hope Aunt Dicksie feeds
us well."

In the end, they bought for her a pot of caviare ;

a box of Basil's favourite water biscuits ; an electric hair-brush (this had intrigued Easter); a black hand-bag delightfully and expensively monogrammed ; and a book called, *Why I love my garden.*

It was very hot in London that afternoon, heat of the grey, pulsing variety that pressed upon you unforgivingly, and rose up from the pavements to smite. On an island in Piccadilly, Basil standing behind an overheated female with a vast folding neck, thought with sudden longing leaping towards its near fulfilment, of the river at Puppetstown—the river like a young hound, a silver hound, a black hound, and the thought was so unbearably wild and pure, he put it quickly out of his mind lest it should suffer a change at this thronging, ugly moment. They were making their way towards Lilywhite's, where Easter wished to purchase a tennis racquet, and tennis racquets reminding Basil of snow-shoes, he tried on many pairs because to do so gave him cold thoughts. Easter, however, firmly refused to buy him a pair, and quite rejected the idea of their suitability as a gift for Aunt Dicksie. He rather enjoyed Easter when she was being firm, and liked providing her with occasions for a little mild bullying.

In the lounge of the hotel where they came at last to rest for tea, they met one of Easter's lovely young girl friends. She was so beautifully dressed that it seemed almost unholy to look at her, and her little wonderful face was painted with the boldest cunning.

" I'm so te'ibly tired," she said, " and so is
Reginald te'ibly tired." Reginald was her escort.
" We've been at Susie's wedding. I think it was the
most te'ibly nice wedding I can remember, but
te'ibly tiring."

" Have another drink with us," Basil proposed ;
" we're *terribly* thirsty."

" Well, it's te'ibly nice of you. Reginald said I
was drunk, so perhaps I oughn't to. When I'm drunk,
I'm mad for love, and Reginald says it's all too
te'ibly tiring. What are you doing to-night ? "

" We're going to Ireland."

" Oh, how te'ibly—nice for you. We're going to
St. Raphael later ; Mamma is mad for a sunburn.
Won't you be at Lord's next week then ?
Not ? "

" No," said Basil, and it struck him now mercifully
he would not be at Lord's next week then. He
looked across at Easter. She was like a thin green
wood-cut beside this fairy. He looked at her brown,
nervous hands with their unvarnished nails, and
from them again to those other hands as placid as
the paws of a little animal—an ivory little cat he
thought of, with its nails dipped in linnet's blood.
Extravagant, perhaps, but there was exactly the
same fine suppleness and placidity.

" How old is she ? " he asked Easter when the
pair had made their fatigued adieux.

" Who ? Oh, Flower. She must be quite eighteen.
I knew her at school in France. She was a nice

person then. I remember she put a bad orange down
a drain and told the most thumping lies about it.
Really lovely lies. And she knew more vulgar
stories than any of the girls there. But do you know,
the other day, Tommy Burrows told quite a mild one
—I laughed like anything, but Flower *simply*
couldn't see the point. Isn't it astonishing how
people change when they leave school ? "

" Or do they ? " Basil pondered.

" Well, I can't cope with Flower now a bit, and
we used to be rather friends."

" I shouldn't grieve, darling. The thing is not to
give a blast for people. Places and horses and pieces
matter——"

". . . And pieces ? "

" Pieces of China or Pieces of Eight or even a
Piece of your Mind. But I've told you all this before
and will again, I shouldn't wonder."

" Don't you think Flower attractive then ? "

" Not te'ibly," Basil murmured. " No, I think
she's an unmoral little Nit-wit. But not so nit-
witted as she's unmoral."

" Gawd ! " Easter sucked a front tooth and they
both laughed. " You are devastating, dear."

" Are you going to change, Easter ? "

" Oh, it's too hot. I can wear a coat. Shall we
have dinner on the train or here ? "

" It will be too early to eat here and too nasty
to eat on the train. Isn't it frightful to think we've
added this further problem to life by deciding to

live in Ireland ? It's going to annoy us every time
we go back there from here."

" Well, it may be quite good on the train and
then you'll be done out of your difficulty."

" Of course it won't be good on the train, and
besides I can quite easily think of another difficulty
just as bad or worse."

Dinner was bad on the train and the journey entirely
unenjoyable, but the crossing was duly brightened for
Easter by the charming manners of the stewardess.

" Indeed I'm sorry to leave you so long," she said,
coming into Easter's cabin when the shores of
England, or more properly speaking, of Wales, were
some miles behind them ; " but sure what could
I do ? I was tending the Countess of Loughlin.
She have a secretary with her," she continued in
hushed narration, " and a lady's maid and a little
dog ; she's very exact in all ways. Wait till I tell
you ; there's a parcel outside her door now, addressed
to the Honourable Mrs. John Downing, and I don't
know what's in it. Don't say a word and I'll let
you have a look at it."

Easter's years in England had not quite deadened
a something within the very core of her being that
entirely sympathised with any manifestations of
irrepressible curiosity, and encouraged them whether
they were her own or another's, towards complete
gratification. Now she looked at the large flat parcel
that the stewardess brought in with wondering
speculation.

"I think it's a little golf coat," the stewardess hazarded at last, after she had read the address aloud and turned the package over and over in her hands.

"Well, *I* think it's a picture," Easter contributed, simply because this was the last thing to which the parcel bore any resemblance.

"Well, now I *wonder* is it?" Oh, the drama to be enjoyed, given only that one is endowed with a proper interest in matters that are strictly other people's business. "I wonder would she like a picture?"

"Who? Mrs. John Downing?"

"D'ye know her? Did ye never see her? I tell you then that's a lovely girl. Oh, she knows me well. Now if you ever meet her say 'Kehoe' to her and that's all ye need say. She'll know me on the minute."

"I suppose you know practically every one in Ireland," Easter said, "going backwards and forwards."

"Well, I do. Indeed they never forget me, they're very good. But I think"—there was a gleam in her eye comparable only to that which had illuminated the examination of the Honourable Mrs. John Downing's parcel, "I think I never seen you before, only ye're the one stamp as Lady Slaney Strahart, that's the Duke o' Wexford's daughter, and she's a nice girl, oh, *very* nice."

"She may be, but she's no relation of mine,"

Easter disowned the aristocratic connection with regretful firmness. " My name is Chevington."

" Chevingtons of Puppetstown. Indeed, that's a lovely family. I'd know by ye ye were one o' the real gentry—d'ye know what I mean ?—the real bloody gentry. I'm on this line now going on thirty years, and I recall poor young Mrs. Chevington that died, and Mrs. Curtis that was Miss Chevington, and the two lovely twins she had. . . . God, I must go ! That's her Ladyship the Countess reaching. Ah, I'd know every one o' thim with me two eyes shut——" With which last ghastly boast of her intimacy with Ireland's nobility she faded blandly from Easter's cabin.

It was evening on the next day before they came near to Puppetstown. And the day had been spent in blind wrestling with the vagaries of a railway that saw no necessity for their deliverance from its slow toils. Basil was silent and Easter was weary. She had nearly forgotten the morning and the thrilling sweet of mild voices, and the smallness of the trains and the mountains that seemed to set their feet in the sea, and the way of a wide shining morning river, plumed by clove-brown reeds and their glass-green sharp leaves. She was tired and a sad humour was on her when the little train at last dropped them at Puppetstown's station. Small and ugly it seemed, the station that had once been to them all the grand termination of the sober life they knew, and the gate to the world outside that they knew not. When they told the driver of an unbelievably shaky and filthy car to take them to Puppetstown, he gazed at them for a moment in unaffected surprise.

"Well, I will," he said slowly, "I'll take ye as far as the gates in any case. But they'll surely be locked on us. Only for that," he added, with a flourish of generosity, "I'd lave yez above at the door."

Basil looked at Easter and Easter a little shakily looked back at Basil. "*Locked?*" said she, with a drop in her voice.

"Well, can't you go round by the wood avenue gate?" Basil asked their driver.

"I can, of course, but ye'll meet locks any place ye'll go in it, that's one sure thing."

"Oh, we can leave the luggage at the lodge and walk up."

"The lodges is empty. Indeed," the young man continued informatively, "there's no life about the place at all."

"If the gate is locked you can wait there while we go up to the house and fetch the key," Basil announced, with weighty decision which the settling of any trivial matter calls for in Ireland, and followed Easter into the car. Their actual arrival was shaping rather blankly now and perhaps, he thought, it had been a bit theatrical not to send a wire to announce their coming. Locked gates. Empty gate lodges. And Easter in her thin tweed coat, tired and vexed but mercifully silent beside him.

The evening was a little grey and bitter, as an evening can be in July. A wind blew up the dust in skirling clouds and bellied in the tattered side curtains of the car, dragging them from their anchorages of rusty safety pins. There was a summer's growth on all the fences, and Basil and Easter, looking out at them, thought to themselves secretly that indeed they had forgotten what unaccountable looking obstacles banks were. Old women in donkey carts and children playing in the dust had as good a right to the road as any motorist, and so had stray asses and white wandering goats, while their driver slowed down almost to a stop for every cur dog (and there was one at each dirty little house they passed) that crossed his wheels, hysterical and furious. Far away the mountains held as it seemed their hands over their faces to commune a little heavily among themselves alone. A small old wood, with black soapy tree-stems growing out of a toil of dark greenery and the low flash of water seen through its distances, was not kind or friendly either.

" The Hunt ruz a fox within in that wood," said their driver, nodding his head towards it, " in the month o' Febooary, gave thim a right chase. From Knocknaskeogh to Tomanool there was huntsmin puckin' out through the country and the dogs yowling out before thim always, and the trumpeteer in a red coat going first and he bugling. I declare to God that was the greatest fox-chase I ever seen.

I was as riz in meself I took out through the country on me two feet to folly the horses. Indeed I was as tired as a dog that same night. But in regard o' the two commercial gentlemen I had in the car along with me, they were mad for catching the mail to Dublin, and every Jesus they called down on me when it should go from them at the station I wouldn't care to repeat. But for all "—he paused a swinging moment—" I'd lose me life at any time for a fox-chase, I'd take a hell of a delight in it, God knows I would. Here ye are now—what did I tell ye ? "

He stopped the car before the gates of Puppets-town, and indeed they were fast locked ; while through the flat windows they could see the lodge was dark as a bottle in its emptiness. The geraniums that had once been kept in green window boxes had reverted to a wild small hardiness, and their occasional flowers glimmered like lighted candle-wicks against the window panes, and their thin, tree-like stems cracked dry joints against the glass.

Basil and Easter climbed out of the car and looked at the locked gates, and in through their wrought iron-work down the long straight avenue to where the house, informed with a certain eldritch air of abiding cunning and distrust, waited their coming. There was no smoke from any chimney and the long lines of blinded windows were like so many inturned, indifferent eyes.

Basil did not care for this business of peering at the house through the shut gates. " Come on," he

said, " we'll get over the wall by the old fox track."
And silently Easter followed him down the dusty
road and dropped behind him into the long arm
of beech wood that grew the length of the demesne
wall.

" I *am* so glad," Basil said, as they set off across
the intervening field for the avenue, " that you
forgot to make me carry your new dressing-case."

Young horses were feeding in the distance and
raised their blood-like heads to stare, and cocked
their small ears to listen as the strangers' voices
reached them. They trotted forward, cresting
curving necks, then wheeling, galloped with manes
and tails flying like dark cloaks away into the
evening.

Basil stared after them in a rhapsody. " Look at
that chestnut colt," he said. " Easter, he's a
wonderful mover, and look at the size of him."

" I think he grew too big," Easter said, " I like
that little brown thing far better."

" Yes, because she's made to carry you, that's
why you like her. Let's try to walk up to them
again."

" But Basil, that fellow will probably drive back
to the station with our luggage if we don't send
some one down to him soon to unlock the gate."

" P'raps you're right." Basil turned regretfully
away. They climbed through the railings and
followed the avenue up towards the house.

Portugal laurels, once trimmed, had grown with

the dark thrusting hardiness of their kind, and stooped heavily across half the way. The scent of distant lime blossom trailed a faint arpeggio on the weighty dusk. On their right hand they could hear the young horses galloping still, and before them the house stood as if entranced, its eyelids steadily lowered. The faint arrowy lines of the grass-grown ruts led up to the door and wheeled away round towards the stable-yard. Not even one dog came out to bark, but there was a white fox-hound bitch, grown so old that she knew not friend or stranger, lying stretched beneath a great scented bush of syringa, and she did not stir as they walked up the granite steps and between the high granite pillars to peer in on the forgotten familiarity of the hall.

How forgotten it was and how familiar, and how unfriendly. The slope of the evening light set the same splashing narrow stain from the same window to the very spot on the floor that it had crested with red and blue since they ever remembered. The doors at the end of the hall were shut fast in their high arches. The corner table that had once been sacred to whips and sticks now held, besides those things that they remembered, an assortment of gardening tools; a light spade, two small hoes, a rake, a trowel, a hand-fork. Old gloves so stiffened by mud that a hand might still be stuffing them out lay on another table, with a regiment of horses' hoofs mounted in silver and inscribed with the ghost-like names of dead hunters. On the floor

squares and triangles of bulbs were laid out to dry,
and on the long Heppelwhite sofa too, but yellowing
sheets of newspaper had been set between the bulbs
and the faint, rotten brocade.

Easter and Basil stood together in the hall through
which they had gone out and come in for so many
childish years. Now the faint grey chill, the mustiness
of bulbs, paper peeling damply from the wall, and
the little wind that came turning sharply round a
broken pane in the shallow fan-light above the door,
all disallowed the free and uncareful happiness they
remembered and in a moment sank their spirits and
their hopes. There they stood, the pair of them,
having tried so confidently to sail their ships into
the harbour of Yesterday, only to find that harbour
filled and silted up against their anchorage; and now:

" Basil, what *is* that peculiar noise ? " Easter
stood back a little towards the door. " It's hissing
like a snake," she said ; " do be careful, darling.
I think I'll ring the bell, d'you know. Wouldn't
it seem more natural ? Oh, there's that noise again.
Basil, come outside the door. Oh, *why* is this so
awful ? "

" It's a turkey hen," Basil announced, rejoining
her after a slightly nervous tour of exploration,
" sitting on eggs in the *Breton* cradle. It hisses like
a snake and I bet it'd bite like a dog if it got the
chance."

The turkey hen, rearing its pale head like a
horrid weed in that dark corner of the hall had

shaken him queerly. It was an insult to their Puppetstown—a lousy bird that hissed and stank. And now
the old white bitch came stiffly up the steps to peer
at them out of her sunken eyes, and raise a hoarse
clamour when her slow mind had taken in their
strangeness.

Basil lifted the stiff, heavy door knocker, clapping
it boldly up and down. "Aunt Dicksie!" they
called. "Aunt Dicksie!" And clapped the knocker
furiously. It was as though they blew a trumpet
and shouted without the walls of silence; and in
token that the walls fell down before them, the
turkey hen rose from her corner and her pregnant
eggs, with blind, tearing noises and a rattle of dry
feathers. She flew desperately out in their faces
and ran, hooping her tortoise back, away down the
avenue to the laurels.

"Forrid-on now!" In the hall again, his eyes
blazing, a wreath in them as of triumph, Basil
snatched a dented slim horn from the medley of
gloves and whips. The doubled notes he blew on
it were a shattering insult to this silence. Standing
straight as a rush beside him, Easter crooked a
sudden finger to her ear and holloaed as good as
any man, and howled like a dog after (her two
chiefest accomplishments). Thus they claimed
Puppetstown for their own.

A door wheezed and banged in the distance, feet
came hurrying, and before them stood a thin, pale
young man with a little black beard and strange

pointed ears. There was a faded salmon fly stuck
under the lapel of his blue coat, and his eyes lit
up, clouded with doubt, and lit again as he looked
at them.

" Miss Easter ? " he said. " Master Basil, it is ?
Would ye recall me, sir ? Patsy Roche, sir. I wonder
would you ? "

" I wonder would we ? " Basil dropped easily
back into the tongue of his young holidays. " Indeed
we would, Patsy. But that's a frightful disguise
you've grown on your chin. How are you ? "

" Right well, sir, thank God. And Miss Chevington
the same."

" Where is she, Patsy ? "

" Within in the dining-room ating her dinner,
Miss Easter. Will ye go in to her, till I'll get a bit
ready for yersels. I'll hop it in now on the red
raw minyute."

But as he sped back towards the kitchen, Patsy's
ingenuity for once sent no respondent spark to
kindle endeavour. " In God's name where should I
go for it ? " he asked of the shelves that yielded
nothing further calculated to solve the situation
than dairy salt and lavatory paper. " A bit o'
slack salmon and a crow—that was her dinner and
what length would it go between them ? May God
pity me if I had as much as an egg itself I'd knock
out a kageree with the heel o' the poor salmon. Be
the Holy ! " said he, with the inspiration that sometimes lightens beleaguered moments. " I'll nip out

a couple from in under the turkey is nistin' in the hall. Sure she's not a week lying on thim and isn't it all one when they'll be hard-boiléd ? " And he was off for them, flying down the passages in his queer, light-footed poaching way.

.   .   .   .   .   .

" Hallo, Aunt Dicksie ! " said Basil.

" Hallo, Aunt Dicksie ! " echoed Easter.

Side by side like returning travellers in a play they smiled at her shyly down at the distant foot of the table where, stuck like a little idol in her chair, she seemed to diminish under their eyes as they looked at her for what seemed a very long moment.

A long and sinking moment it was for Aunt Dicksie too. Since she had heard them racketing at the door and heard them blowing horns and shouting in their pride, she had known that the time was at hand for her lonely, passionate watch on Puppetstown to end. Young and greedy and unkind, the children had come back, not to her, but to Puppetstown, to take it from her for their own.

Now she came towards them and kissed them both in the grave, chilly way that they kiss who have other than human ties and likings. Her face that had always been so clear was brown as mould now, with a faint moustache mossing her mouth and chin. Her calm eyes were holden secretly. She smelt, Easter thought, just like an old bush. How did she dare to be so unlike the graceful, useful aunt they remembered ? And was it necessary for

her to wear men's laced and hooked boots, and
a long purple skirt that very nearly had a
bustle ?

" This," Aunt Dicksie said, " is quite a surprise.
Your mother forgot to let me know you were coming.
But sit down and have some dinner. A little salmon,
Easter ? Or game pie ? And how is your mother ?
And Evelyn ? "

Basil, with the green foot of a rook curling grimly
on his plate, made such suitable answers as the
occasion demanded, but Easter drank a glass of
water in painful gulps and said very little.

" Patsy," said Aunt Dicksie as he came in with
a kedgeree in which the slack salmon had been
heartened and the turkey eggs deadened by a
prodigious use of red pepper, " see that Miss Easter's
room is ready for her, please, and Master Basil's.
I know you would like to go to bed early," she said
to the children, and Easter wondered whether she
would mention half-past nine as the appropriate
hour. But she did not. They followed her into the
drawing-room feeling that they had been let off
only because it was their first night, like the first
night of the holidays.

In the drawing-room one shaded reading lamp
alone pricked the darkness. Small the light it gave
out, but potent the smell. A jackdaw's nest had
fallen into the steel dog-grate, adding a faint,
stuffy whiff of soot to the struggling scents of
lacquer and paraffin oil. Outside the summer wind

had died and the air was very still. Inside the drawing-room it was very still too.

"Well," said Aunt Dicksie at last desperately, "I have a lot to hear, haven't I?"

"Yes. We have a lot to tell you, haven't we?" they echoed almost in despair.

"Is Fortune here still?" Basil asked, lighting a cigarette.

"Yes, Fortune is here still."

"And John O'Regan?"

"No. O'Regan is dead, I am sorry to say. And the chrysanthemums have never been the same since. Not quite the same."

"Aunt Dicksie, there are some nice young horses out there." Easter nodded her head towards the un-shuttered windows. "Very nice indeed," she added, with a dictating little air of knowing something about the matter that Aunt Dicksie found in-sufferable.

"And which did you like?" she asked. "And what did you like about them?"

"I like that little bay mare," Easter said; "she looks like galloping, doesn't she?"

"Indeed, I'm afraid"—Aunt Dicksie's voice was very vague and coaxing—"that is about all she does look like. A bad, weedy little thing, I'm glad to say I haven't many more like her." And how, she thought a moment afterwards, could she have been so unkind and so rude, really, to the child. Poor little Easter—a nice little girl she looked, if only

she had stayed in England. Aunt Dicksie's heart
hurried her. Everything was slipping from her.
The silence of years was gone. The pretence that she
was keeping Puppetstown for these children was
gone, and Puppetstown itself was turning from her—
she knew it would. There would be no kindness
anywhere for her. Money would spend itself like
water after all her years of carefulness, when life
had been so simple and devoted, when she had been
at so little trouble to herself and at no thanks to
anybody. The long thin roots of her being gripped
fibrously into Puppetstown and her heart was nearly
breaking, as she sat and talked through that long
hour to the children she had once so loved.

" Let me see," she was thinking in between every
stiff little phrase, " I must send a list to the grocer
to-morrow. . . . And I suppose they will take
Fortune away from the garden . . . and Patsy will
never be able to cook for such a quantity of people.
. . . And I must stay here or I must die. If only
I was really brave I would go and leave them. . . ."
Shuddering she drew herself together and away
from the thought, it was not bearable. Basil was so
grave like the little boy she remembered. Hitting
his pony and holding it. She could see him when he
was told he must not jump such a fence out hunting :
" God, I'll go ! God, I _will_ go." And he had gone
too. Would they laugh if she told them the story,
and how they had always been in trouble for saying,
" God, I will," like the maids. On the whole she

decided not to risk it. She was too much on the defensive against Easter's grave young womanhood, and too afraid of her own silly, unhappy tears, tears preposterously unexplainable. So that when at last it was ten o'clock and Easter rose to her narrow, balanced height and picked up the bag that matched her coat, and the tidy little hat that matched her bag, and said : " I really am *dreadfully* tired." Aunt Dicksie rose too, her long skirt whisking about her boots and did all in her power to encourage the notion of bed for each of them.

Alert and fashionable in the dead and drowning elegance of that drawing-room, Easter was staring into the mirror that hung above the mantel-shelf. Conceited too, Aunt Dicksie thought, conceited and self-possessed. But it was not her own trim, unwanted little face that Easter saw, not her own self so alone as she was, but red carnations blotted in the glass against the deep reflection of the night sky. Full red carnations against an unstarry sky. Romantic, passionate, Spanish was the sight, and it flew to Easter's heart, flooding her with a terrible wine of self-pity.

Why had she come and why had she not stayed ? Basil had persuaded her with words that were nothing, slyly persuaded her away from her love, exciting her to find again a time that was past, that perhaps had never existed at all. Puppetstown had always been like this—stale and still, she thought, as they lit their candles in the hall. Smelling

of damp and cats, she thought, as she climbed the
stairs by the small stately light of her candle. And
falling in pieces, she thought, as she caught her foot
in a perfect crevasse in the floor of the landing,
and saw a basin glimmering low in the darkness,
set to catch a leak, she supposed, and months ago—
to judge by the dark slime beneath the water it still
held.

" Good-night, Aunt Dicksie," she said, at the
door of her room ; " is Basil in his old room ? "

" Yes, my dear. Where else should he be ? Now
I hope you will sleep well and be properly rested in
the morning." Again that cold, unearthly kiss, and
Aunt Dicksie was gone away down the dark straight
length of the passage, her candle flame flickering and
bobbing as she went. Easter turned the handle and
stopped confounded in the open doorway. Her
room indeed she knew it to be. There on the wall
the hunting pictures she had thought once so potent
of the very spirit of that dear sport to which all
others yield, and there too were dreadfully
familiar and faded photographs, bent and peeling
from age and damp. But it was not the sight of
these ancient familiars that so caught her mind,
not the absence of that horse of dreadful beauty,
not even the sour ashes of a long-dead fire in her
grate ; it was instead the numbers, the massed and
countless quantities and varieties of *beds* that
crowded each other in horrible proximity round the
room. Some were in pieces, some whole, some

sagging like broken-winged birds towards the floor, and the sight of them in all their crowded dishevelment held her in unhappy wonder.

"To-morrow," thought Easter, steering her way among the beds towards the dressing-table, "I'll go back. All this is more than I can bear."

A broken shutter drooped across the window and she had to climb over several beds before she could wrench it open and drag the wide window up ; and when she had climbed back across the beds to the small floor space where her suit-cases crowded angularly, the window fell shut again with a smashing thump that told of a broken cord and of devilish peversity. A bath at least, thought she desperately. But in the bath dust lay heavily and spiders had webbed the taps which hissed derisively when HOT was turned on, and gurgled vacantly at the more modest suggestion of COLD.

Returning down the passage Easter met Basil armed hopefully with a sponge.

"It's no good," she told him, "there's half a foot of dust in the bath and not even *cold* water. Oh, Basil, it's too awful, don't you think so ? Aunt Dicksie hates us—obviously. We can't even have a bath. The house is squalid and filthy. I'm so *hungry*, my dear—that foul slack is making me feel so ill too, and oh, *Basil* ! " her voice rose hysterically, " there are nineteen beds in my room, there are, I've counted."

"Well," said Basil, " there are nineteen of what

ought to be under them in mine, darling, and I'm
terribly hungry, just the same as you are. So don't
give way or I'll cry too. Be a brave woman now,
Easter. Scour your body with face-lotion, put on
your pyjamas and dressing-gown and come to my
room for eatings and talkings."

" *Food?* Really ? "

" Yes, darling. Truly. Really. Aunt Dicksie's
caviare. It's so nasty of her not to have baths like
a lady should. I don't think she's worthy of this
rich gift of caviare, do you ? "

" No, my dear, of course she's not. Do let's eat it.
And I tell you what, I'll brush my hair with that
electric hair-brush I got for her. I don't think she'd
care about it at all and it would be quite a thrill
for me."

" Blast her, anyway," said Basil, comfortably
condemnatory and they parted. They parted to
meet, Easter cleansed and tautened by the spirituous
tang of face-lotion, and tingling about the head after
Aunt Dicksie's hair-brush in Basil's room, there to
eat biscuits spread lusciously with that most god-like
nourishment for the greed of man.

" All the same, Basil," said Easter, much comforted and rather cheered from her love and despair,
" it's not one bit what we expected it to be, is it ? "

" No, it's *not*," Basil agreed, returning from a
fruitless search for water to drink on his wash-stand.
" It's so different that I don't even quite remember
what I expected, do you ? "

" We expected it to be larger and heartier, and servants to look after us, and Aunt Dicksie delighted to see us and everything like it always was. We didn't expect to find a turkey sitting on eggs in the hall, nor all those bulbs, or that frightful slack—that was only fit to be put down a rabbit-hole—for dinner, or the smell of cats, or no water, *or* nineteen beds in my room, *or* nineteen——"

" Yes. Well, if I can overlook them, darling, you ought to be able to. And listen, Easter—it's just as frightful as you say and worse, definitely worse. But the thing is, *don't* you see, we might have rather more sport putting it all right, putting it back to what it was, than we'd have had if it had been all complete and ready for us. Look out," said Basil, leaning from his open window, " at the woods and——"

" Well, I won't really, Basil, and if I were you I wouldn't either. The window cords in my room were rotten and they probably are here too, and one of those windows would hurt so awfully if it crashed on me, don't you think ? "

" I just meant "—Basil removed his person from this new danger—" that if the house is in this mess, think what the rides in the woods are like ! We'll have to cut them out before the winter, and I should think there must be five and six-year old horses out there that have never had a thing done with them. And, Easter, my dear, the house could be so absolutely lovely. I'd forgotten the ceilings, had

you ? and the fireplaces, and I simply can't wait to
tear the pictures off that Chinese paper in the
drawing-room."

" Basil," said Easter slowly, " I'm not sure that
it's not going to be rather fun. I've always wanted
to do things to houses. But shall I make hideous
mistakes ? "

" Well, I wonder ? Where would you start ? "

" With the leaks in the roof," Easter answered
promptly.

" No, you will make no mistakes, darling ; you
will make it a lovely and habitable house, I can see.
And while you're at it, I will make little beginnings
with the horses. But you must buy something really
safe to give me confidence over the country—the
sort of thing you would mount a little only child
on, I'd like."

" I think a green bathroom," Easter said, " or,"
she pondered, " yellow perhaps. So *gay*. Electric
light," said she with an eye on her sinking candle,
" and new boots for Aunt Dicksie."

" Well," Basil yawned, " bed now."

" Yes. Could you please come and make my
window open ? "

They padded together down the high, empty
corridor. Far below in the dank well of the hall a
cat squalled hideously. It seemed to Basil as
though the evil of decay that had set its fungus
in his Puppetstown cried out against them
both in that riven, dreadful voice. They had

come to find a refuge and had found instead
Adventure.

   .   .   .   .   .   .

There rang through Puppetstown now the tingling
beat of hammers, the volcanic jutting of blow-lamps,
the click of trowel on stone, and occasionally the
slyly modest shrieks of the cook that Easter and
Basil had imported from Dublin, as she dallied
hopefully with the plumber—a man of parts and of
means, and the only link that held her to Puppetstown.

On a morning in September, a morning bloomed
like a blue plum, a morning when the sky soaked
the heather from the mountains and the mountains
fainted to the changes of the sky, Easter stood
without her house, Puppetstown, and wept.

The murmurous buzz of the men at work and this
ringing of their tools deafened her mind, and inclined her towards melancholy. She was all beset
by this business that she had undertaken, loosing
as she did so such waves and torrents of cares and
responsibilities upon her own guidance, and solving
as she had never dreamed of. For what did she care
what happened to the scullery sink? And it was
just by such small decisions as these that her day
was ridden.

" For whatever change should come on it," said the
plumber who had uprooted the sink in obedience,
Easter suspected, to the whim of the Dublin cook,
" it could as well be there as to stop where it was."

Anyhow, the finality of the statement so mesmerised
Easter that she agreed and forgot to inquire why the
bathroom, the supposed work of the moment, should
stand neglected while the scullery sink enjoyed the
attentions of no less than three workmen.

"And what," said the Dublin cook, encountering
her with artless skill as she made her escape from
the scullery, " will I give the min for their dinners ? "

" Beef ? " suggested Easter, flinching from this
new difficulty.

" Beef ? On a Friday ? " The Dublin cook
threatened to become temperamental at the mere
suggestion. " Will there be no fish man around ? "
she inquired with a *distrait* haughtiness that Easter
found difficult to stomach, knowing that the cook
knew as well as she did that there would be no
fish man round, nor ever had been nor was there
likely to be.

" Eggs, I suppose," said Easter then.

" There's not above three eggs in the house.
Unless you'd send for them. Indeed, I'm sure the
plumber would go on his bicycle—he's a very nice,
obliging man."

" Is he ? " said Easter, while it came over her
like a wave that the plumber should even now be
at work in her green bathroom. " Please understand
the plumber is to be left at his work. I won't have
him sent away on absurd messages, I simply won't
have it."

" Well, I've lived with ladies all me life "—there

was a hysterical break in the cook's voice—" and I never met such treatment as I got since I come in this place. Ye wouldn't see what food ye'd get in it," she yelled, " neither eggs nor fish nor a bloody ha'porth on a fast day. Nor a fire to cook a bit on if ye had it itself." She indicated the range, black and dour indeed, at the plumber's request, and mysteriously dripping water. " Get out from me kitchen," she screamed, suddenly and horridly losing all control of her unpleasant temper. " God knows ye quit the place like rats when the Republic boys was in the sway. Two more years," she prophesied, " and ye'll be undther the grass and yer toes cocked in the grave " (she cocked her two thumbs in grisly pantomime), " and not another word more about ye—God damn ye ! "

It was at this prophetic moment that the plumber's face was thrust gently forward through a deep and dark hole at the back of the range and " excuse me," said the plumber's gentle voice. " Have y'a a pin ? " Easter chose the moment for immediate flight.

Half-way down the passage towards the front of the house she remembered that she should, of course, have given the cook notice, but she was far too much afraid of her to go back. In her room she found Patsy making the bed.

" Patsy," she said, " where is Bridie ? "

" Miss Dicksie bid her gather the windfalls in the garden, miss, and she's without there now."

Bridie was another of Easter's innovations, and
that she should be thus snatched from her rightful
morning duties (and only yesterday Easter had
printed those duties and the hours at which they
were to be performed on a card which Bridie had
accepted with a reverence rather augmented than
impaired by the fact that she could not read a word
of it) to tend Aunt Dicksie in the garden was a bitter
and crooked matter. But one could not argue it
with Patsy.

A wind blew in at her window, and a clean, thin
wind, little and unfriendly, it was from the mountains. " Patsy," said Easter, suddenly caught about
in the breath of it, " where is that horse, do you
know, that I used to have on my mantel-shelf ? "

" I think Miss Chevington have it put by, Miss
Easter. I couldn't rightly say, but I'm nearly sure
I seen it in the big china cupboard."

" Oh." Easter went out of her room (emptied now
of all the assorted beds). Why then had Aunt
Dicksie disclaimed all knowledge or even remembrance of that horse when Easter had asked
about it on the night before ? Why, a thousand
times why, about Aunt Dicksie. " Certainly," she
had said to everything the children proposed. " Do
just as you like." And then retired to the garden
to attend to the violet frames from which Fortune
had so gladly exchanged to the stables once more.
To toil and dig and dream, that at least was left
to her, with the jewelled splendour of the dahlias

now in September, and the smoky heights of
Michaelmas daisies, little fires to feed on garden
rubbish and their smoke to enjoy. And not only
on garden rubbish were they fed, but surreptitiously
and a little day by day on a book called *Why I Love
My Garden*. Oh, those children, so hard and efficient,
so friendly and cool, how they had hurt her by their
gift of that dreadful and sentimental book; by the
swift and unconcerned way in which they had taken
Puppetstown out of her keeping; by their wholesale
devouring of the plums—which she could have sold
for one-and-three a pound; by their lusty appetites
and lustier gramophone, to which they would dance
strangely and briefly; which they would play by
the hour, while they read, while they talked, while
they wrote letters, while they played cards—at any
time and all times. In the morning-room where
they sat now (the drawing-room was all uprooted
and thrown about) its dreadful tongue was never
silent. No wonder that Aunt Dicksie, who for six
years and more had heard no other discords than
birds' sweet ravings, should stay out the day long
in her garden, and sit silent in the evening, nor join
in condemnation of the plumber nor in enthusiasm
for the progress of a young horse she had indeed
bred, but in which it seemed she had no further
interest. She would be neither let nor hindrance to
those children, but neither would she give the help
that was not asked for nor the counsel that was
unsought. Let them leave her the garden. In their

reformatory zeal for the rest of Puppetstown, let that be spared to her at least, a place where she would be alone and away from them. Away from Easter's cool directness and distant good manners, and from Basil's shy coaxing ways to which she could never respond because he was not a little boy now, but strange and charming young man. More than ever like one of her white peacocks, retreating to a dark fastness of the shrubbery, there to hunch itself, afraid and unattractive in its fear, she was, as she turned her face from the children who did not need her help and set her hands to the garden that always needed her, changelessly loving, unforgiving of forgetfulness. She who had kept Puppetstown for them through these years, when but for her it had been sold and broken and deserted, never more for them, their river, their horses, their woodcock in the proper coverts and the woods a stronghold for foxes, never more but for her, an obstinate old woman holding to the place, her fingers scrutched in the very bone of it, had Puppetstown been there for them when they came to claim it. But of this they seemed not to be aware at all, these cruel, cold children. It was as though they rescued Puppetstown from her evil keeping, that was how they compassed their works about the place. Although they never directly blamed her for its decay, she could feel them unreasonably condemnatory.

"We'll have to do more of the roof than they

thought, Basil; the rain has been coming in for so long, the beams are quite rotten." Thus Easter. Or Basil; "That's a grand horse, that brown four-year old. Terrible pity about that blemish on the fetlock, must have got tied up in wire some time. I'd never have a *strand* of wire near young horses, personally. We'll have every inch on the place down, Easter." Things like that they would say— Basil sitting with his dark, clipped head in the sunlight and his legs crossed over the arm of a chair, long stick-like legs with jhodpurs gartered below the knee and large dull shoes, pale socks, and a handkerchief tied small and neat round his neck. Yes, even their clothes were strange to Aunt Dicksie; Easter's she thought as ugly and as simple as her dancing, and Basil's like a groom's.

.   .   .   .   .   .

And now Easter was in tears. In tears for the world was against her; the cook was against her, violent and unruly. The plumber was so pliably unbiddable that she did not know where to have him; Patsy was upstairs making the beds that Bridie should have finished two hours ago; Aunt Dicksie for her own trifling and idiotic purposes had ordered Bridie to the garden. Aunt Dicksie had hidden her Ming horse. Aunt Dicksie with her genius for mismanagement and her suave ignoring of dirt and squalor, her silent tolerance of their presence at Puppetstown, was the ultimate and final object of her angry tears.

As she stood there Aunt Dicksie came towards her, running towards her, flushed and angry and hurrying with all she had to say.

" Are you aware, Easter, is it possible that you are aware, that the plumber's men have dug a drain straight through my precious bushes of *Daphne Mezereon* ? There they are—torn up, lying on the ground—six of them. And the white ones, too——" Past tears, stricken and grieved as a child might be, wild for a joint and human condemnation of the plumber's evil doing, Aunt Dicksie faced Easter.

" Can't they be planted again ? " said Easter.

" Planted again ? Do you know how many years they take to establish ? Do you know they are the slowest growing things in this world ? I don't suppose you do know," said Aunt Dicksie, " or care one single thing about them. But let me tell you they are. And they didn't like this soil and they didn't like anything about this place and I made them grow, and now, *look* at them——" She spread out her hands as though she threw their mutilated corpses at Easter's guilty feet. " Their scent," she said, "and in February——" It was as though their blood flowed out on the ground as she said it, the white scented blood of the *Daphne Mezereon*.

" I am sorry," said Easter. Her own tears were all stilled and chilled away by this childish outburst on the part of Aunt Dicksie. " I suppose if the pipes went that way they couldn't help it, could they ? "

" Oh, it's too much," Aunt Dicksie lamented.

" It's heartbreaking. Six—and the white ones too. If I had even known they were going to dig there I could have had them taken up without disturbing their roots, but now they're broken and destroyed. Even my garden—no, it's impossible. Oh dear, even my garden, and the *white* Daphne——" She went sadly into the house, lifting her feet in their heavy boots slowly from step to step. Even her long, many times quartered skirt did not conceal the patches on those awful boots.

The world was spinning on an axis of crowded, trival miseries—raging cooks, weeping aunts, pierced shrubs, plumbers, painters, and masons—all, all abominable. What, wondered Easter, could one do to disentangle this web of littleness that was life day by day. She followed a path that tunnelled into the black-green heart of the shrubberies and hoped that no one would find her with further report of iniquity and difficulty.

Rank the shrubberies and overgrown, and with such uglinesses as broken china thrown out in their dank depths. Stooping idly, Easter saw the blackish shine of a broken Waterford finger-bowl thrown there in the green ivy. Green glass and ivy. How absolutely typical, she thought, remembering the charming, narrow sideboard that she had found scoured white by constant sun and thrust away in a grimy corner of the disused laundry. "Sure that's broke," Patsy had said, "this long time." And her cleaning and oiling and polishing of such outcast furniture he looked on as a more eccentric form of economy than Miss Dicksie's years of meanness. " Though indeed," he allowed indulgently, " the way it is these days ye wouldn't see what furniture ye'd buy for a thousan' pounds—ye wouldn't hardly know it was in it."

Easter picked up the old finger-bowl and looked about on the ground, not quite despairingly, for the piece which was out of its lip. She heard Basil calling outside and answered, " I'm here. . . . Here —Basil," though a moment ago she had fled to be alone.

" My dear." Basil stooped under the arch of laurel and sat down on the ivy-grown, ivy-smelling edge of the path. " I've cut the leg off that chestnut colt. I think it's so awful of me. Fortune didn't want me to school where I went either—said there were stones in it. Damn." He rested his cheek on his hand and looked at her miserably. " Isn't it frightful. I've wired for the vet."

" Probably it's nothing like as bad as you think." Easter was not even surprised at this new catastrophe.

" Oh, I know it is. And look here—I've had the most frightening letter from Mamma—written in blood-red ink on sky-blue paper. I think she's really more annoyed at Evelyn's being engaged to Sarah than at anything."

" Oh," said Easter, looking into the deeps of the little Waterford bowl as fixedly as if it had been a crystal, " oh—yes ? "

" And she's wild with us too. But I can't make out quite whether I'm compromising you or you are compromising me."

" Neither of us can be compromised with Aunt Dicksie here."

" No, my dear. But the awful thing is I met her on the stairs just now and she said she was going over to stay at Tattingham. She looked as if she'd been drowned. But she was quite calm and brief about it. You might think she'd paid us a twice-yearly visit all this time."

" Aunt Dicksie's mad," Easter stated unimaginatively. " Quite mad."

" That's not the point." Basil was very earnest. " I don't mind how mad she is, I don't mind if she's so mad that we have to chain her to the leg of her bed, so long as she'll stay here. Because if she goes everything will be most difficult. They may even try to make us marry each other, and we don't want to do that."

" No—we don't, indeed," said Easter in a shocked little voice. " But do you think she really means to go ? It's all because the plumbing went through the end of her garden and they rooted up some shrubs. She was in a shocking state about it."

" Oh, Easter, it's *not* that—not really—it's every-thing. It's us changing the house, I think, and us coming back. She's frightened of us, I think, Easter. I expect we've changed terribly more than she has."

" Of course, we've grown up."

" And she's grown old—much worse."

" But I don't know what to *say* to her. She's so sour. She's as difficult as—as the house is. She's worse than the plumbers. She doesn't want us any more than the place wanted us. Luck's against us, Basil, everything has gone wrong, even this young horse now. I don't think she wishes us luck somehow. And I can't tell you how frightful the cook was to-day—the things she said to me—she'll have to go. Only Patsy and Fortune want us here. Nothing will ever be finished in the house, except the scullery. I *am* so unhappy."

" You've been working too hard and I've been having all the fun with the horses ; that's what's the matter with you, poor Easter. We'll go out schooling this afternoon—after the vet has come——"

But when the vet had given his verdict Basil was in no great humour to go out and school another horse. A bad job, the vet said, and a long one, if the horse would ever be really right, he didn't know. " And I beg your pardon, Master Basil," said Fortune as he was about to leave the yard ; " could you send into the town for another bottle o' iodine and a roll o' wool ? "

Slowly round by the front of the house Basil walked. His head was sunk and unhappy. Aunt Dicksie saw him out of her bedroom window as she packed and unpacked, and twisted and folded clothes in and out of a large trunk. She could not make up her mind about what to take and what to leave,

or if she was really going away or if it was all a
terrible dream that would resolve from her into
blessed, blessed unreality. How unhappy Basil
looked as he stood there pondering on something.
Why so unhappy, when he had come and taken all
that his young need saw good? He turned towards
the house with sudden resolve, saw her at her
window and waved as though the sight of her
assured him more firmly in his intention. She heard
him after a minute coming upstairs, and said,
" Come in," as he knocked at her door.

" Hallo, Aunt Dicksie—you aren't packing, are
you? "

" Just putting a few things away——" Aunt
Dicksie stooped over her cavernous trunk.

" But you aren't really going over to Tattingham,
are you? "

" I don't know—I think so. I had a letter from
your mother to-day."

" Yes, so did I have a letter from my mother
to-day."

" She's very lonely, I think, because of Evelyn's
engagement and you and Easter having come here."

Basil was lying face downwards on her bed,
staring at her disconcertingly, his chin in his
hand.

" What did she say about Sarah? " he asked.

" Oh, nothing *against* her, of course—— "

" No, that's the trouble; she's so definitely
suitable. The fondest mother couldn't crab Sarah.

But, Aunt Dicksie, what did she say about Easter and me ? Very grieved ? "

" Yes," said Aunt Dicksie, surprised into the admission. " I mean," she added, " she doesn't think you should have run away here together and she quite blames me for it—blames *me* ! " She gave an odd little burst of laughter.

" And if you go away to Tattingham it won't be quite respectable, so we'll either have to leave or—or do something about it ! *Don't you go*, Aunt Dicksie," said Basil, with sudden urgency. " It's only one of darling Mamma's little plans for getting just what she wants."

" *Basil !* "

" Listen, Aunt Dicksie, we need you awfully, Easter and I do. We couldn't bear Puppetstown without you. We never thought of living here without you. It was my fault that Easter came. She was so unhappy and I thought you would be wonderful with her, and the house and all the things outside would be such a help to her. So comforting, you know, she'd forget. But it hasn't been the same, has it ? No, but has it ? "

" How could things be the same, my dear ? I'm an old woman. Puppetstown's been alone for more than six years—nobody caring, only one jealous old woman struggling along here as best as she could. No wonder you find Puppetstown—changed. I should think it *was* changed."

" I wouldn't mind Puppetstown seeming so

different," Basil said reasonably; "but I resent
the change in you rather. You could be so lovely
and attractive, Aunt Dicksie—and look at you—
difficult and tiresome. And *must* you wear Granny's
clothes and what look like Patsy's cast-off boots?
I hate you to."

"Basil, how dare you speak to me like that?"
Amazement flooding her, and narrow in the flood
a silver line of delight, Aunt Dicksie faced him.
Faint carnation triangles in her high cheek bones,
her eyes startled from their inward turning. Her
lovely tired hands seemed to wake from a drouse
of inhumanity, and she leaned towards him, her
fingers nipped on the curling wood of the bed-post.
"What d'you mean, Basil?"

"Well, quite frankly I know you'll say I'm mad
if I tell you. But I'm so queer in my mind about
houses and places. I know things. For instance,
people belong to houses—not the other way about
—either living people or dead. Easter and I've just
been staying at a house that belonged to ghosts—
it was *so* awful. Now we've come here, and Puppetstown and you belong and we've no share at all in
either of you—you won't let us in."

Again: "What do you mean?" Aunt Dicksie said
in a little whispering voice.

"I just mean that. I mean that we'll never do
any good at Puppetstown—your Puppetstown, not
ours—with your ill-wish. Nothing'll go right for us.
Nothing can. Horses nor house nor anything else.

We'll never be happy, Aunt Dicksie, unless you
help us."

"You didn't want me," said Aunt Dicksie. "I
couldn't interfere, could I? Not when I wasn't
wanted."

"Oh, Aunt Dicksie, and we came *back* to you."

"Not to me at all—to Puppetstown."

"To you both—we never saw Puppetstown
without you. Some one said to Easter, why did you
live here alone and she was so amazed—she never
thought of Puppetstown without you." Basil slipped
off the bed and stood there, dark and doggish and
cute and embarrassed a little, he had said so much,
but his embarrassment was cute of him too. "Dear
Aunt Dicksie," he said, "do be nice to us, we can't
bear it if you aren't." He kissed her suddenly and
left her.

"Easter," she heard him calling through the
house; "Easter, Easter." A silence, and then:
"Come into Bunclody with me. You must. Come
on." A pause, and then: "I won't go without you,
darling Easter, and the horse will die and then I
will blame myself." They were gone. She heard
their car starting and the engine failing fainter in
the distance.

Six o'clock and a silence settling heavy as the
mason's dust on Puppetstown. All the workers who
had brought their changes there had left. Aunt
Dicksie was alone with her house, and a flame leaped
in her. This her house to give the children.

Unhappily the children had come back to her, not assured and grasping as she in her shyness and strangeness to them had thought. From her window she saw the young horses she had bred for them, moving in all their strong beauty of action against the soaking gold of the evening. She saw the children, strong, beautiful and brave, riding a hunt on them. Almost she heard on that summer evening the crash of hounds' voices, and saw the little wildness of foxy places. And the children coming back to her and Puppetstown when their day was over and fulfilled. Friendly, dependent children. Excitement flowed within her. Certainty and delight were hers, strong from this power of keeping or of giving. With beautiful deliberation Aunt Dicksie sat her down and took off those offences in the shape of boots. Her way was chosen.

.　　.　　.　　.　　.　　.

"What have you been doing, Basil?" Easter was driving their car towards Bunclody, a town where two rivers met and from which small roads led to mountainy places.

"I've been exorcising, Easter. Very tiring." He leant back again in his seat, smiling to himself and very silent all the rest of the way. "What will you do with yourself, Easter? I must get things done to the car," he asked, when they stopped in the unattractive market-place of that town with the lovely name.

"I don't know. Wait here, I suppose."

"Go for a walk."

" Yes, I might do that. Will you be long, d'you think ? "

" Hours, I should say. Would you like to see the smallest house in Ireland ? I'll tell you where it is if you would."

" Would I like it, Basil ? "

" Yes, love it. Go up Patrick Street, past the Rathgarry road and take the first turning to the left. Good-bye, darling."

Up Patrick Street, past the Rathgarry road and the Place of the little Crosses, Easter went. Bunclody was below her now. Her feet were set on the road for the smallest house. A little and winding road it was too, and a stiff way to climb. To the left and right of her as she went along were small fields, grey and close as sheep folds, the shadows of their stone walls lapping gigantically across them in the evening. Little airy wild flowers and late, slight foxgloves grew at small, gentle distances apart from each other. Mountain and sky were pale as green glass, and in the nearer foothills that climbed up to that greater loneliness there was no colour at all.

A dim little road Easter was on now, uncertain and full of apology for where, after all, was it leading but to the smallest house ? The low stone walls saw no more reason now to protect the way from the trespass of goats and lean calves. They abandoned their road to the mercy of the hills so that it fought for its own narrow life between the close, dark green of the gorse bushes.

Up, still up, and would she, Easter wondered, ever see this house. And was it here at all? Quite capable, Basil was, of sending her to look for it and saying when she returned: " Oh, I had a nice thought that it might be there." Or : " What sport for you, darling, thinking every minute you were going to see it."

Again the little walls sprang low on either hand, the lichened stones a green silver and sloe-black in the holes between them. Two white goats, spancelled and smelling dreadfully, clanked solemnly on before her. Now the untidy hand of use was on the wild path. She was coming very near to the smallest house. Round the steep corner where the bare rock shouldered out through the road and she was upon it.

No wonder it hid from her. No wonder it stowed itself away in this far, forgotten place—little shameful slut of a house. What had Basil sent her so far to see? What was this talk of a house that had brought her here?

Built in against a sod and stone bank was a lean-to shelter, nothing more. Rough-barked boards ; a roof of dark birch twigs. A place for the goats off the mountains. A very poor lodging for the few hens that picked round in the narrow road. But no, certainly it was a house. It was a house because, built solid of mud and stones, rising square above the birch-thatched roof, there was a chimney. A real chimney ; standing not ten feet from the

ground, its little smoke had scarcely breath enough
to live, but it was a chimney without a doubt for,
with indescribable jauntiness and spirit, a weather-
cock reared itself bravely two feet above its topmost
stone, witness irrefutable to the hand and habitation
of man. Here, it said, you see a house, a dwelling for
man, built by a man to house his love. The winds
blowing off the mountains had clipped the N. and
the E. from the iron weather-cock, but the gallant
bird did his small best, pointing west and south
with a will.

Easter knew who it was that had built this smallest
house. Now she remembered ; Patsy had told her.
Those were his goats that marched before her. Those
were his few sorry hens. That was his long white
dog, curled like a snake against the door-post, with
an eye malignant upon her. Where was the woman
for whose sake he had built the house and with whom
he lived there, she remembered—alas !—in sin.

Yes, they were a scandalous pair, as Patsy had
told her, who lived here in this sorry backwards
place. The disgrace of the parish, they were, and
thorns in the sides of priest and curate. Hasn't
Maggie Foley a husband a soldier in the British
army ? And wasn't Jimmy Connor the common
outlaw of three town-lands ? Only he was the great
warrant to play a flute at a dance or a wedding,
there's no decent person would go next or nigh him.
There they may live and there they may die, the
two light-o'-loves in the hills. No one would dare

to let, lend or sell them a house. Didn't the Priest put the Great Curse of God on them, and what luck can they have after that ?

Not much luck about it, Easter thought, hurrying away from the dirty little house, guarded only by its lean dog. Spy she had been, bringing her curiosity to this smallest house of sin. Up in the hills, farther —higher, she would forget the queer distress this little house had left to hang heavily about her heart. How long, she wondered, before Romance failed there and died ? But what was Romance, she wondered, and where ? In a tale forgotten ? In a kiss not given ? In no known and friendly thing but set in wildness for a snare and a delight and a beckoning thereto ?

Down the little road Easter turned later on that still evening, back past the smallest house. The snakey white dog went slinking past her, blue-white in the dusk. The one square window was an orange flat of light far in below the stooping birch thatch, and from the chimney of the smallest house, turf-smoke went up, incense to the single beauty of a star. Shrill sweet music piped out a quick twisting tune. Easter's feet hurried past to the catch in the dancing music ; a dark, bold-faced little man played it in the doorway of his house, while, solemn and elfin in the steep road, his love-child danced to the tune.

.   .   .   .

" Car's ready. Will you drive, Easter ? "

" No. No." Easter shook her head mumly. She had found the end of a charm again. She must hold it with careful, infinite gentleness and secrecy ; if she told a thing it was lost to her, lost to her. Now as they drove there was a cold chill taste and the smell of burning weeds in the air. Deep and narrow these roads home from the mountains. Little white houses squatted low behind their burdened fuschia hedges. Easter's heart was ringed about with a hoop of flame. The darkness of Puppetstown's woods was secrecy, and her dim, lovely gates grave and certain in their beauty. A thin wind was biting the jewels of the dahlias in the garden and the evening was welling towards the house with the first cold breath of autumn. And the cold breath turned back blue from the lighted house—there were candles in the hall, small and stately amongst all the crowded disorder and Aunt Dicksie came out of the morning-room, saying :

" Children, children, I've had such fatal words with the cook and I've sent her away, and the plumber's gone too. He's going to marry her. Easter, darling, I feel we're really now revenged on both of them so completely. But you mustn't bother because there's a much better plumber I know of, and Patsy has cooked dinner for us."

" Has she really gone ? " Easter almost whispered in her relief. " *And* the plumber ? That's too good to be true."

" Yes, both gone. Don't change, Easter," said

Aunt Dicksie, complacently regarding the army of diamond brooches which she had clapped on her garden clothes. " It's so late, darling. Unless you want to."

" No, I'll be down in a minute."

But Easter's minute was long indeed. There in the centre of her mantel-shelf, god-like, entrancing and felicitous, was her Ming horse restored to her for her delight, to charm her always. And without, Mandoran, Mooncoin and the Black Stair leaned nearer than a dream, wilder than the strangest dancing. The charming spell was laid on her again. She was entranced and delight and excitement sang in her when at last she went downstairs again.

All the gaiety and wildness that had been silent so long at Puppetstown were present in Aunt Dicksie's voice ; in the rings on her fingers ; it was there in the fire that went singing and whispering up the chimney of the morning-room, and in the mists of amethyst flowers that smoked against the mirror over the mantel-shelf. From nothing had Aunt Dicksie brought forth this graciousness of beauty. From flowers and fire, from strange rings on her fingers and a sudden passion for life in her voice.

" Oh, Aunt Dicksie, what a heavenly fire ! "

" Laurel, my dear—it makes a hotter fire even than ash. And you know, ' ash-green, fire for a queen.' "

" Ash-green, fire for a queen," it sang in Easter's

head through dinner. Dinner with the windows
uncurtained to the night—stars stretched like a
broken net between the dark, formal draping of
the curtains. Soup and snipe and a cheese omelette
for dinner. "Fire for a queen. Fire for a queen." The
small, pretty words hummed still at the back of
Easter's mind. And when dinner was over, Patsy
laid down the liqueur glasses beside each plate (now
these were the most treasured of all the glass at
Puppetstown ; they were heavy and small, and of a
strange oval shape and without a base to stand on
their stems ending sharply—" no heel-taps " they
were called) and filled each glass with a brandy of
calm forgotten ecstasy. Basil lifting his glass looked
over the table to Easter. He would have liked to say :
" Puppetstown," but his love for Puppetstown was
too shy.

Across the table Easter, the heavy, small glass
balanced delightfully to her hand, knew a vivid
moment. It was as of a glimpse of far-off bright
things, like a sudden slit through her thoughts,
showing her the fun and the truth of life. Herself
and Basil, in love with only Puppetstown, both of
them. " And never," said Basil, with his dark,
friendly smile, " need we be married—never while
we can keep Aunt Dicksie alive." They turned and
drained their glasses to Aunt Dicksie with a very
simple grandeur.